For my little Victoire.

Chapter One: Life Worth Living

If he ran he wouldn't last. He might possibly give out, he thought, but he ran anyway. The color of the spring nighttime was dark blackberry, and the side streets were vacant, except for the spots of dim white lights hanging overhead, which were usual that time of the morning, after 3AM, in 1975.

He turns a corner and stops in a doorway beside a store with its protection gate down. All six feet of his twenty two year old coffee dark body remained motionless in there as a white and sky blue police car sails by on the cross street, searchingly. He waited for the car to turn from view before leaving.

Walking out of that doorway he calmly walks fast down the block, hearing left and right instead of looking that way. He heads for the subway station at the end of the block and entered it.

Later that morning. The sunshine brightly showed the commercial and residential areas of Roberts Street. Commercial/residential, because of the division of both districts, by the narrow one-way street known as Roberts.

On one side you had fire house red or heavy cream colored brick houses for two or three families, while the other side had business concerns like Linda's Hair Salon, and Lee Chung's Fish Market, and Lady Tee's Tarot Readings.

Awakening from sleep the young man's eyes opened wide suddenly and his torso rose quick like a nightmare. His one room apartment had the sunlight raying through the window on the sparseness in there: a chestnut colored small desk, a smudged gray fourteen inch Philco black & white tv (portable) on top of it, a black push button phone that looked like a rotary in the corner, a black waste paper basket.

Three bangs on the door!

He rises from the flat bed he slept on and gets up to answer it. On the other side of the threshold stands a five-nine balding perfect circle headed man with Greek features, bordering sixty years old. He gets right to it:

"Listen... There's gonna be guys workin' in the building this month 'cause I'm renovatin' the place. If yous're stayin', the rent's gonna be double. So that'll be one thousand and two a month. If yous don't plan on payin' it, ya got thirty days ta move out." And he turns and walks away down the stairs with his back showing a huge sweat stain on his white tee-shirt.

The young man stands there just a bit shocked, but not enough not to close the door, which he did. Before he goes over to plop himself back down on the bed, two knocks are heard on the door now. He turns back around to go open it.

There on the other side stands a five foot seven inch twenty year old caramel tan colored man. "What happened?" he says to the other, who was letting him in.

Closing the door but not realizing it (staring at a wall) he answers, "The fuckin' guy declares thirty days for me to pack up and go, if I don't have the new rent, which is a thousand and two a month now. For me, that's a million and two a month."

"C'mon Dice!" the other says, "Is he the fantasy man?... He must be the fantasy man, right?"

Dice still stands not facing the questioner but the wall. "The fuckin' guy," he repeats, bracing himself, "...declares, that I got thirty fuckin' days, like, Oh!-- okay! Let me pack up now, and I'll be out! Pronto!"

"That's what I'm sayin'," replies the other. "He must be the fantasy man!... But it ain't like you didn't know it was comin' tho."

"Yeah I know," Dice says. "Soon has become now with a dagger sticking in its mouth. Diplomatically of course-- there's no need to be caustic. "

"So, what happened to the other thing? You went down there?"

"Yeah, I went down there, and when I got there I got real locomotive and left. I thought they were in there and spotted me first. There'll be none of that I said." He plops his rear on the bed, reaching for a cigarette and lighting it. "And besides, like I told you Spike, I wasn't gonna hang around long enough to get caught anyway."

Spike sits next to him and takes one of Dice's cigarettes from the pack that was on the bed, then looks all around. "I thought you said you were gonna pick up a box? You got a ban on entertainment in here."

"I know. No music, no radio... I was gonna get something before, but what's the point now? This guy might change the channel and flip me out tomorrow for all I know. Real life ain't like fiction at all."

"So what happened when you went up there last night?"

"I was a star. A Hollywood leading man," Dice explains. "A swashbuckler. I had in my mind right from the start I was goin' in there and confront shit. So, outside of the front of the club there's the usual line--"

"Right."

"--from here to Venice, only thinner. Now, how many dudes you think they had at the door, waitin' for me."

"I dunno. Two? Three?"

"Five!"

"What??"

"Five angels standing there waitin', and one of them knows me already, and he tells the others it's me, shifting his head, ya know?"

"Right."

"And I'm like, fuck it-- I ain't carrying no kind of persuasion for silence. I'm not the master of my destiny tonight by any stretch of the libido, ya know? So I had to get locomotive real fast, before they started revvin' up their engines behind me, like biker dudes."

"Like what?"

"Like the Apocalypse. Frightening."

"Terror men."

"Exactly," Dice says, as he gets up and steps over to the window to look out of it. He sighed a slow sigh inside his head and mourned out, "You seen Rosie yesterday at all?"

"Nah," returns Spike, not looking at him.

As Dice looks out his second floor window he sees the passers-by moderately walking to and fro. He turns to Spike like he had an idea and says "Let's go outside and see what's happenin'," and they proceed to do that.

Once outside, Dice and Spike talk and walk casually in and out through the pedestrians. The crowd looked like spring, with their coats on, coats off, no coats, and light jackets. The anticipation of summer was around, thick and inevitable.

The ladies are resplendent with beauty and Spike responds to that, saying,"You can tell summer's coming," as he stares each one of them down while Dice is thinking about something else. Then Spike says, "Check this out. I was talkin' to Moose the other day. Tell me this ain't serial killeresh..."

"Go 'head."
"Awright. You remember Bob Randerson?-- he's trying to call this guy--"
"Right."
"--and he keeps callin' and callin', leaving messages with the guy's wife and the guy never calls him back?"
"Hmm."
"So, what d'you think Bob did? He puts all his energy into waiting for the guy to get off work. I mean, he's waiting for him at his subway stop and everything. And then he finally sees him coming down the stairs at his station?"
"So don't tell me."
"And he grabs him by the neck and starts choking him!"
"Get outta here!"
"I swear ta God, he starts chokin' him right in the station, shaking him 'n shit like a ragdoll. Goin', 'You didn't call me back muthafucka!! You didn't call me back!!'"
"Get outta here!-- who you said told you that, Rosie?"
"Nah, Moose. Moose!"
"Oh! Yeah, he always has some wild stories to share with mankind."
"So wait a minute, the guy's still choking this guy. Then he stops and pulls out a butcher knife and starts stabbing the guy all over the place with punctures 'n shit."
"Unbelievable. So you think the guy calls back now?"
"Nah, he's probably dead now."

And the two bust out laughing out of control.

They look at a coffee shop across the street. "Let's go there," Dice says, as if he knew Spike's answer would be "okay" already. And they head over that way.

Before them, girls and women stroll back and forth, and the guys' eyes follow each one of them, as the sun's light slaps against their faces from the moving cars.

Commotion was the layered sound of voices and auto motors, and crowded passing buses with heat exhaust, while the other buses passing were scant with people.

"When was the last time I told you I talked to Rosie?" Dice asks his friend.

"I don't know. I think it was last Monday."

They walk into the coffee shop, which is as crowded as the outside, with chairs full of people. Dishes are clanging dull against each other here and there, as waitresses are seen all over the place walking with them in their hands, some carry trays filled with food, others painted with the stains from it.

Dice steps up to the take-out counter to the spice-brown waitress there. "Let me have a cup of java and a jelly donut."

She gives her nose a quick twitch up, twice. "A cup of what??"

"I was being nostalgic. Uh, just make it coffee. Instead."

She goes to get it not amused. Suddenly, a loud metallic crash explodes inside and everybody turns to the left to see a tall thin man standing up-- his hair rampaging stalk standing high. His powder grayish complexion is sixtyish in age and he has on a gray overcoat. A gray tweed overcoat! (Spring.) He's angry and he shouts:

"What kinda hospital is this? Where's the hospitality??" and he steps up on to his chair and stands tall there, looking around searchingly. "Where's the damn help around here??"

Everyone is staring in shock. Dice and Spike turn back around to the waitress.

"Hey," says Dice. "What about the coffee?"

The waitress stares at him opened mouth as the gray man now unzips his pants and flings out his penis.

"Where the fuck are they I ask!!" the man shouts, as women now scramble out of the place, hysterically.

The waitress at the counter utters "Oh shit," and Dice and Spike are impatient now waiting for the coffee. "C'mon, sweetheart" Dice complains.

The gray man's eyes search each running woman while he casually starts to masturbate. Back and forth rhythmically he pulls it back, pushes it forward, with a mean look on his face, as the counter waitress starts laughing and says "Oh shit" again.

Dice reminds her, "You gonna get me that coffee?" She looks at him, then quickly pours him some coffee while looking back at the gray man and chuckling as the people still run out.

Spike asks her, "There ain't no guy or nothin' to restore the nation to order here?"

She replies, "He's probably downstairs. Fuck him. He'll come up. It's his store. I ain't tellin' him shit. That motherfucka wants me to master minimum wage. I don't have my degree yet."

The gray man is jerking himself off faster and faster now, and faster still, then shoots his orgasmic semen out onto the customer counter.

Dice, Spike and the waitress scream, "Whoa!" together at the accomplishment, and laugh as a short, slick, India ink black, shiny haired man storms out from the back with a white short-sleeved buttoned shirt and a fat black rayon tie.

Dice and the others watch him as he approaches the gray man, who now plops himself down in a chair and begins to silently weep in his open hands.

The short man shouts at him. "What the fuck're you doin'!! You from the IRS?? Is this a new tactic?"

The gray man sobs "I Am a Fugitive from a Chain Gang?... You seen it?... You seen the movie??..."

"What the fuck are you talkin' about?"

Dice and Spike are laughing along with the waitress.

The gray man says, "The movie.. You seen, th... the movie??"

"NO!! I didn't see it, ya trash! I'm gonna sell you to the gut busters in prison, you fuck! I"m gonna change legislation on your balls, you fuckin' heretic! Heretic!!"

Spike laughs out loud with the waitress and Dice. A police siren is heard approaching in sound. The man in the white shirt grabs up the gray man's coat collar and Dice and Spike laugh more.

"You're history fella!" the white shirted man tells his gray prisoner as he tries to pull him up now off the chair, but forgets he's not tall enough to lift him, so he loses his balance, stumbles and falls backwards on the floor. Dice and the others laugh harder as the gray man drops his head in his opened hands and starts weeping again.

Two policemen bust into the place-- guns drawn. One of them demands "Don't move!" and Dice and the rest don't move as the other officer spots the weeping gray man on the chair, with the white shirted man getting up off the floor behind him.

The gray man looks up to see the officer standing in front of him, now lowering his weapon.

"C'mon buddy," the officer says, "Let's go."

The gray man looks up at him. "I... I've seen the movie." Dice and Spike start snickering. The officer in front of them orders, "Outside people. Let's go," and the waitress, Spike and Dice walk outside and stand in front of the coffee shop, which is now half-crowded with onlookers.

Spike, standing with the others, comments to Dice and the waitress, "That guy's created a spectacle with a sense of humor. And he's outrageous."

"Yeah," Dice adds, "but I think he's sincere."

The waitress wonders, "Oh shit-- maybe I won't have to go back to work."

"Fat chance," Dice says. "That's the movies."
"What?" she turns to him in what-did-you-say style. "I don't believe I like your tone."
"Tone? I'm tryin' to be factual baby."
"Hey, hold up! You got some kind of medical record?..."
"I ain't got no problem at all! I--"

Spike grabs him. "Hey, we gotta go check out that thing man," and nudges Dice with his elbow to Let's go. Dice looks at him. Then he gets it, as the waitress says, "I hate snotty motherfuckas like you."

"I should go tell that guy in the coffee shop to fuck you. Go tell that guy in there you wanna be received, bitch."
"Kiss my ass. Go die in the subway, on the tracks, in urine."
"C'mon, let's move man," Spike says.

And Dice stares at her as he walks away with Spike. Then he remembers, "I didn't even get my damn coffee 'n shit." The waitress is not looking at him deliberately.

"Now that bitch right there?" Dice continues while they walk. "The nut in there, should've been shootin' his manhood right up in her. She acts like a real authentic cunt."
"True. She was troubled. I'll say that."

"Damn females make me sick. It's always something. I hate when three quarters of my brain is soaking up their image, then, they turn out to be turnips instead of ice cream, so you go to the bathroom to try to shit 'em out, and do they come out in the stool??... No!..."
"Let's check out that park up there."

As they begin to head up that way leaving the little crowd craning their necks at the coffee shop, Dice continues, "I sit on that toilet and strain and strain, and all that ever comes out is food waste. Not female waste."

"Maybe you can get some herbal tea for that, or something," Spike says.

The jigsaw shaped lime green trees surround tall the benches in the park, wagon train style, as the two walk into it, and between them. Several people are on the benches, here and there. On one of them is a light coffee tanned thirtyish looking man with wooden crutches. The smoke oozes from his mouth and slowly rises and swerves above his walnut brown closely cropped hair, as he turns and spots the two coming in. He waves.

"What's happenin' Martino," Dice says to him, reaching in his pocket for a cigarette. "What ju doin' down this way man?"
"Eh," Martino starts, "I felt like gettin' out the neighborhood for a little bit. You know... What's going on down there?" he asks, gesturing to the coffee shop.
"This old guy freaked out in there," Spike tells him. "You should've seen it."
"Yeah," Dice adds, "but it would never be a tv sit-com. It's too realistic. Who wants to be reminded of shit you see everyday."

The two drop themselves down on the bench to sit next to Martino. The smell of the marijuana Martino is smoking is pungent like a hard punch in the chest, and Dice comments on that aspect with a pleasing frown as he reaches for the joint when Martino hands it to him.

Spike says to him, "Guess what?"

"What?"
"Dice has been given somethin' sort of like a death sentence."
"Yeah," Dice agrees. "I'll set up a scenario for you."
"Awright," says Martino, waiting.
"Suppose your landlord came to your house banging on your door earthquake style, and you open it real quick and he tells you, 'You got thirty days to get out.' Now, would you summarize that as just having the beginnings of a bad day? or the beginning of a bad year?..."

Martino takes his joint from Spike, who just took a couple of drags from it, and thinks about Dice's question. "Hmm," he slowly moans. "That's what happened to you?..."

"Yep... You still sell guns?—Nah, forget it. What's that old sayin', Death is no solution?"
"Yeah," says Martino thinking, "but everybody does that now anyway. That ain't no Broadway production."

Spike agrees. "Yeah. Somebody's gotta come up with new forms of punishment. Punishment that means something to the psyche. Like lynchings."

"I tell you what," says Dice, sitting up taller on the bench as he takes the joint from Martino and takes a long drag on it. "I bet it wouldn't take me an eternity to think of something like that. If you've got an object that's diabolical enough, you can think of something. I wouldn't have poverty of thought on that one, I doubt it."
"Yeah," agrees Martino, thinking. "Sometimes... sometimes murder can be effective... but it's gotta be at the moment the guy's celebrating some kind of happiness... You know?..."

"Hey Mar," Spike says, turning and taking the joint from Dice, then handing it to Martino. "You don't have a degree in that do you?"
"Not exactly," Martino answers. "But... I got a friend, who's doing life upstate. He hipped me a little bit to how something like that is done... He's something like a politician. I mean he was into that... A lot..."

Dice kind of chuckles to himself. "How'd he get in there then? He didn't do a good job studying his favorite subject."

"I know... But, when you kill some guy who's got a campaign goin' to run for an Assembly District... it's kinda hard to treat it like you just killed some guy, who worked a hundred and sixty hours a week... on minimum wage."

Dice and Spike together, almost at the same time, nod their heads in "Hmmm" fashion agreeing with him.

After some time the two decide to move on. The joint that was once whole has moved on completely up to smoke and new dimensions as Dice and Spike slowly stand to stretch their limbs. Dice looks around a bit pausing for something, then he says to Martino, "Hey Mar, did you see Rosie around before you left the way?"

"Nah," Martino answers, staring across the street. "Hey, you see that female over there across the street?..."

Dice and Spike both look to see a five foot eight inch chestnut colored young lady twentyish in age, with celluloid black shoulder length hair and a polka dot black and white above-the-knee pleated dress. She walks steady with the movement of the calm wind, floating.

Martino reveals, "Everytime I see shit like that I say thank God for creation! No accident can make something so fuckin' beautiful like that again and again from time to time."

Then Dice asks Martino, "You know if Rosie went to her brother's in L.A. or not?"
"Nah. I don't know."
"Hmm... Yeah... so... we're gonna get up outta here," and Dice stretches his hand out to Martino for a handshake. Martino braces himself on his crutches to stand and when he's up, he gives Dice and Spike a shake of the hand.

"So I'll check you guys later," he says as he begins to walk, the longest leg taking the first step, while the other one just hangs above the ground. "I'm a head back around the way... You should come back around the way if ya gotta get out of your place Dice, you know?..."
"Where am I gonna stay at? With you and Darlene?"
"You come down there everyday anyway man."
"Nah. I been living alright with that as my past, like kindergarten. I've been my own man for five years now. If I settle my ass back down over there my progress will be as progressive as this asshole ordering me out of my place."
"Five years... It don't seem like you moved out only five years ago."

Dice begins to walk out of the park along with his friends. Martino heads in one direction and says "Later" to Spike and Dice while the two of them turn and head in the opposite direction. Then, a thud is heard. Dice and Spike both turn around quick to look.

They see Martino facedown on the ground with his crutches beside him. Dice and Spike just look at him without concern. Martino gradually begins to grab the crutches and raises himself up with them slowly. "I haven't smoked in a while," he reveals, laughing.

Dice is surprised. "I didn't know that. What, you were on some type of hiatus or something? I thought you kinda invented this smoking weed thing."

"Nah," Martino says, finally on his feet. "Sometimes... sometimes you have to relax the brain. But only for a second. If you go too long without thinking you can become nothing, or something that pretty much amounts to the same thing."

Dice and Spike proceed to wave good-bye to Martino again as he proceeds to step away a step at a time. They themselves head again in the opposite direction.

The evening returns quietly and soft, like the last one the night before when Dice was facing the Nix Club. This evening, he is before the Nix Club again-- a converted 1890s depot that once loaded grain and food goods. In the sun's day light, the exterior of the place is cranberry brown, but the night makes it look black like a non-lit tunnel.

The line to get in is orderly and roped single file in front of the place, with several bouncers towering above them by the length of a head. They look up and over the line as if they were shorter.

On the side of the club, where the sparseness in club goers and passersby are, Dice inches up casually beside the club's exterior wall. He watches the line slide up one quick step closer to the entrance of the club, but makes sure his image is not visible to the bouncers that are there.

A man passes by him and he slightly flinches a tad that wasn't noticeable. Still, Dice wonders now if he wasn't showing an obvious shade of apprehension, as he continues to watch the front of the place.

The bouncers there still stretch their necks to look at the crowd and over it, continuing to not spot Dice.

Dice himself stretches his chin closer towards the club's front door to get a better look. Then, an elbow swings over his head around his neck. One male figure in the darkness behind Dice, drags him backwards while continuing the hold him around his neck. Another male figure moves backwards along beside them.

Dice struggles wildly to get away as the two males drag him to a ghost town empty side of the street, strewn with broken glass bottles. The man then lets Dice go, dropping him down on his buttocks on the ground. He looks up at them.

One man has unruly dust brown hair with a matching complexion, while the other one's complexion imitated strawberry milk, with freckles splashed across his nose and carrot-tinged buzz cut hair.

They stand over Dice and look down at him. Dice, looking up, spits, "Awright! Granted! So here I am. This better be good, mothafucka."

The freckled one glares down hard at Dice to throw him some words. "I fuckin' think you're in the ultra wrong position to be mutterin' shit," he says, then looks over at his partner and asks, "Right?"

"Sí," the dust brown haired man answers, then laughs hyena-style without conviction.

Dice slowly stands himself up as if gathering his limbs up from different places. His eyes stay looking down at the ground as he raises himself. "Tell me this," he says to them. "Can any of you make yourself useful and tell me if you know where I can find an apartment?... Cheap, mothafucka?"

The men turn to each other and stare shocked. Then the freckled one asks, "Is he funnin' with us too much now?... Ain't he on trial here?..."

And as they still look at each other, Dice grabs a half broken quart of beer bottle beside him on the ground. Thrusts it forward, plunging the jagged edges of it into the freckled one's neck-- the back of it.

He (the freckled one) freezes shocked, gagging and flailing his arms wildly behind his head, grabbing the back of his neck, and bringing his hands back in front of him to see the thick blood drowning them. The dust brown colored man is shocked at the sight of his friend's bloodied hands and his gagging. He stands there.

Dice still has the empty half bottle in his hand watching him for a move, and the freckled man drops to his knees, with the blood drip dropping from his neck, the way melted ice cream does.

The dust brown man snaps out of his shock enough to realize he can get away. Dice gets ready, not knowing what to expect. Then the dust brown man looks at his friend in disbelief, calling "Jay!... Jay!..." Then, he runs out and away desperately.

Dice turns to the freckled one now, whose right side is down on the ground, while the left side is up, with the left hand thick with blood, holding the back of his neck, grunting.

Dice inches over to the front of him anxiously, stooping down a bit in front of him. His eyes bulge out mean now. "I need an apartment, mothafucka," he sprays through his teeth. "Can you, assist me, you scum drop?..."

The freckled man appears to try to answer him, breathing through his mouth, opened wide, loud and caustic. He tries to look at Dice but turns his head sideways, and stops midway before achieving that in full.

Dice still stares at him. "Can you help me?" he asks, getting a bit closer in his face.

The freckled man, still trying to answer with great effort, slowly takes his blood soaked hand away from his neck. He gradually moves it down slow along his left side, and, swipes out (quick) the nine millimeter automatic from the back of his belt.

Shocked, Dice stares a second at it, then at the freckled one-- who's struggling to get a good handle on the gun. Then Dice kicks the gun high out his hand, which lands and slides on the ground away from them, and he surprised himself at the effectiveness of the kick.

So he stands up now proudly and looks down at the freckled man struggling to do something. Then he takes his foot and kicks the freckled man's chin, who flips on his back now, tired from the gasping. He pants as his neck makes an additional puddle of blood on the ground.

Dice lowers himself down to his knees on the side of the freckled man's head to look at him. He stares at him hard, and sees that his eyes are closed now, half conscious.

"I said, I need an apartment. Can you help me live civilized, and not get thrown out?..." Dice asks him not expecting an answer, but just to get the pleasure of seeing him flat on his back.

Then, he notices a quarter inch piece of broken glass from the bottle he had on the ground. He picks it up right away, then places his left hand on the freckled man's forehead.

With the other hand, he slides the glass between his fingers and carefully places it underneath the freckled man's right eye, and now begins to scrape the skin off from underneath it with precision in downstrokes.

Five, six, seven times he strokes, scraping off the skin there, and keeps stroking, with the unconscious freckled man seeming to feel nothing, though he tries to shift his head from left to right in slow molasses movements.

Dice has now scraped off enough skin so that the slit shaped eye length scraping is now stark pink. He continues. Scraping in careful downstrokes, he takes his time as he scrapes-- the skin from it curls backwards and tumbles to the ground as a few blowing car horns are heard in the echoed distance.

The spot under the freckled man's eye is now glistening bloodshot red. Dice stands immediately up, dropping the glass in the blood puddle that's underneath the freckled man's head. The puddle is expanding at crawl-speed now, to the tips of Dice's dense black work boots.

Looking down at the freckled one, Dice unzips his pants like a military drill and whips out his penis. Carefully aiming at the freckled one's eye, he begins to urinate right on the spot under his eye where the scraping was made. The excess urine splashes upon the freckled man's eyes and brow, mimicking rain on concrete in sound. He moves not.

Chapter Two: Wut?

The next day, raindrops stampede the ground, cars and windowpanes, with its exuberance bordering on anger. The metal gray sky outside Dice's window looks painted and dirty from soot this nine o' clock morning, as he sits on the bed staring at the phone in the corner.

He stays staring at it, wondering something that wasn't enough to move him just yet to do anything, but stay staring at the phone. A few minutes pass before he finally gets up and walks over to it, backing against the wall and sliding himself down to the floor next to it.

He sighs deep unconsciously, as if waiting for something to happen. Then, he grabs the phone's receiver. He begins to dial a number. As he hears the other phone's ringing in the receiver he breathes deep inside, waiting for the ringing to end. On the third ring, a female answers with "Hello?"

"Hello," Dice says firmly, then nothing.

A moment of silence is hanging in the air for seconds until the female says, "Well... you've got nothing to say?..."

"I got something to say," Dice replies with a certain subtly. "Thanks for callin'."

She says nothing which allows silence to rule for more seconds. Then Dice proceeds, "I guess you feel I ain't nobody now."

"No," she says, as if that was unusually incorrect.
"That must be the deal. I can't remember when I heard your voice! My phone's still working."
"Well, I was gonna call you, but I knew you were gonna get into the same thing again if I did."
"And what's that, that I wanna see you?... Send the assassins then."
"Right. Ha, ha, ha. I'm dyin'."
"Send 'em. It must be a crime of some sort if I just wanna see you."
"But you don't wanna just see me. That's the thing."
"So now you're sorry you ever met me I guess. Right?"
"You're writing the dialog for me here."
"I'm the first dude I ever heard of who ever said the things that I said to a girl like you, Rosie."
"Hmmm."
"That oughta prove something."

Rosie pauses for seconds before saying, "But I can't see you."

"I know," Dice reminds himself. "I don't know what to say about that. Everything's all mixed up."
"You should just wait till I settle things with him like I said. He's due out soon, you know that."
"Five years-- he shoulda got twenty for misrepresentin' manhood."
"Don't even think about it."
"...slappin' around women..."
"She's lucky she's alive."
"...and for ten dollars, at that!..."
"Most people get killed."
"...ten dollars... How cool is that?"
"Not very."
"Listen... I'ma go, awright?"
"Alright."
"But you're still not gonna call me."
"I told you, I want things to be clean with me and him, and settled."
"But I said I don't care."
"But I do. And you should."
"Why."
"Oh, you don't care if I'm married? Then you don't care if nobody else is married either."
"What nobody else? This ain't no novel!"
"I don't want it to be."
"I'm not no gigolo or nothing. I don't do this for sport-- you think I do this for sport??"

"You're writing the dialog here."
"Well I don't do this-- look, what can I do to make you believe I'm serious? I've looked you right in the eyes. I've told you how I felt..."
"If you don't know how I feel by now then maybe you don't deserve me."
"I made up my mind already. You're mine, and I don't need a state law or decree to tell me if Tuesday is Tuesday. To-day is fucking Tuesday, and it is a rainy day!"
"Bye-bye Dice..."
"Awright. Bye."

And he hangs up the phone proudly as if he made an important point. Then he stands up and immediately shouts, "SHE WANTS TO BE FUCKIN' PURE!!!!..." and walks over to the closet, saying, "She is fuckin' pure!..."

Towards middle morning, the rain stayed stopped with the sky outside remaining painted blue gray. Dice is casually heading down the block to the neighborhood McDonald's for the breakfast special there.

The place inside is semi-filled with people, with some of them standing for orders while the rest of them are sitting and eating. Once Dice comes in (knowing he wants the Egg McMuffin special) he orders and receives his food, and searches the area for table sitting. Then he spots a guy with a Panama hat (brim turned up), munching away on his food, with his head down, reading something as he does this. Dice is glad to see the guy there, and onward he goes heading over to him.

With tray in hand, Dice happily sits in front of him. "What's happenin', Rue!" he says.

Rue looks up with a quick astonished smile, and sticks his hand out. "Where you been?" he asks, not intrusively but abrupt.

"Ehhh I been around," replies Dice, beginning his meal now after saying that. "But you, you've camouflaged yourself. Tell me how many times I've seen you this year."
"Probably more times not seen than seen," Rue responds while chewing. "I been upstate for a couple a years. You know, a little body laxative maintenance type cleaning, to get my non-dependent body functions back, like they were at the time of my birth 'n shit."
"Two years, huh," Dice replies, not wanting to reply. "It must be weird learning how to walk again I guess."
"It's like swearing before God you'll never say the word 'no' again, in every single sentence that you utter."
"Aww you'll be awright."

Rue finishes swallowing his chewed morsel before saying, "So... look at this..." He gestures to the paper cup of orange juice on his tray. Then he resumes, "Ain't you glad they serve this shit in paper cups instead of glass?..." Dice starts smiling knowingly to himself, saying nothing but eating.

Rue continues, "That glass... I can see people knocking that shit over all the time and breaking it on the floor... people, sliding on the pieces, bustin' their asses 'n shit... And we ain't even talkin' about what jagged pieces of glass can do."

Dice throws his hands up laughing. "Awright officer. You got me."

"Those were the guys that did it?"

"Nah," Dice replies while chewing. "The other guy that was there ran out."

Rue laughs out, not loud, but throwing his head back to do it. Then he repeats, "The other one ran out. Victory is comic too, huh?"

"Yeah but those weren't the guys that shot my brother anyway."
"Nah?"
"Nah. They were just playing enforcers... And I've been going back from time to time to that club to check for them too."
"Yeah, they probably shot outta town after doing that shit."
"I know... But I keep thinking maybe not. Life is serious and absurd."
"Right."
"So I figure... maybe shit can go just totally wacky as far as this goes, and the guys'll be in the same club they used to work at before they shot my brother."

Rue takes a gulp of his orange juice, and then after swallowing, "How's your grandma been holding out?"

"She's holding out okay I guess. But you know, she has always been between ham sandwiches and watercress soup. And she'll shout doctrine at you quicker than the 'up' in 'uprising.'"

The two laugh together in agreement. They both finish eating about the same time and just sit there. To change the subject a bit, Dice asks Rue, "You still drawing and painting?"

"Yeah, when I fit time in," Rue says as he still thinks his answer. "I do something now tho and it seems more macabre than Vincent Price. I feel like the coffin is closing and -- here they come! They got the nails! They gonna nail it now!"

"Hey how'd you find out about that?"

"About what?"

"The jagged glass asphalt alley behind the neck nightti--"

"Well look, you figure, you figure... that anybody from the Foxx Club, that gets wounded or fixed up in any way, everybody's gonna naturally assume it's you, just from the calculations alone."

"You heard people talking?"

"People talk. Naturally."

"Well, I don't give a fuck about that. Some people mourn differently you know. And besides that, I gotta get outta my apartment before the month's out. So right now, my anger matches a dude that's still mad, 'cause he had to eat mayonnaise sandwiches everyday for lunch and dinner, when he was living in the projects."

"You gettin' kicked out?"

"On top of death, an eviction is the meat sauce on top of the spaghetti."

"Damn. They're using you for target practice maybe."

"Maybe. That's why I've been thinking I've been showing too much of the playground side of me up to now."

"Maybe others might see it like that."

Dice stands up and gives his hands a napkin wiping. "Yeah," he finishes, "maybe I should get more serious about things."

"Like Stalin?" Rue asks, standing now, also wiping his hands.

Dice, in you-gotta-be-kidding fashion, looks at him and throws his hand get-outta-here style. "C'mon," he shoots. "Better than that. Juvenile I ain't."

The two walk out of McDonald's with their stomachs satisfied. Rue turns to Dice as they stand in front of the place and asks him, "Well, so what you gonna do?"

"About everything?" returns Dice. "I dunno. Right now I guess... I dunno. I gotta get a place somewhere real soon, that's law. But I also gotta find those guys. But with that, I'm almost sure they're gonna fall right into my hands anyway like rain falls on my head. And it always rains. Eventually it will rain, so why worry really."

Nighttime comes again, and this evening, in a half-wooded suburban area, with faint wood frame houses behind the stationary green leaves and bushes of spring, stands two native African-looking men about six feet in height, with statures like ancient warriors.

On their torsos are long-sleeved, dark dyed ink blue polyester shirts, with flower prints (both print shirts are different in the arrangement of the flower designs). The two are standing there off the dirt road that is before them.

In their hands they each have an end of a bright solid white cord. Neither appears nervous or hurried in the silence as they begin to stand apart more to extend the cord.

The largest bush between them is what they step closer to, still holding the cord, but tightening the stretch of it so that it is firm-- they step further back to align themselves with the bush.

Officially they raise the cord up and simultaneously lower themselves lower than the bush itself, which makes them unseen. They stay down there for a few more seconds before rising up again, without the cord.

The two step forward now, over the shrubbery to the dirt road. They stop and stand there casually, looking pleasant, appearing to be waiting for something. They are patient, and they say nothing to each other.

A few seconds later, a white 1953 Buick Skylark convertible (matador red interior, black top up) pulls up in front of the two. They both climb into the back of the car with routine casualness that borders on mechanical. The car then drives off, leaving the area even more silent than its previous silence.

Back in the city, Dice is at the end of a cashier's line in one of the huge electronic store chains, and standing in front of him is a short, four eleven eightyish, elderly woman. Her straight silver gray hair has not one strand standing up alone as it goes all the way back into the bun behind her head, and her skin has wrinkles of wisdom. Her look is Native American.

Dice has a package of blank audio tapes in one hand, and the other one he places on the woman's shoulder. "Stand back Grandma," Dice says to her. But as soon as the customer in front of her receives his packages and change from the cashier girl and walks away, and as soon as the cashier girl turns her back to rummage through something on a shelf in front of her, Dice's grandmother reaches over the counter and deliberately mashes all the keys on the cash register there.

"Grandma!" Dice busts out.

Grandma turns to him childlike and laughs hiccup style, showing the rot in the few yellow teeth that she has left in her mouth. "I like to screw up their system every chance I get," she says, and laughs her hiccup laugh out again with the look of mischievous satisfaction.

Dice grabs his grandma's elbow. "C'mon grandma," he says, ushering her away after he gets his package and change from the cashier. Grandma is chuckling at the thought of her insurrection as she leaves the store with her grandson.

Outside in front of the place is where the two stop for Dice to advise her. "Ma," he begins. "You're gonna get us thrown behind bars, or if not that, just plain harassed."

"I don't care," spurts Grandma. "I like to see authority's reaction to truth. You should've let me see the girl react."

"Ma," Dice patiently explains, "she was just a cashier. A regular worker. What kinda wisdom would she have? She's probably just trying to eat."

"Pooh! That's no excuse." She hiccups her laugh out again. "If she has any brains, she would care about things like that. Hurrah!"

"Hurrah Grandma," Dice utters as he loosely guides his grandmother (who walks perfectly without the need for it) across the street.

They walk down sidewalks filled with stores and shoppers on the outside and inside of them. Fish markets and discount spots abound here, and the street has parked and double-parked cars sitting still-- the heat scent from their running engines fill the atmosphere, as Dice and his grandmother walk past them.

"Your brother," Grandma begins to point out, "God rest his soul but he was an asshole, you know that, right?"

Dice sighs before he says, "It still don't make it right for somebody to just come along and pop him."

"You're right," Grandma agrees. "Granted. He still was an asshole. How many times have I told him to not hang around with the stupidies. How many times have I told him that? How many?"

"Trying to count is unnecessary."

"That's right. Look at him now. He makes me so angry lying in that damn ground like that. I could kill him! When you mother asked me to take care of the both of you before she died, what d'you think she would've told me if she was looking at his outcome in a crystal ball while she was in the hospital?"

Dice hunches his shoulders for I don't know.

"Well," Grandma continues, "she would've said Pooh!... If that's the outcome, then I drop him on his head. Hurrah."

"C'mon Grandma. She wouldn't have said that."
"Like that no good father of yours. Quick!-- who is he? What's his name?"
"I stopped looking for that in grade school."
"Well who can blame ya... There's no point in it. He means only something to your mother as a one-night stand."

They continue past stores and passerby shoppers until they turn a corner, where residential two-story copper brown brick houses line the sidewalks. Grandma changes the subject by asking Dice, "How's your place? Your apartment, how is it?"

"It's awright ma," he says with a brush.
"You let me in only one time since you've been there... You got bodies buried there?..."
"No."
"Oh... You got... you got, some kind of embarrassment thing going on with Grandma?..."
"No ma, of course not... You know how it is. A guy wants his space and all that."
"You're not clandestine are you? I can't stomach that. That's why things are the way they are now."
"Nah ma, I ain't clandestine."

They both turn and head towards the front of one of the houses. Dice sticks his hand out to Grandma as if he always does this, and she immediately hands him her keys in the same way. Dice sticks a key in the door's keyhole right away and opens it.

They stop by the staircase in the foyer while Dice opens another door with the keys. He then enters through that one with Grandma sliding her feet behind him following.

Grandma's apartment is small and lit dingy, due to the grease-filmed lampshades on the two oval end table lamps that are colored pineapple. The place is splashed with 1950s flower prints on the lightbulb dim wallpaper, and a forest green armchair. Three gold colored cats and a kitten scatter about not too wildly as they come in. "Stop making a ruckus," Grandma says to them as she slides her feet over to the hulking burnished red sculptured dining table to sit.

Dice looks the place over as she does, walking from here to there, looking at this and that. "You got enough here to eat, ma?..."

"Say that I'm stupid," she replies. "Give me no credit for any kind of brain work."
"C'mon Grandma..."
"Faculties?... Pooh!-- I've got faculties! You can't accuse me of Milton Berleisms in real life by any stretch of the imagination."

Two tap knocks are heard on the door. Dice immediately goes over to answer it and sees an elderly fish gray haired woman, standing about five feet. She moves no muscle with a serious expression, but before Dice can question her or his grandmother, she shoots out a sliver of spit that almost lands on Dice's chest completely.

She looks up at him and announces, "You mother, she no play fair. She play like mobster."

Grandma is craning her neck now over there to see who it is, then slaps her hand on the table to rise up quick. "Who's that!!" she fires. "Is that Angie??... Stay the hell outta the bingo hall!!"

    "She no play fair" the woman continues (Dice standing there stunned). "Mobster! Mobster lady!"
    "Is that Angie??... Angie!... Stay the hell outta the bingo hall!. You, politician!!..."
    "You son, he is unlucky! I have pity for him, you witch."
    "I'm gonna wring your neck you spy! See what my penalty is for sore losing!..."

And she takes a step forward to get her but Dice swiftly slams the door before she does. The elderly woman is still standing there behind it, saying "Hey mobster lady!..." and tapping her knocks against the door again.

Dice is holding back Grandma, who is now steamed with agitation. "Come back here you swine!! she attacks. "You wanna act like you're running for office with me??... Hurrah! Let me strike you off the record!..."

Dice still holds Grandma as she flails and grapples to get the door's knob to open it. Then he yells at the door, "Lady, go home!" but her two taps are heard on it again. And Grandma yells out, "Re-elect yourself and come back in here! I'll show you how to stay out the bingo hall!..."

The woman returns, "You, carpetbagger!" as Dice begs her, "Lady! Please go away!"

Grandma still struggles to break away from Dice. "She's not gonna go away," she balks at the door. Dice then holds his hand up for her to quiet down, as he listens to the door for a few moments. "I think she left," he practically whispers.

Then, he gradually eases his hand over to the doorknob and opens the door gradually. The two of them see nothing but space where the woman was standing.

    "Look ma," Dice says, closing the door relieved. "You see? She's gone now finally."

"Gone?" Grandma says with disbelief. "I wanted her to come in, so I could twist her political exactness around her neck!"
"C'mon and sit back down Grandma," he says, ushering her back to the table. "And that far right son of hers... I'll tell them all he's a fascist! along with herself!"

As he sits her back down he stoops down beside her. "Look Grandma, you really gotta start controlling yourself more. What's everybody gonna start saying-- 'Oh, she should be put away. He should put her away.' Everybody's gonna start suggesting that if you don't calm yourself more. And then they're gonna look at me."

"Pooh! What do they know? They know nothing, that's what they know! They know how to continue to serve the government master. Just serve it. Serve the government master and leave me alone, that's what I say. What do they know?... They're only as good as what they're told to be good at. The nerve of them..."

"Look ma... You can't tackle on every major issue of importance that's bothering you. Just the ones that's trying to make you less than yourself. But that woman was hardly an agent, or even political for that matter."

"Everything's political! I bet ya your landlord's affiliated with some ridiculous party or thought that wants to assassinate your peace."

"Why'd you say landlord?"

"It's all the same. What difference does it make? If I had a said girlfriend, what difference does it make? Pooh!-- rebellion is rebellion. No matter who it's against..."

"Yeah... I guess they're all authority when you boil it down."

Chapter Three: Who Sez I Ain't?

The next day which is morning, Dice awakes to the sounds of clanging metal, hammers hitting on wood, and distant male voices downstairs underneath. And with that, he rises from bed and heads down the stairs.

The clanging comes closer to his ears as he trots downstairs, and there!-- at the foot of the staircase stands four white T-shirted men, cigarette smoke from them climbing wiggly up through the air, as they hammer and talk and hammer and laugh, and rip out sections of the wood inside.

Dice stands there for a second looking at them as they don't look at him. For a second he thinks about saying what's going on, but doesn't. "What's the point," he says under his nose. Then he heads back upstairs through the destruction of banging and the mist of plaster powder.

Back in his place Dice stares out the window for a moment, then plops himself down on the floor next to the phone. He picks up the receiver and starts to dial a number but changes his mind. Then he looks at the wall. An iron thump from downstairs jolts him, but he remembers there are workers down there. He immediately stands, then walks out the door of his place to the outside's morning.

In the half-wooded suburban area where the two native African-looking men had appeared with the white cord, the morning's sunlight aims at the spot where the men stood, which is now supplied with the body of a twentyish Latino male, hanging up high from a horizontal brilliant white cord. The cord: one end is tied to a telephone pole, the middle of it wrapped around the man's neck, while the other end is tied to a tree.

The corpse, drooped, slow swings a bit forward and back, lethargic like the morning's wind. And the emptiness of spectators remained nil at the sight and proved that the morning was too early for viewers to be there. But after a few eternal moments, the first scream for the day (a woman's) is heard in the distance.

Dice on the other hand, is walking through an area which is known as a worker's ghost town. Behind and in front of him (as well as the sides) stand the buildings which served as factories in the region at one time, all now closed.

As he walks, the emptiness provides nothing but the sound of his footsteps against the concrete. The facades of the buildings wear chipped lily pad green paint, and some of the buildings of seven stories have wooden barn-type doors the same color, showing their turn of the century style.

Dice walks on and pays no attention to the demise of one-time production here. He walks, staring one way as he does.

Behind him he hears the sound of a car's engine approaching, but doesn't turn around. There's a battleship gray 1971 Dodge Dart pulling up beside him now.

Inside the car is a mid-twenties man with charcoal dark eyebrows and a shaved bald head. The diamond earring in his left earlobe sparkles and flashes against Dice's eye as the man asks him, "Hey baby, you gotta match?..."

Dice stops and looks, checks his pockets, and pulls out a lighter. He comes closer to the man to hand him the lighter and asks, "What happened, the car's lighter is dead?"

The man lights his cigarette with no expression to indicate if he will answer Dice or not. But now Dice is staring at him in disbelief, seeming to recognize him.

The man however answers. "Yeah," he moans out, then taking a long drag on the cigarette to light it. "The shit is out."

"Oh shit!" Dice exclaims. "You look like my girl's cousin!... Check it out, do you know this girl?..." And Dice reaches in his back pocket again while the man curiously waits there-- his head stuck out the window.

Dice swipes a short bright white cord out his pocket. The man's eyes flash open stunned as Dice, swiftly swings it around his neck and pulls it hard, choking him. "Is my brother in heaven mothafucka??..."

The man winds his neck around to get it away and his cigarette tips out his mouth. Dice pulls the cord harder and harder, his mind drifting away somewhere else now distant. He strengthens his pull on the cord and hears the faint sound of someone gasping for air far away. He feels like he's off the ground and moving.

He is moving!-- the man's foot is pressed on the accelerator as Dice sees the two of them rocketing towards a building. Dice releases the cord and lands in the street on his back. The car smashes head-on into the building like a stock car race.

Dice now springs himself up and scrambles to run away and does-- heading down a thin cobblestone side street, he keeps going, unseen. The car explodes and he hears it while he runs.

Spike's bedroom is cramped with things and crowded with clothes. Things like broken irons, reclining pole lamps long in demise, and above the calf sweat socks.

Crusty speckled ash brown work boots crookedly support themselves up in the corner, next to a mound high pile of sheets. Spike sits on that as he listens to Dice, who's sitting on top of a dingy white broken 1964 portable Zenith tv.

Dice says with importance, "That was one of them tho, that's all that counts."

"You think he saw white before he crashed or after?" Spike wonders.
"Don't matter now really," Dice decides. "All that matters is one more left is better than having forty more left. I'm in real life, and life for me at this point means an eye for an eye."
"When you had the rope around his neck, was he like... 'Lawd ham mercy!... Lawd ham mercy!...'" Spike tumbles over letting his giggles spill out.

Dice thinks about the question for a few seconds. "Nah," he says proudly. "He was quite sincere about his end."

"You should say that with a British accent."

Dice clears his throat, and prepares his British accent. "Um, I say... he was quite sincere about his end..." and the two of them cackle laugh, moving their limbs rubbery like rubber.

They settle down now and Dice stands up to look out the window there, where baby shoe boxes filled with old G.I. Joe soldiers are piled. "The point," he details, "is the word'll go around that I'm an assassin, or some shit that's equally bizarre."

"True."
"A very American conclusion and assumption... that I'm some kind of assassin or some shit."
"Of course... People like to look up to something I guess."
"Yeah well, I'm on a different mission... Actions have gotta have a purpose as far as I'm concerned."
"Don't you think it would've been better to just plain ol' shoot his ass, like everybody else does?..."
"Eh-- I don't know."
"After all, death is only death."
"Yeah, I know," Dice moans. "I'm at a stage now where getting the job done is the most important."

After a moment of wondering, Spike goes over to the window and says to Dice, "You think a lot of people around here are gonna think you did that?"

"Well, you know how things get. Somebody's gonna put two and six together around there somewhere and assume."
"Yeah. But they'll probably be a scared a you, Mister Dice."

Dice thinks about that as Spike continues. "They're probably gonna think maybe, he could have my head removed or something... Hey!-- you think he got decapitated in the car crash?..."

Dice shrugs disregard. "Eh... Fuck him..." Then he plops himself back down on the tv. "What the hell am I gonna do about this landlord, man?"

"You giving him a graveyard too?"
"Nah. And at that point, I might as well be professional at it then if I'm gonna do that."
"That's sharp. How much can you get for ending people?"
"I dunno. This fuckin' landlord... I can't believe I gotta take my mind, and place it somewhere to work, in an area that should already be settled as far as peace goes. The last thing I should be thinking about is where I'm gonna be living next month."

"Hey, but if you were doing a bounty hunter profession, would that be special, salary-wise?"

"Probably. Death is a good business, legal or otherwise."

Suddenly a commotion is heard outside. Dice and Spike do abrupt looks at each other. Then they both lean forward and look out the window.

Downstairs they see a crowd of teenagers in front of a playground situated in the middle of the block. Two teenage males are in the center of the crowd, and the two of them trumpet their voices at each other back and forth with force.

Seconds grow on and more thunder creeps into the tone of their voices as they continue throwing them at each other. Then, one swings a roundhouse punch at the other, landing it with an explosion thump on the guy's chin.

The struck man falls back backwards on the ground. The crowd oohs and ahhs. Then the hitter reaches behind his back and pulls out a small white silver automatic pistol. No one moves back.

He fires the gun twice, hitting the other on the ground. The crowd individually says "Oh shit" while Dice and Spike say "Oh shit" simultaneously in the window.

The man who fired his weapon officially pockets it now and walks away, with a few members of the crowd following him. The several remaining crowd members stay with the grounded wounded man, standing over him.

Dice asks Spike as they still watch, "Who was that guy?"

"I don't know," Spike says squinting. "I think it was Raymond... wasn't it?..."
"I don't know. I don't live around here anymore. I don't know who the hell these new subjects are."
"Let's go down and check it out," Spike says. They both then quickly leave the place.

Downstairs outside a few more people have gathered at the spot where the young man was shot. They talk amongst themselves, rapidly moving their hands with vigor, explaining, describing in multitudes like the pitter-patter of rain.

Dice and Spike step up to the group with Dice stretching his neck a bit up to get a good look at the victim down there. "Anybody called the ambulance yet," he asks anybody.

A short fortyish man with a white/gray tweed cap answers. "Ambulance?... When they'd last come here when somebody called?" he asks.

A large round sixtyish woman with a shabby house dress proclaims, "They ain't comin'. What they comin' for? And when they do come, it be too late-- is he dead?..."

Beside the wounded teen, a young woman kneels and places her hand underneath his nose. "He's barely breathing," she reveals, and moves her hand away quick, to not get something.

"Well," the large woman continues, "watch how long they gon' take if they do get here," she declares, nodding her head once for exactness.

A tall thin man in auto mechanics clothes (leaning against the fence there) suggests, "Well if they do come late, they oughta answer for it."

Towards the end of the fence, a medium height woman with cornrow braids beyond her shoulders, and black rimmed glasses, instructs the man with, "That wouldn't be wise brother, to do that. If we did that they would never come anymore."

And the large woman jumps in with "They don't come now! What's the point??"

The woman with the braids calmly enunciates, "The point being, that we just can't go chargin' off to war every time some kind of injustice is breathing down our necks."

Two other male teens-- one holding a large green portable radio-- laugh while the other says "A point well taken..." and switches the radio on, which thrusts out funk music that jumps out of the speakers, and blares over everyone's voices. The teens immediately turn and head away chuckling. Folks look at them.

Finally the ambulance pulls up with no siren, only the usual circling red light, circling patiently around, lighting the spectators' faces red in flickers as it circles around, with the vehicle creep-rolling onto the block as it goes.

The large woman points one of the two ambulance attendants in the truck to the victim on the ground, yelling "He's over here!" to him as if he were totally unable to see him.

He gets out and strolls over to the victim. The man in the mechanic's uniform stares down at him sarcastically. "Take ya time now. Don't walk too fast..."

The attendant, who has a medium sized Afro, stops. He turns slow like oozing syrup to the man. "What the fuck did you say diarrhea?"

"Aww shit," the mechanic stamps the palm of his hand on the fence. He looks at everybody looking at him. "Now what am I supposed to do about something like that?..." he asks actually waiting for an answer.

The attendant is standing there waiting, looking at him. The mechanic drops his head down, not shamefully but down— turns himself back around like all is forgotten.

The attendant then giggles sudden and uncontrollably. "What an artifact!" he releases, walking and heading now to the shot victim on the ground.

Wham! on the back of the head (the mechanic hits him there). The crowd individually sighs "Oh shit," as the attendant sinks down to his knees on the ground.

The mechanic looks down at him (hand on hip) and heaves a "Ha!" holding a wrench in his other hand. "Where you think you at customer, Mayberry?..."

The attendant is on his hands and knees. He shakes his head violently to the left, right, left right-- trying to get the kinks out. Then, he slowly climbs to his feet with everyone's eyes painted wide open behind him and around him.

He glares at the mechanic who still looks at him. Swaying and almost wobbly, he snarls, "I'm gonna hang your ass you fuck!" and tries to swing a feeble punch at the mechanic, who blocks it with the wrench-- it makes a thud sound on the attendant's arm, hurting him.

The crowd groans "Oooh!" at that, as the second attendant finally jumps out of the ambulance, blinding with rage. His short stature storms over to the mechanic, and he raises his hand, armed with a mirrored silver flashlight long in length.

The mechanic sees him coming. The first attendant is acting like his arm is broken, holding it. The second attendant volumes a scream at the mechanic, emphasizing with his flashlight, "You bastard!!... You devious bastard!!..."

He leaps on the mechanic and they both crash to the ground and roll. The crowd spews excitement like playground laughter, and the voices are stadium orders and commands.

A woman in the back horns out, "Ooh Lord-- they breakin'!" as the flashlight and wrench lie dead on the ground now and the mechanic wrestles with the second attendant, and wrestling, they roll over the shot victim. The blood puddles that lay on the ground from the victim become mashed and expanded from the rolling.

The crowd is a vocal orchestra of voices, mingled with rooting styles and mangled with some laughter. The mechanic is on his back and the second attendant jumps on him. He punches the mechanic's face hard once, and then again, twice, sending the mechanic's awareness to unconsciousness.

The crowd hoots "Oooh!" in almost approval as the second attendant reaches in his back pocket. He pulls out a small two inch pocket knife and takes his fingernail inserting it in the groove on the blade to pull it out. He slides it out.

He takes it in his index finger with pained glee, inches himself over to the mechanic's head, and gets up closer nose to nose to the mechanic as the crowd watches.

He takes the pocket knife (using the flat part) and places it under the mechanic's left eye and carefully begins to scrape the skin underneath it. A male voice from behind declares "He's acting like a child!"

The second attendant begins to carefully scrape the skin under the mechanic's eye (who continues to be out cold). The crowd grows more silent and interested as he continues scraping, carefully peeling the skin off there as it curls backwards and slides jaggedly down the mechanic's cheek.

The second attendant scrapes very carefully underneath the mechanic's eye as the heads of the crowd moves closer to get a better look. He scrapes the skin there until the outer layer is removed, exposing the pink glistening layer that lay underneath it.

Suddenly he stands up and the crowd rears their heads back when he does this. Dice is frowning at the second attendant, as he sees him unzip his pants. Dice then turns to Spike. "C'mon," he spurts, "let's go. All we got is copycats around here!"

As Dice and Spike turn and head away from the crowd, a simultaneous "Ohhh shit!" yell is heard from them as the two continue to walk through the housing project, not looking back. Spike says, "What now?"

"About what, about everything?" asks Dice.
"Yep."
"I dunno. I still think everybody's tryin' to challenge my good nature. Put any warrior in my position and what the fuck you think they'd do, sing?..."
"Unlikely," says Spike, as his eyes attach themselves to a shapely female walking.
"See, people think an eye for an eye means revenge. Incorrect. An eye for an eye means education."
"Yeah, I get ja."
"'Cause even if you're life is going before you while it's ending, you're getting the education that you can't do that shit and get away with it, whatever it is."
"Right, right."

"And the bonus... If reincarnation's a reality, hallelujah!-- the next time around you'll fuckin' know better."
"Here here."

They continue walking through the neighborhood, aiming themselves no where in particular until Dice suggests, "You wanna see the future of the working class?"

"Alright," Spike replies. "I'll bite."

Dice then gives his friend a head gesture to make a turn with him at the Chinese restaurant at the corner, and he does.

A few minutes later the two are standing in front of Dice's building, listening to the destruction going on inside. Dice turns to Spike and tells him, "The reception's better inside." Taking out his keys he opens the door and they enter.

The mist white dust inside touches their faces like breath against a glass in the winter. Wood and metal bangs drown out thought. Pieces of plaster drop hard on the floor while the male workers talk excitedly like a Greek chorus untrained in meter and music.

Dice just stares at the scene helplessly. "It's a wonder of humanity ain't it? Shit don't get better than this occasion."

"I feel like my life's in danger here," Spike says.
"You wanna get a better sound of it?..." And before Spike answers, Dice heads up the staircase to his place with his friend following.

The noise and din inside Dice's apartment replicates the clamor heard down the stairs when they come in. Spike looks up at Dice to say, "I'm stumped. This quiz tells me I'm hearing the same shit."

"The same??... Nah, the shit is louder in here. My eardrums are like sixties demonstrators, protestin'."
"Well either way, it's loud," Spike remarks, heading for the door, wanting to leave.

Dice is just standing there looking helpless at the ceiling. Spike suggests "Hey, let's go check out Bob or something, man. You got a critical situation in this land."

"I know. Anarchy is living here... I thought a man had some kind of justification for destruction when he does it. But look at this shit."
"Let's just get outta here."
"Here... Just think, I live here."
"For now."

"True... For now."

The two leave Dice's place and step out of the building showing looks of shell shock. After some seconds pass Dice snaps out of it. "You still wanna check out Bob?"

"Yeah, we ain't seen him in a while," Spike says with a start.
"Yeah, I guess... But Bob has a habit of creatin' drama all the damn time. Guess who's had enough of that?"
"I hear ya."

They begin walking away from Dice's building. Moderately they continue down the block which contrasts Roberts Street, showing the sparseness of empty store front three-story buildings inhabited there.

Here comes a cop car cruising up behind them, pulling up slowly to a stop-- Dice and Spike turn around and see it, but turn back around with disregard.

One wide-sized alabaster color officer standing six-three gets out and says "Hey" to them, closing the car door. Dice and Spike stop, while a shorter officer with a Mexican tinge also gets out of the car.

The friends stand there waiting as the six-three cop comes closer, smiling at Dice only. The shorter one approaches also. He smiles at both Dice and Spike.

The six-three cop addresses Dice. "Where you boys heading?" he says, then looks down at where Dice's penis is.

"We're going to a friend's house," Dice responds with another thought in his head.

The shorter cop grins at his partner.

The six-three cop says, "Uhh..." looking Dice in the eye, then staring back down at where his penis is. He looks back up at Dice and wipe-licks his upper lip quick. "You got fuckin' I.D.?"

"Yeah," Dice says, and starts reaching in his back pocket.

The short cop utters "Easy now" to Dice, smiling.

Dice slides his wallet out slow and careful not to alarm the officers and hands it to the six-three one, who takes it, looks at it for a few seconds, and hands it back.

"You know," he begins, glancing at Dice's penis area, "we've been gettin' a lot of complaints about--" he stops himself abruptly, his eyes up in the air, wondering. "Are you guys responsible for all that shit going on in the projects right now?..."

"No," Dice explains. "We were there before, today, but that's because my friend lives there," and he's pointing his finger at Spike.

Spike says "Yeah, I live there," to the officers, who seem not to care.

The six-three cop waves his hand "no" side to side. "That's not the point that interests me" he balks. Then he gets closer to Dice's face. "There's some shit goin' on in that animal project down there, and I wanna know if yous know anything about it..."

The short officer giggles as Dice and Spike both say "no," with Dice adding, "We don't know about it."

The six-three cop then rolls his head back seeming satisfied. He does a quick glance at Dice's penis area again but turns quick to his partner. "What d'you wanna do?" he asks.

The shorter officer almost bursts out with laughter but holds it in. "Let's... let's tell 'em a secret," he says back to him, resting his palm on his gun handle. He smiles halting his giggle.

The tall cop angers back "No!" to him, and heads immediately back to the car, throwing open the door. The short cop still stands in front of the doom-expecting friends, not completely suppressing his giggles.

The six-three officer (in the car now) yells "C'mon, Tim!" to the shorter one, and he, Tim, looking at the friends, says in verifying tone, "See?... I'm traditional," and walks over to the patrol car, getting in.

Dice and Spike stand there watching as the patrol car pulls off down the street, cruising in the manner that it came. Dice's eyes are still on the fading car leaving as he says, "You see that fuckin' shit?"

"Yep," agrees Spike.
"And then they have wonders about what's wrong with the town." Then he starts emulating, 'They don't let us protect them. They throw bottles at us.'"
"What the hell was the plan, Dice?"
"I don't wanna guess. I'm puttin' a ban on it. What good will it do?"
"None. No good."

They return to walking back down the block as before. Spike looks at Dice and wonders, "What's to stop them from coming back around? You think they gonna do that?"

"They can do anything. It's been proven."

The two reach the corner where fortysomething men stand around in conversation, the gestures from them slow in motion, moving clumsily to make some points. Dice and Spike walk past them, turning the corner. Dice then asks, "So whudya think, you think I should release this landlord's bowels or what?"

"You professional now?" returns Spike.
"Somehow the thought is combing my hair back, It's tugging at me now for some reason."
"Maybe it has something to do with our enforcement confrontation."
"It might."
"Cops make a lot of things unnecessary."

Dice shoots a clump of yellow spit out on the ground. "Year after year," he says, "I get the impression that I'm on the wrong track."

Spike hums a "Hmm," listening.

"I think maybe I should consider something that'll give me leverage in life."
"Hmm."
"Maybe I should get a steady job or something."
"What, you got connections?"
"Connections..." Dice reflects, reaching for his pack of cigarettes with disgust. "Connections in this episode mean Smith & Wesson."
"Maybe you can get hooked up with the post office again?"
"Nah, fuck that. I ain't goin' back there. I made my money, saved it, left. That's it. It served its purpose."
"I hear that."
"While everybody was busy participating in the fashion show entering the joint every fuckin' day, I was putting my dough in hiding."
"I remember."
"I wasn't gonna sit around in there forever, thinking they were gonna serve me, forever, or even offer me a package."
"I know. Better to show wisdom than an asshole."
"And wisdom's not natural... You gotta work at gettin' it... Maybe get a few bruises and knocks in the head cowboy style."
"Indeed."
"You gotta earn it, that's for sure. The shit don't come natural, that's certain."
"Right, right."

"So fuck goin' back there. That's like tampering with a natural phenomenon whose intentions are good."
"Hmm."
"I made my money, therefore I am."
"And now, you gotta get a new place," Spike adds with a frustrated sound.

Dice looks at him. Thinks about it. He returns no answer.

The two walk past scores of young men standing on the store- filled blocks, which is in another housing project district. Talk and laughter ride over passing car engine sounds and various dance music sounds emanating from diverse directions and places.

They walk past liquor stores lit and decorated with a.m. alcoholics, while requests for passerby change come from those smiling with hands out, or frowning with hands in pockets.

Their requests were in demand tones, and a couple of the guys approach Dice and Spike in that manner, nearly bumping into the two native African looking men who had the white cord, who now walk past Dice and Spike, casually.

One of the guys asking for change aims himself at Dice, saying, "Hey brother..."

Dice immediately declares. "No money, man. I'm thinking about servicing funeral parlors right now."

The native African looking guys hear that-- looking at each other. They glance behind at Dice while still walking.

The guy asking for change tells Dice, "You better be careful now, bruh. They got instruments out here causin' casualties, walking--"

"I know, man," Dice cuts. "We just ran into some of them."
"Right," the guy replies, hard-scratching the right side of his head, then hesitantly adding, "So listen bruh, all I need is a quarter--"
"We're busted man" Dice declares with a hard wave of the hand.

Spike slows his walking a bit reaching in his pocket, pulling out a dime and handing it to the guy. "It's a dime, bro," he says, keeping pace with his friend.

The guy stands there speechless but satisfied as Dice and Spike continue down the block away from him. The two native African looking men are still in front of the two, looking back at them.

Spike tells Dice, "We got fans in front of us. You know those guys?"

"Nah," he says with quickness in it. "I never seen 'em before."

Everyone continues walking a few steps until the second African looking man on the right turns completely around, stops in front of Dice (abruptly halting him in his tracks) with Spike and the first African looking man on the left stopping along for measure.

The second African addresses Dice. "Excuse me, my brother," he begins, in politeness bred outside of America. Dice is standing there expecting the next unknown with eyes wide open. Spike is standing there waiting and wondering also.

Continuing, the second African goes on, "Forgive me for overhearing the conversation you were having with the gentleman."

Dice looks at Spike and asks pointing, "Who, him?"

"No no," the second African corrects. "The gentleman back there who was in need."

Dice thinks a second or two, then remembers. "Oh. You mean my man back there."

"Yes... yes, that's right."
"Well... what did you hear, what about him?"
"On the contrary, it is nothing about him that I am concerned with."
"So, what's happenin"?"

The second African does a slight chuckle. "Again I must say forgive me, but it sounded like we might have the same interests lying inside us..."

Dice thinks for more seconds. "I don't know what you're talking about brother man," he carefully utters. "This conversation hasn't even lasted a minute yet, and to this point is how much we know each other."

"Indeed you are correct. But something in the reality of funeral parlors, always incites my interest... Especially when it touches on me and my brother's profession." And he points to the first African looking man who smiles teeth at Dice.

Dice reflects a second glancing at Spike, who stares numbness on what should be said. He then says to the second African, "Oh, I see. Are you also like an employer? And do you employ equally, as far as opportunity goes?"

Both Africans smile at each other with understanding, then the second one responds to Dice, saying, "Perhaps we can talk in a place that is more favorable to seclusion?"

And the Africans along with Dice and Spike turn, walking in another direction with Dice leading.

Down a side street they head where one side is occupied by an old folks home in cinnamon brick construction (taking up the length of the block in capacity) while the other side of the street bears a park that contains spaciousness and emptiness from people. The group goes inside the park and take seats on benches.

The second African admits to Dice, "I am quite impressed with your willingness to exchange our interests."

"That depends," Dice answers. "While we were walking up here you were talking about reasons for carrying out orders. What, that makes you able to do your assignments without thoughts of divine payback?"

The African just smiles at him. "Why should I talk with you about this?"..."

Dice can't believe what he hears as he looks at Spike (who also can't believe it) and the first African, who smiles his pearly whites again in his direction. Then Dice fires, "Wait a minute! You summoned my fuckin' interest. I was just ho-humming the day in negative thought on how I was gonna live beyond animal status."

"Ha haa!" the second African roars. "I see you have emotion! That is not a good thing. It makes you vulnerable to capture, and ultimately incarceration."

Dice reflects on that. "What makes you think I wanna divvy up with your operation? And what is it anyway? Don't think I don't know the history of setting up set-ups in this country."

"I am sure that you do. But you will admit that I am correct about my statement on emotion?"
"How would I know that?"
"Because look at me..." The second African takes his hand and sweep-gestures to himself from head to toe. "I am the picture of calmness, and I am sure I have returned more flesh to the soil than you yourself have."
"How do I know that? What's verification in your eyes?"
"Very well..."

The African then looks down at the ground of the park while the others look on with wait in their eyes. He then spots a squirrel moving around a small area of trees. Looking at everyone, the second African tells them "Observe..." and gradually stands, casually strolling over to where the squirrel is.

Quick! like lightning he grabs the squirrel's tail. Hoists him up (his little paws kick frantic scurrying). He grabs the squirrel's head, palms it. Twists it around quick (a chicken bone crack is heard). Then he drops the squirrel's body on the ground, headless-- blood pumps out in gulps from it on the ground, paws and legs kicking, slowing to a stop. Then with the squirrel's head in his hand, he takes it, and throws it high, high, high and away a far away distance.

Smiling, the second African returns to the bench, pulling a handkerchief out of his back pocket, wiping the blood off his hands while the first African stands and applauds him. "Bravo! Bravo!" that one says, showing all of his teeth this time.

Spike is impressed. "That's astounding!" he says, while Dice stays stationary in the face trying to show no emotion. The second African sits back down looking at Dice for a reaction.

Spike says to the second African, "Damn!-- so you must be the king of your castle where you come from."

The African replies, "King?... I am a professional my brother. Titles are words that have meaning only on paper..."

Dice now carefully stands up-- everyone looks at him as he says nothing walking over to where the headless dead squirrel lies (blood still pumping out of it slowly there). He stoops down, picks it up and turns to face the others. Everyone is looking. Waiting.

Dice then takes the squirrel and brings it up to his face, throws his head back, opens his mouth and pours the blood from it down his throat, gulping, one, two, three times, then throwing it down on the ground. He wipes his mouth with the back of his hand.

The Africans are astonished along with Spike (who looks the same way) as Dice walks back over to the bench. He takes some tissue out of his pants pocket to wipe his hands as he stands in front of the second African.

The second African now stands with amazement in his motion. "I have truly misjudged you my brother. You have much strength!"

The first African agrees, showing his teeth vibrantly, shaking Dice's hands up and down up and down. "Yes! Yes!" he pierces. "He has displayed much valor!"

The second one suggests, "Come. Accompany us to our quarters. We can talk more freely there."

And everyone begins to walk out of the park now, with Dice walking behind the group as they leave. Then he says suddenly, "Go ahead. I have to take a leak," and immediately goes over to the locked rust brick lavatory house in the center of the park, walking behind it. Everyone continues heading down the block while Dice is stooped over behind the lavatory house, silently throwing up on the ground-- the splatter of vomit only heard.

Inside a small one room place, lit dim yellow with one oval light hanging overhead, a 1940s dark oak table, designed carved, with four chairs manufactured the same way. Dice, Spike and the two Africans are in the room, each sitting in a chair at the table. A dresser in the same furniture style as the rest sits in the corner with a small color tv on top, showing unfocussed pictures.

They talk. The second African says to Dice, "We think it would be very profitable for you to become a part of our little business organization."

Dice out loud wonders, "Why tho? What's the real attraction?"

"Attraction, is not the proper word," the second African explains. "Our concern is international."

The first African talks, interjecting with "Yes. We are truly interested in expanding our little operation."

Dice reveals, "Eh well, I'm not really interested in going global man. I haven't put much brain energy into that."

The second African declares, "Ah, but you should, my friend. Your will appears to be very concrete. Have you not considered how much money can be made as an eliminator?"

"I'm not a eliminator, man" Dice says with distaste. "I only wanna take care of a few things that were wronged to me on the family side of things."
"But if it is your will to take care of that, why not put it to good use financially?"
"Eh..."
"Let me explain to you the scope of this opportunity. We have too much death by contract orders."

The first African smiles agreement and states, "Yes."

The second one continues, "And because of this, we cannot take on such demand to remove people the way we would like."

The first African agrees, "Yes. It is so big for us. So much opportunity."

The second one goes on. "Right. It is quite difficult. The demand is high, and we would like to meet it, but it is difficult... And, you see, we offer what you call here, a cut rate, to do these jobs..."

The first one shows his teeth and repeats, "Yes. A cut rate."

Dice expresses more non interest by throwing his hand up. "Eh... How come y'all didn't approach some other brothers from the Motherland or somethin'?... Why you ask me?"

The second African moves his head closer to Dice for emphasis. "Because, we were on a job here in this country. My brother and I have just finished a job, and, we have met you and admire your courage."

The first African agrees smiling. "Yes, we admire your courage."

The second one continues, "You see, if we were working back home, or perhaps somewhere in Europe, and we came into contact with someone else who displayed as much courage as you yourself... well, we would perhaps make the same offer to that person..."

Dice just looks down at the table. "Well... I appreciate the offer, but I'ma put as much politeness into saying no as possible."

"Oh, I understand" the second African says with his tone in slight disappointment. The first African stops smiling. Then the second one stands and extends his hand to Dice. "Very well," he says. Dice then stands and shakes his hand, then the first African's, whose smile continues to be lost.

Dice prepares to leave the place with Spike, who also lacks a pleasant expression on his face. Dice reaches the door but turns to the second African. "Thanks a lot again for the offer."

The second African labors a smile. "Yes. Yes. Good luck to you my brother," and Dice and Spike walk out of the place with their heads sort of down.

They were in a hotel, and coming out of it, litter dances around the entrance with dingy balled papers that shift when people walk past. Dice and Spike pass the loiterers standing there, and as Dice walks through the littered papers that are shifting, he reaches in his pocket for a cigarette, shaking one out and handing it to a dazed Spike.

Dice says, "What a presentation. I think they were authentic. Were they authentic?..." They both turn a corner.

"I dunno man." Spike hollows out. "They seemed legit to me."
"Yeah?... Yeah, they were legit."
"They were legit."
"I can't see myself going all over the Earth subtracting people from the land."
"That had a sound of a lot of money to me."
"Yeah, but I have my own agenda, really."
"That would've took care of your landlord and all that shit tho."
"True. But what kind of fantasy would I look like, traveling all over foreign lands, erasing this one, erasing that one... And I'm over there and I don't know where the hell I am."
"What about me tho?"
"What chu mean?"
"Well, I'd be with you, right?... It wouldn't be like you're alone with no contact."
"Hey, you thinking about elimination as a profession?..."
"Well... You know... I was thinkin'--"
"Spike, I'm only thinking right now about fixing up other people's fate, according to natural law. I just wanna settle this family style, right now."
"Yeah, but just think of all the other people all over the circumference that have fate to straighten out with opponents and villains or whatever, and can't do that shit..."
"I got wisdom on that. But--"
"And then, to put a cherry on top of it, they pay good money for that type of stuff."
"True."
"You could say, 'Landlord?... I spit on your grave! Now here's two thousand dollars. Go fuck your mother's asshole.'"
"You got blood in your guts?"
"I'm just sayin'... I could get it."
"Nah man you gotta have it."
" I can get that way."
"How ? You're too comfortable, man. You're still in your mom's house. Danger and destitution is only what you hear and read about."
"Awright. Well--"
"You haven't been denied nothing essential yet."
"Well..."
"Knowledge this... You got five dollars in your pocket right now."

"Awright."

"Now, with that five dollars, you gotta figure out how to eat dinner, buy toilet tissue, and maybe have car fare to go somewhere important."

"It can't be done."

"Right. It can't be done. So, if you have a situation like that everyday, and, just add on more stuff to what you gotta do with that five dollars, and suppose you had some kids--"

"You ain't got kids."

"Exactly, but suppose, or just think of the people out there that're in that kind of situation, that do. Well, when it's like that, your insides become enamel... Torture is like, 'What, torture?'..." And Dice throws his hand in the style of get outta here.

Spike keeps walking with nothing to say yet. Dice goes on. "You ain't recognized the true meaning of elimination until you can't pay for living. You gotta pay for this, and the price of not payin' is dyin'."

"I hear that."

"And those that get dead by another hand sometimes deserve it."

"Well, that's what I'm sayin' too. If somebody deserves nighttime I can give 'em nighttime."

Dice smiles at him. "Ain't nobody sayin' you're drenched or anything. I know you got grit in your heart."

They both turn a corner with Dice saying, "Yeah I'm just saying, this is my little conundrum actually. You know, I don't wanna get no friends involved in any of my shit..."

"But that's what I meant before... You gonna have to get a place soon, man. How you gonna get one?... Those brothers sounded like they practically knew how to manufacture dollars and get away with it."

Dice replies reluctance to talk about it. "I dunno. I guess I should think more about finances... I plum forgot about it for a second."

"That's what I'm sayin'. Financial security is what we left back there."

"Don't worry. I got plans. I just wanna make sure they're permanent like carvings. You're thinking's on the right track tho Spike."

They continue heading down the block with no more discussion.

Later that day, a .32 ACP caliber cartridge in a hand is shoved into a semi-automatic Colt 1903 Pocket Hammerless pistol. Once used by Al Capone, Bonnie Parker, John Dillinger and Willie Sutton, its blued metal finish looks spring storm cloudy. The walnut grip panel handle of it fits inside the hand of a man, in the day that is now slowly becoming night.

The hand belongs to Dice, who is lying on his stomach on top of a roof. The roof is on a building that is across the street from the one where he lives. He looks at the front door of it.

Night is hinting at the full coming of itself while slight numbers of passersby walk past Dice's place as he waits. He grips the semi-automatic tight as he aims at the front door of his building.

Some car horns blow sparsely and people walk here and there, underneath the unseen Dice who's aiming at the door across the street over their heads. He tries to control the rhythm of his breathing and the sound of it. Checking to make sure, he turns his head to look behind him up there. No one is there.

Seeing his front door opening he grips the handle tighter now, waiting for who he's waiting for to exit. He waits. The door opens now. The pistol glares dim.

The workers walk out of the building (those involved in the renovation) and Dice loosens the grip now on the handle of his gun, as he still semi-aims at the door. The language of their talking is heard boisterously as they walk down the block and away. Dice watches them while he aims at the door still.

Seconds dissolve as the time passes into minutes while Dice waits. He allows no thoughts to interfere in his head and his eyes stay stuck on the image of his front door. Then out comes his balding landlord.

Dice's insides move ready now, grabbing the Colt handle firmly he holds it, tightly. The aim is straight and he shakes not, moves not. Steady as she goes, he closes the one eye now looking at the landlord closing the door behind him.

The landlord, into his pants pocket, pulls out the keys and locks the door. Dice puts his index finger on the trigger of the gun, fitting it softly on the concave trigger like a puzzle piece. The landlord locks the door. Turns. Dice fires.

The shot echoes like a crack bouncing against everywhere. He missed! The landlord stop looks-- scared rabbit eyes (who what when where) drops to his knees on the ground, horrified. Dice whispers out, "Shit!!"

He rolls over and over on the roof, rolling till he reaches the exit to go down. A man's horrified yelling is heard. It quivers and vibrates like a motor as Dice (on the staircase in the exit) stands up, hush-stepping down the stairs, to not make a peep.

A tenement building is where Dice comes out of the exit and appears in the doorway. He sees various people running over to his building to assist the landlord who is doing that yelling.

People take the landlord's elbows to raise him up easy as he still yells, quaking his vocal chords, yelling even louder now. (An elderly woman tries consoling him with gestures of the hand.)

Dice stares at the scene across the street from the side of the tenement building where he stands in the entrance, as the landlord still yells and yells-- the ending of it never coming and sounding like a girl's to Dice, as he becomes aroused and entranced staring at the scene.

A police patrol car pulls up and stops, with the officers getting out of it. The landlord is yelling even more louder now as Dice gradually moves his hand down to his penis and massages it slowly to the girl-sounding yelling, staring at the commotion.

The landlord's body is limply flunking to the ground as he still yells while the officers and others try to help him to his feet. Dice stands there still watching, his hand still occasionally moving his penis back and forth in his pants, as the landlord's yell finally begins to subside in the strength of its volume. Dice puts his hand in his pocket now.

He stands in the same spot on the side of the tenement building for fifteen to twenty minutes, all the time it takes for the landlord to be driven away in the patrol car, and for the people who were trying to help, to evaporate from the building as if they were never there. Dice grabs his penis with the pocket that his hand is in, and immediately heads on over to his building as night declares itself.

Once inside his place, Dice immediately goes into his bathroom, takes handfuls of toilet tissue from the roll, takes his penis out of his pants quick and impatiently. He wraps the tissue around his penis and vigorously masturbates himself. After achieving orgasm, he takes his fist and angrily punches a hole in the wall there.

The next day, Dice is standing before a door and knocking on it a few times. The peep hole opens and closes, and the door is opened right after that. A beautiful young beige woman in her early twenties opens the door: eyes the shape of almonds with black brown hair missing her shoulders. She stares surprised at him, glad to see him but not. "You're walkin' a thin line doing this," she says to him.

"I don't care," he replies, and pushes her inside her apartment, closing the door behind him. Both inside now, he grabs her and they both embrace like desperation, and passionately kiss a long time, as the experience itself drowns them pleasantly.

They stop for half seconds between kisses to take deep breaths to kiss more and do so, forgetting all that exists on the inside of the apartment or Earth itself.

She finally realizes that she must make him stop, so she faintly takes the palms of her hands and slowly, pushes him back (and he stops suddenly, looking at her) and back some more. She says to him, "You must think you got the right to do--" and Dice puts his hand up, shushing her.

He goes into the living room there which is furnished with pillow shaped soft black leather sofas and easy chairs, which he plops himself into. "Listen Rosie," he begins. "It ain't like I don't care about what you said... I just think it's time to declare ourselves as a couple, despite the circumstances and consequences..."

"You wanna eat?" Rosie says with a bit of exasperation.
"Yeah, okay."

Walking into the kitchen, which has paint freshly appearing white and bright in color, he sits at the table there, which is matching the white of the walls. It bears a low lateral design that equals a Frank Lloyd Wright.

Rosie comes over to the table with a plate of biscuits. "I just took these out of the oven," she says to him, placing it on the table in the center.

He takes one. "So I guess you think I'm fucked up and hate me now..."

"You're always developing my feelings for me. Maybe I should think you're fucked up. Would that be happiness for you?"
"Don't be a stoop."
"You act like it."
"The biscuits are good."
"I know. I know I can cook and do other things too, like intellectualize and analyze your ass when I have to."
"Look who's talking..."
"Yeah, but I'm just playing with you. Sometimes when you say the shit you say to me, I get mixed up with your reality and mine."

"Eh, I just wanna be with you, that's all." After a bite of biscuit he says, "Guess what my landlord delivered to me?"
"Finally?... You know that was gonna happen. When you gonna find a place?"
"That's gonna be like hitting a lottery."
"You ain't tried yet."
"I know. I gotta get money tho."
"Don't even wonder about it."
"C'mon! I'm not gonna ask you for nothin' like that. That's not what I want from you."
"I hope not."
"I don't... I got ways. I got methods and ways to sooth those puzzles."
"Honestly I hope."
"Honestly. Honestly... what's honest these days anyway? If I say 'honest,' should it mean survival, or should it mean honest?"
"I don't know," Rosie says, sitting down at the table facing him. "Honest is honest as far as I'm concerned. I hope that doesn't mean you're gonna be a pissed off guy all the time now."
"What, 'cause I gotta find another place?"
"Mm hmmm."

Dice eats and thinks about it with his eyes aiming up a bit. "I should be pissed off tho right? I got reasons justified to be pissed off, right?"

Rosie's eyes show a wandering thought as she wonders. "I guess so," she admits. "But you shouldn't."

"Shouldn't smudn't... What would you do if I told you I just blew my landlord's brains out?... Would you still care?..."
"Care, smare... I would just think, that you fuckin' lost your mind."
"Would you hate me, like, severe?..."
"No... I would just feel bad... For us..."
"Oh."

Dice stands up now from the table as Rosie adds, "You gotta start thinking about serious solutions tho."

"Yeah, I know,." He walks over to her side of the table, bends down and gives her lips a full kiss with some tongue (which she opens her mouth for pleasantly). After a few seconds of that he raises his torso. "I really got some good ideas to push things along better."

"Mm hmmm," Rosie hums, like she knows some secret. "I hope they're good ideas and not nursery ones."

"My ideas are logical." Dice says, correcting her. "Their personalities are besides the point."

Later on that day, Dice re-enters his home finding workers there in full demolition force, removing tubs of plaster and wood. The barrage of noise floods all hearing of anything else inside.

As Dice climbs the stairs to his place, he sees that the workers have now splashed onto the second floor, as he passes them with frustration coating his face.

No other sound is sound but the noise, and the noise overrules all sounds that would be, as Dice enters his apartment, not even hearing the sound of his footsteps and not hearing the sound of his key unlocking the door. He barely hears the door closing when he does it.

The thoughts of what to do inside lie dormant somewhere outside Dice's head, for the clamor and din overrides the possibility of retrieving them. He paces the floor a few times. Stops. Decides to turn the tv on. Does so. Then he remembers he won't hear it. He snatches it off with a twist.

The banging and knocking goes on with violence in its volume, and Dice's skin becomes warm as he turns around twice. He heads to the window to look out of it. Changes his mind. Changes it again. A louder knock makes him jump, having the sound of something that fell more than a knock.

"I need some justification," he says to himself as the hammering on wood now, the hammering, becomes more forceful, with a sound in its intention of possibly coming through the wall. Dice immediately goes back over to the tv. Switches it back on.

The flickering black and white images appear as Dice turns up the tv's volume. Faintly the audio appears in the air somewhere but not there enough for Dice's ears. He turns it up some more.

The tv images move and scatter in some scene on the screen without volume, without sound (it seems) because of the revolt with noise from the workers against the reality of silence-- weak and feeble in its warfare, with Dice failing as its commander. Like a flash Dice snatches the tv off again.

Miraculously four knocks on the door can be heard, and Dice is surprised he can hear them as he goes over to open the door. The landlord stands there. Right away he gets to it, shouting above the uproar demolition. "You're still here?... This month's gonna be over soon. Yous got a few weeks at best left."

Dice with force to be heard shouts "Yeah. I know. I know."

Raising his voice higher the landlord delivers. "They're gonna need this room soon, so yous better be quick about gettin' your stuff out." And he turns his back quick and leaves the front of Dice's door with no desire for a response-- heading back downstairs with plaster flying off from the walls beside him from the banging.

Dice stands there watching him go as plaster dust floats towards and past his face. The blood inside him turns warm from thinking of the landlord's remarks and comments. He takes his hand and pushes the door hard so it slams closed.

"Fuckin' bastido," he says beneath the loud thump bumping, aiming his words at the door. "Fuckin' big clumpo... Fuckin'... stupido, blobbito... Ya big shit face. Fuckin' toilet neck... scum. Ya scummo stain. Ya fuckin' plump ass neck slob, slobbo... Slobbito... Snot tissue. Shit fuckito face snot tissue... Fuckin' producto, stupida. Ya big, fuckin', stupida... Piss mouth... Stain from my crack... Ya big shit stain on my drawers..."

Back on the other side of town in the projects, Spike comes out of a small grocery store holding a pint container of orange juice in his hands. He stops in front of the entrance before taking another step and takes a sip of orange juice.

To the right of him heading for the store, a dark tan young woman approaches-- rail thin she looks, raven haired and decked with a thin black full-length leather coat. She holds her head tilted from a chance of recognition, which fails when Spike recognizes her.

"Joanie. Is that you??..."

The woman tilts her head up and smiles sheepishly, with the right side of her face a swollen mountain of orange blackberry hue. "Hi Spike," she says with a tad of embarrassment.

Spike is wounded. "Joanie! What happened??..."

Her eyes roll down to the ground trying not to let her ailing smile show. "I'm alright," she tells him. "It really looks worse than it is."

"What??" jumps Spike. "Hey, I ain't laughing!... I'm ready to call the authorities lookin' at you."
"Really... I'm alright."
"Bullshit! You look like you're lucky to be alive even, and all that shit. I can't believe I'm looking at you like this."

Joanie's insides sink along with her demeanor now, and solemnity washes over her facial features.

Spike realizes they're in front of the store, and takes her by the arm to the side street away from its corner.

He looks at her closely now, and winces as he moves his hand up to the abuse on her face to touch it, but changes his mind. "This is like some Spanish Inquisition shit Joanie!"

"I know... I must be a sight."
"So this is what your husband rehabilitated to?..."

She shrugs her shoulders quick with an embarrassed chuckle. Spike is outraged. "This don't make no sense! I know people that fight intentionally and don't look like that."

"We both know people like that," Joanie says with the calmness of a new born kitten.
"Well..." Spike addresses with demand. "What're you gonna do about this?..."

Joanie shrugs her shoulders not knowing an answer to give. Spike replies, "I hope you got plans on living more days... Maybe see your kids grow up and have grandkids and stuff like that."

Tears now roll downstream down Joanie's cheeks and Spike begins to realize his comments may be too harsh. "Hey," (he floats his words out now) "I don't mean to be rough about it. It's just that this kind of injustice needs roughness for an answer. Don't you think?"

Joanie once again shrugs confused I-don't-know shrugs almost promptly, as Spike looks at her face wound eagerly now. "Listen," he says, in a secretive tone. "What's your money situation like?"

She jumps almost startled from the thought of his asking. To make sure what she hears she says "What did you say?..."

"I said, what's your money situation lookin' like?..."

Joanie shrugs her shrug again. "I dunno... I could probably lend you some I guess, if you need it."

"Nah, nah. I don't need it. I asked you because, that thing on your face is a crime against humanity."

Joanie sadly turns her head away and looks across the street. "Damn Spike, I didn't realize I could get frostbitten talking to you."

"I'm sorry. I guess I don't have a flair for softness at all. But what I'm sayin' is I know how you can be remedied for this situation you're in. But it's gonna take money."

"What kind of money? Why?"

"Listen" and he moves a bit closer to her in confidential manner. "Those Order of Protection routines and any cousins they might have-- that shit don't work. These guys go around, they say they're gonna kill ya, you tell the cops they're gonna kill ya, they make you fill out some papers, you think you're protected now, then bam!-- the fuckin' guy comes and kills ya anyway. Then the cops say, 'I'm sorry.' Is that a way for a person like you to go?..."

Joanie looks speechless from the detail Spike gave her. "I ain't never thought about it that deeply before. But what's money got to do with it?"

"Look, I can make it so that Prince Charming of yours, never lays a finger on you, not even in the afterlife."

Joanie wonders a bit as if she thinks she knows what he's talking about. "I don't understand," she frowns. "What's money got to do with it?"

"Listen ... You know Dice, right?"
"Of course."
"Well, when I see Dice later, I'ma tell him to come see you. Or maybe you can meet him somewhere?"
"Maybe. But what's Dice got to do with--"
"Dice is gonna be able to help you. But I gotta talk to him first."
"Help me with what tho?"
"Your husband... Don't you wanna apply real rehabilitation to your problem?... Only money can buy you that, if you're spending it wisely."
"Oh," Joanie hums out with slight discombobulation.
"Look, I'ma go tell Dice about it right now, okay? I wanna try to make life breathable for you as soon as possible... This shit don't make no sense, man."
"Oh... Okay... So, Dice is gonna come see me, about my husband's--"
"He's gonna see you. I'm gonna see him right now, so don't worry."
"Oh... Okay, then."

"So I'll see you later."
"Awright then... Okay..."

And Spike gallop-walks away, for his legs try to run to hurry to Dice, but Spike is restraining them (he thinks) to look normal walking away.

Joanie is still standing there watching him walk with more diagrams of confusion on her face than before.

Later that day Spike went to get Dice at his clamor-ridden place, and the two of them headed back to the park where they sat with the two native African men. The two friends sit there now on the same bench where they sat before when the Africans were with them.

Dice stares blank but looks attentive as he pours cashew nuts into his mouth from the slender pack he's holding in his hand. Spike speaks enthusiastically to him, saying, "I think it's a good way for us to begin business, man."

"You do, huh" Dice says, chewing without feeling.
"I mean, you gonna be the man in this, but I can help you."
"Hey Spike, I ain't got no kind of apprehensions or anything about you helping me man, if I decide to do this."
"Oh I know that man. I know."
"I mean we go way back and all that."
"True."
"So don't think otherwise. I mean, this is a serious decision I gotta make."
"I know. And I'ma help you make it."
"You know death?"
"I think I can issue it."
"How?"
"With precision. I think I can be precise."
"You can't think tho man. You gotta execute like a man with balls."
"What, you think I don't have balls?"
"I never deemed you that way."
"So damn, why you said that?"
"You're kinda agitated unnecessarily man."
"Oh shit!-- I come and bring you some business--"
"I don't need you to bring me business Spike. I got capabilities."
"I know you got that man."
"You kinda hungry man, huh?"
"What chu mean?"
"I mean, you've been pushing towards this destination for a long time."

"I'm just trying to help."
"You're just trying to help... You're just, trying to fucking help!... You act like I don't know nothin' man!... You act real hungry like I said. Suppose I had fear and I didn't really wanna do this."
"Then I wouldn't bring it up, man."
"Nah, you're acting like it's all about your future, man."
"Damn, I didn't know you felt that way about it."

Both stare ahead now silent, looking at the air in front of them. A few minutes pass by quietly sailing without Dice and Spike giving in to talking urges.

Finally Dice says, "Look man..." and he stands up to slide his hands in his pockets (with the pack of cashews) and looks around. "I'ma check with you later..." He then immediately begins to head out of the park.

Spike looks up stunned at him. "Awright man, leave! You wanna stay pissed man?... You pissed man? I'm sorry. Shit! That's all I gotta say."

"Apologies wasn't requested man. I'm just going to clear my fuckin' head," Dice says, on his way out now.
"Go ahead! Go fuckin' ahead!... That's the last time I try to bring good tidings to you."

Dice is waving his hand yeah, alright, okay, whatever, if that's the way you feel about it-- walking and not looking back as he does so.

Spike remains on the bench and shoves his hands in his pockets, shaking his stretched out crossed legs as if frost has settled in them. Then he jumps up abruptly, and walks out of the park in a huff.

He walks down the street fast and hard not looking around, not shifting the eyes this way or that. Gradually appearing around him as he walks are Catholic school girls, walking and talking, apparently just getting out of school. Their laughter and talk seems to creep up to Spike as he storms down the street-- a couple of girls to his left, two couples on his right behind him.

He crosses a street, not checking whether he has the go ahead light or not, but just walking anyway. He walks and more groups of Catholic school girls approach behind him, giggling and talking amongst themselves as he walks vigorously down the street.

Spike turns the corner there and heads down a more narrow street with less people. He sweep-wipes his brow with the back of his hand as the girls seem to follow him almost, talking amongst themselves, laughing playfully, speaking on top of each other.

He steps forward hard, walking, seeing nothing ahead of him it seems. He almost walks into the few people that approach him, walking.

Spike spits and treads hard on the ground while the street becomes less populated with passers-by and buildings. Walking, he passes barren lots emptied of parked cars but filled with auto wreckage. The lots become more extensive as he walks the same pace he walked since leaving the park. Two Catholic school girls are left from the groups that were behind him.

Spike still walks hard and sharp, spitting with force again on the sidewalk as he walks, taking the back of his hand again, wiping the sweat off his brow with a vengeance. The mounds of dirt in the extensive lots beside him become hills as he passes them. The laughter and chatter from the Catholic school girls have ceased, as only one girl behind Spike now, about twelve years old with a cocoa complexion and no expression, catches up beside him trying to pass.

Spike quickly turns to look at her, angered. He shifts his eyes to look at her auburn hair, which falls down to her shoulders in little sea waves, and at the thigh skirted Catholic school uniform she wears. Then he glares at her.

He looks around quick to see nothing but unpeopled lots with dirt hills and strewn dead auto parts. Under his breath he says, "Look at this fuckin' prostitute!..." Then grabs the girl, slaps his hand atop her mouth, lifts her body up (her legs kick up, struggling).

He carries her into the nearest lot beside him quickly, having trouble holding her wrestling body, but managing. He throws her back on the tan colored dirt behind a diesel truck fender. Angrily mashes her head down to hold it with the palm of his hand.

He takes his other hand, reaches under her skirt and snatches her panties off with one rip. "Fuckin' bitch! Whatchu doin' gettin' my dick hard??" he says under his breath again as he takes the same hand to unzip his pants, pulls his penis out and jam it inside her. The girl's eyes flash no emotion.

Minutes later, Spike walks out of the lot by himself. He stops at the block's curb, looks around calmly, then decides to walk back up the same way he came, and he does so, casually.

Chapter Four: I Yam Wot I Yam!

Standing six foot three but appearing to be shorter, a slender mid-twentyish man with a black medium-sized Afro, is walking down a street through staring pedestrian traffic whose eyes are pasted on him. He is unconcerned as he walks and smokes his cigarette with elegance.

People nearly stop in their tracks to stare at the young man as he walks with pride, wearing black shoe polish all over his brown-skinned face, except for the area on and around his mouth, which is painted baking flour white with white grease paint. Through his nose (amazingly so), is a stereotypical dog's bone, like the kind drawn with dogs in comics and cartoons.

He proudly walks and smokes looking straight ahead, as others stare straight at him, reading his black sweat shirt. The white lettering on the front of it reads: "Kill all the inscrutable white people." It reads the same thing on the back.

He precisely turns the corner of the block where Dice lives, as the sun melts down its orange hue behind the community of residential buildings. Reaching Dice's building, he doesn't have to ring the door bell, for the workers are seen leaving the place, so in he goes through the door, as the last worker holds it open for him, staring bug-eyed.

The young man climbs the stairs inside to Dice's apartment through the white plaster mist which has lingered. When he reaches Dice's door, he gives it two knocks and Dice answers with a yell of "Come in."

The man opens the door and finds Dice, perfectly standing on his head against a wall. Seeing him standing there, Dice replies, "Hey, what's happenin' Lube? Come in."

Lube, the young man, comes in closing the door behind him as he looks at Dice with obvious admiration. "Dice," Lube begins, "I see you have been examining the wonders of Eastern relaxation," and he takes his hand and taps the end of his bone, as if trying to scratch his nose.

Dice flips himself over right-side up on his feet, extending his hand to him. "So what's happenin'," Dice says as they shake.

"Nothing of significance really," Lube responds as he sits down informally on the floor and lets his back hit the wall. "How long have you engaged yourself in such practices?..."

Dice at first expresses his not knowing of what Lube is talking about with his face (for a second), then he busts out with "Oh... Nah, I was just standing on my head to make a decision, really."

"If that utilization was an appropriate one, I trust that you have made your decision," Lube says with assuredness.
"Well, I really had made my decision earlier. But I was with Spike--"
"Good man that Spike."
"Yeah, but he's pissed at me."

Lube takes his finger tips and taps his cheeks, to see if his black make-up is still on his face. He sees the polish on the tips of his fingers and feels satisfied before responding. "Yeah? What is Spike pissed at, primarily?"

"Ehh, he's pissed because I noticed his wishes," Dice says, plopping himself down on the floor next to Lube. "We all have our moments I guess. I'll tell him it was normal for us to be normal."
"Was there much dissent in your conversation with him?" Lube asks, wiggling his nose with the bone a bit, as if it irritated him.
"Nah, just a difference of opinion."
"Oh... Say, you know, I am actually quite hungry. Shall we travel to the store to purchase something for our stomachs?"
"Right."

And the two almost simultaneously get up and prepare to leave. Before leaving the place however, Lube stops in the bathroom and looks in the medicine chest mirror. He checks both sides of his painted face and taps his bone twice. Then they leave.

Heading down the street towards the Burger King, Dice pays no attention to the scores of stares and gasps at Lube from various passers-by. Every set of eyes in cars or on foot are cast on Lube, who walks with his straight ahead gate.

When reaching Burger King, the two step inside with everyone seated at their tables, stopping in mid-bite to stare at Lube. Their eyes follow him as he walks up to the counter with Dice to place their orders.

The young men and women at the counter are shocked statues looking at Lube. Stepping up to one register, Lube looks up at the hanging neon menu while the waiting female cashier seems nervous with apprehension waiting. Two male counter workers in the corner start to giggle after reading his "Kill all the inscrutable white people" sweat shirt. Lube looks at them quick. "Is there trouble here?" he asks perturbed.

The two men pull down serious expressions over their faces, and turn away to attend to business. Lube continues addressing them. "I want to make sure everyone is reminded, do you mind?..."

Most of the counter people hold their heads down now as Dice tells Lube. "Can you get me two Whoppers with cheese, and a Coke?... I'll pay you back later."

"Sure," Lube says turning to him, then turning back to the female cashier. "Two Whoppers with cheese and a Coke, and I'll have one Whaler, and a cup of tea, if you please."

The cashier nervously acknowledges his order and accidentally drops Lube's money on the floor.

"SHIT!!..." Lube fires, glaring at her as she shakes, rising from picking his money up off the floor.

"Sss, sorry, sorry sir... " she says.

Lube continues to show his anger by staring, but it quickly evaporates into his natural pleasantness. Their orders are almost immediately handed to them, and the two proceed to find a table. The cashiers stare at Lube and whisper amongst themselves. A few restrain their giggles.

Sitting down at a table, Lube asks Dice, "So, despite the impending eviction, how does the wonders of life appear?..."

"Well... I tell you... that little incident at the counter just now, made me decide on something... I think I'm gonna start doing bounty work."
"Splendid," Lube responds with pleased emotion. "You mean, like Paladin, and Steve McQueen?"
"Yeah. But it's a financial thing, really."
"Oh, but of course. One must earn one's keep with a vengeance."
"Well you oughta thank God that you ain't been dealing with life's manufactured mechanisms for ten years."
"Well, police brutality can be lucrative if it is won. And I won."
"Understood."
"Indeed, if it were not for that, when would I have gotten my wisdom?... Attaining such knowledge sometimes requires... time."
"True."
"Time, and patience. While the urbanites and the suburbanites are busy trying to decipher me and my motives, I am receiving a paycheck for being attacked by the police for my motives, and for being, let us say, myself."
"Right. Bodily harm-- how long will it be before your award actually runs out?"
"As you are well aware, I subsist on cheapness, and sparingly, as a rule. I would say though, to answer your question, that my acceptable amount will exceed the anti-Christ's reign even. After which, it will probably cease."

Dice stops and in disbelief looks at him. "Nah, you're pulling my leg, Lube. You always got some clandestine humor up your sleeve."

Lube stares at nothing and continues eating with no expression.

Dice continues, "See, the way I figure it--"

"Do you plan to execute your landlord who has decided your future?" Lube asks chewing.
"The thought traveled through me several times... I decided that there ain't no money in that shit tho."
"Here here!" Lube claps his hands rapidly with cautious softness. "Earn your living with a vengeance. That is one of my credos."
"When Spike did see me he was trying to tell me about Joanie. You know a girl named Joanie in the projects?..."

Lube tap wipes his mouth with a napkin, but makes sure the white makeup remains on his lips by lightly touching them with his pinky. He checks his pinky, is satisfied, and responds, "Joanie... Oh yes! Of course I know Joanie."

"Well, seems like Spike's trying to tell me that she's had it with her lawfully wedded husband, and she wants to exchange him for peace by way of peace."
"Oh, but who can blame her? By God, if any existence has to be problematic, then bury the damn thing, is what I say."
"Yeah, well, that's what Spike was tryin' to tell me. But I like to make my own sandwiches, ya know?"
"But of course."
"I mean, a process of acceptance like that is like having a fuckin' mother changing my diapers at this ripe old age I got."
"Surely."
"I mean like, he's my man and all that, and we go back forever."
"How true. We all go back actually."
"Yeah yeah! You know the deal."
"Indeed... What is your opinion about strangulation?"
"Strangulation?... As a method you mean?"
"Absolutely!"
"I dunno... It seems too television oriented to me."
"Really?"
"Yeah. It's straight outta the nineteen fifties or somethin'."
"What?!"
"You agree with strangling?..."
"Absolutely! The mere thought of--"
"Lube... Be cool man. I just asked a question..."
"But of course you did. I assure you there is no ire in my confusion as to why you think strangulation is, old hat, shall we say."
"Eh, it's too much work. You gotta put too much energy into something like that I would think."
"I understand fully."
"I mean, to me, if I'ma do this shit, I wanna do it as quickly as possible. I don't wanna be putting all my energy into something like that... I do the fuckin' job, get paid, get some pussy or whatever recreation and desire after that."
"I fully agree with you Dice. Absolutely."
"Yeah. Well, that's how I'm trying to live anyway."

After finally finishing their food, the two rise from their seats and walk over to the receptacles to empty their trays. The seated customers had slightly forgot about Lube's appearance until he stood up with Dice. Now they go back to staring at him again, along with others, who had walked in the place after the two were at their tables.

Dice and Lube walk out of the Burger King now, with Lube taking both his hands and firmly holding the ends of his bone as they walk, making sure it's still on securely.

Passers-by turn and stare at him (some giggling, some shaking their heads looking at him, reading his sweat shirt). Lube says to Dice, "You know, I was quite surprised when you said that you developed a decision to become a bounty hunter, essentially for the monetary strength of it..."

"How come?" Dice wonders aloud.

"Well, I simply thought your reason would lie more on the death of your brother... I naturally assumed it would be retribution that motivated you. Do you see?..."

"Oh, yeah. Sure, that has a lot to do with it too. But I don't know... Seems like... when you need money for something... thoughts on any other thing go away fading like smoke, ya know?"

"I would say that is true... Yes! I would say with category status, that you are correct!"

As Dice walks with Lube his mind sails to other thoughts. "I guess I better get with Spike and find out about Joanie..."

Later as the darkness comes above Dice in the sky, he heads down the block towards the housing projects to Spike's. Various people walk in pairs and groups communicating quietly like the evening, as they pass him and he passes them, walking.

As the blocks become more vacant and he passes abandoned buildings now, Nuremberg in style and stature like World War II's wake, he only sees a male and female couple ahead of him, embracing and kissing passionately on a parked car. Another car comes down the street towards him as he continues walking. Its headlights illuminate the male as he hugs the girl, his dust brown unruly hair matching his complexion.

Dice passes the two with no one noticing each other. The couple is involved in their passion and Dice is walking. The young girl whispers something in the man's ear and he lets out a hyena style yell of a laugh. Dice stops in his tracks.

He slowly cranes his neck to take a better look at the man. It's one of the men who attacked him in the empty side street some time ago. He nor the girl sees Dice staring at him. Now he walks back over to the couple, pulling up his pants by the waist. He gets right up to the man in closeness and says "Hey..."

The dust brown man turns to him, then shows no clear expression of remembrance. He starts to say a What's happenin' but only gets out a "Wha" when recognizing Dice. The fear in his eyes fill up and spill over enough for the girl to see it and wonder.

Dice clinches the bottom of his own shirt down hard, holding it there. "Remember me mothafucka?..."

The girl stares frightened. "What's this all about??" she asks Dice as he stares at the dust brown man only, whose fear is engraved on his face now.

"You... you got me, you got me wrong, man. I don't know you."

Dice slaps his face hard with his hand (the clap of it echoes above them). The man gapes terror. The girl gasps but stares waiting.

He grabs the man by the collar. "I got a funeral in my pocket right now, mothafucka!... You want a document on where it stands?... You want a reverend?..."

"I... I didn't do nothin' to you man," the dust brown man sputters as his girl looks on.

"I tell you what," Dice goes on. "I got a morbid sense of hearing... You're a fuckin' liar waitin' to be buried. Yes?... Is that what you're sayin'?..."
"No! No!... Please! I didn't mean it!..."

Dice glances at the still shocked girl for a second. Then looking back at the man he says, "I tell you what... Do you think I'm a fair man? No no! Forget that. I'll kill your ass right now."

The girl gasps hard close to a scream while the dust brown man melts scared. Dice continues. "Forget that... This is what I'll do for you mothafucka, sir! If you tell me what the word manumitted means, I'll forget our differences."

"Wwwhat??" the dust brown man slops out. "Wh what's the... I don't--"
"Manumitted. Man-u-mit-ted. Tell me what it means. I'll spare your life."

The dust brown man shakes not knowing what to say, what to do. The girl stares at Dice with her fear diminished in look and expression. Dice looks at her. Then he says to the man, "Watch this..."

Dice snatches the girl's head, stamps a full kiss on her mouth, slides his tongue in and wipes her insides with it quick, then let's her go-- she stands there drenched in all elements of fear, pleasure and confusion.

Dice tells the man, "It means, released from slavery..." Then he lifts up his shirt to show them that he's not armed and says, "See?..." Smiling, he now continues his trek down the block with the dust brown man limply staring at Dice, leaning against the parked car, weak. His girl stares at Dice, leaning against the same parked car, weak with fulfillment.

Later that evening in the dead direct center of acres and acres of a meadow sits Dice, with Spike and Joanie, in the grass on their buttocks, their legs folded underneath them in the lotus style. Joanie looks around at her whereabouts with discomfort. "How can I be sure nobody's watching?" she says to Spike.

Spike looks at Dice, who calmly explains, "Joanie... we're in the middle of vastness right now. If you're sweating at all take calmness as a mate. We're alright."

Spike contributes with, "I wouldn't think of bringing you somewhere where possibilities exist for anything to happen."

"Oh," Joanie coos with remained apprehension.

Dice tries not to show his impatience. "Awright Spike," he says. "Since you wanna aid in this, why don't you speak. Why don't you start with your thoughts."

"Awright. So Joanie, how--"
"I got two hundred dollars right here," she says, reaching in her pocketbook immediately.

Spike holds his hand up. "Whoa! We ain't asked you to shed anything yet."

Dice keeps the money amount in his head. "Two hundred dollars?..."

She replies, "That's all I got right now, Dice. It's not enough?..."

Spike turns to Dice with anxiousness. "Well you know Dice, she can start with that and pay the rest later."

Dice scratches the back of his head. "I don't know Joanie, I don't know. It ain't just the money. I mean, you sure you know what you're doing, I mean, as sure as concrete?..."

Spike looks defensive looking at Joanie. She mourns her words out. "Well... I just don't wanna be wounded no more."

Dice agrees. "I don't blame ya for that. But see Joanie, this is some essentially deep shit I'm embarking on. I want you to be sure you know what you wanna do."

"My two hundred dollars, isn't enough?"
"Well, it's a start."

Spike eagerly adds to Dice, "Yeah, for the experience 'n shit, I guess you gotta start somewhere, huh?..."

"Yeah, something like that."

Joanie looks at him helpfully. "I could get more if you want, Dice."

"Nah nah. That's all right. That's not really what I'm even thinking about. I just want you to be sure."
"I just know too much about pain," she says. "More than I wanna know. All I know is volumes about how to make bruises less noticeable..."

Dice pushes himself up closer to her with a slide. He makes himself prepared with the clap of his hands. "Awright. Tell me what makes him barbaric..."

"Well," Joanie thinks with her eyes down. "He one time took my head, and tried to flush it down the toilet."
"Awright... What else?"
"What else... Let's see... There's so many occasions, I lost the openings where I could breathe without, hurting?..."
"What else Joanie."
"Well... He one time tried to puncture my neck, with... with his screwdriver."
"Okay, what else."
"And he got drunk once... and raped me, with a basketball trophy... from the back tho. He, he like, hammered it in, with his hammer?..."

Spike turns away to look at the lights in a distant office building. Dice says to Joanie with some impatience, "C'mon, what else? What else Joanie."

"Umm... Let's see, he... Oh! He once tried to hang me one time. You know, like a lynching?... It was kinda funny tho, 'cause like the rope broke?... It wasn't strong enough?... It was like a string really. We kinda laughed at that together. Then we made love after that..." She goes into the thought of it looking embarrassed at the dark grass.

Dice becomes a bit more impatient. "C'mon Joanie. I need this. What else? What else?"

"Okay. ...took my earlobe off almost..."
"What?" Dice exclaims, looking at one of her earlobes.
"Oh, but he didn't take it all the way off. I got it sewed back on."

Spike looks in her eyes direct. "Did you ever go to the hospital for any of this stuff Joan?..."

"Oh, no... I didn't go there for anything like that."

Dice continues. "What else Joanie, what else?"

"Hmm... He pushed my head through the window in our house... I got some cuts..."
"What else?"
"He tried to break my leg... That was last night. He bent it backwards, all the way back?..."
"What else?"
"He shoved a toothpick under my fingernail..."

Dice takes a deep breath. "Go ahead."

"He slapped me with a hair brush... It left marks on--"
"Go ahead. What else. What else."
"What else... Umm... He... he made fun of my nose... in front of all my friends..." She slowly begins to weep trying to continue. "...and my mother... Is that abuse?"
"You fuckin' right it's abuse," Dice looks over at Spike who gives his head a quick nod, agreeing. Dice looks back at Joanie and asks, "Anything else?..."

Not looking at them Joanie thinks more and is slightly trembling. "Umm... he took the heal of his hand, and bashed me in the eye..." She giggles to herself. Then she quickly turns to Spike. "You saw that, right Spike?..."

Spike's face shows he doesn't remember before he answers it. "I dunno Joanie. Was that when I saw you at--"

"And... he tried to twist my wrist," she continues, trying to demonstrate, "...all the way around?..." She giggles more trying to show them, trembling more.

Dice says, "That's alright Joanie. You don't have to show us."

Joanie stops but appears to hear nothing. "And he... he actually kicked my ass! D'you know that?..." She openly laughs now, looking at the two of them as she trembles even more.

Spike is looking at Dice before he tells her, "Joanie... You don't have to think about it no more now, okay?"

"Think?!" she retorts hard, actually quaking now. "Is that what you think I'm doing??... I have to, I have to, think about this??... It's in my bones! It's in my, pain!... Think. I don't have to think about this at all!" She laughs and cries as her hand quivers up to wipe her eyes.

Dice puts his arm around her. "It's alright Joanie. I'm gonna take care of it."

Spike echoes him. "Yeah, we'll take care of him Joanie, don't worry."

Joanie's laugh wiggles wild in her tears. "And he... he smashed a lamp on my... on my mouth."

Dice's face forms worriment. "Joanie it's alright. I don't need no more incidents."

"And he kept slapping me one time," Joanie continues as her eyes begin to look tranced. "And he slapped me," she slaps her own face laughing, her thoughts absorbed somewhere else, "...and he slapped me," she slaps her face again, "...and he slapped me," she slaps it again.

Dice instantly grabs hold of her. "STOP it Joanie!" he yells, shaking her. "STOP it I said!" Spike is looking at the two with concern.

She speaks inside the shaking. "YOU DON'T HAVE... ANY iDEA..."

Dice still vices on to her shoulders. "Joanie!! Snap out of it!!"

"YOU DON'T HAVE... you don't have any iDEA, what I... what I have SUFfered, to--"

"JOANIE!" he shouts shaking her harder. She shows exhaustion, breaking down to cry openly.

Spike is looking helpless watching the two. "Dice, what should we do?"

"She's alright," he replies confident. "Joanie!... C'mon! You've got to snap out of this!..."

Joanie sobs hard enough for the two to look worried about her condition. She stops her shaking looking down straight at the grass. She breathes deep, hard sobbing with force. "You... you want MORE?..."

Spike jumps in with "We don't need no more details Joanie."

Dice explains beside her ear. "Joanie... Look, we're gonna help you now."

"It's just so... It's just so... HORRID... It's just so HORRID, the way the sun... LAUGHS at me, for my misTAKES..."

"Joanie... This guy's got a closure coming to him. I'm gonna make it for ya, but I need your help."

Spike chimes in, "Yeah we need your help Joan. We'll take his values away from him, don't worry."

Joanie says, "I don't feel HUman..."

Dice corrects her. "Wrong. You'll be human again."

"I don't feel, HUman..."
"It's gonna change, I swear."
"Can I... Can I, appreciate sunlight again?..."
"You'll see the sun again. I promise. But you gotta help us."
"Help... Help?..."
"We need to know-- Joanie, you understand what I'm talkin' to you about?"
"Understand?... I... I understand..."
"What's my name? Who's this?..."
"Who is this?... I know you Dice. You think I don't know?..."
"Who's that over there? Who's that guy?"
"It's Spike... I know everybody."
"Look Joanie, I gotta make sure you're alright and that you understand you're talking to us... so we can get this thing right, you understand?..."

She looks like she's trying to understand his point. "I understand Dice... I said I have money."

Dice and Spike look at each other. Then Dice says, "Listen Joanie.. What kind of work does your husband do?..."

"Umm... he works for transit."

Spike replies concerned. "Are you sure Joanie?... You sure he works for transit?"

"Of course," she says with surprise at the question.

Dice adds, "Because this thing's gotta be done right."

"I know... I know."

"He works for transit," Dice continues, "so what does he have, like weird hours?..."

Joanie stares back down at the grass hard, not answering. Spike looks alarmed at Dice and calls her. "Joanie!..."

"Hmm?"
"Joanie, c'mon, did you hear Dice?"
"Oh. Um-hmm. I heard him. He does have weird hours tho."

Dice strenuously shows patience. "Okay Joanie, so what times does he get off, like twelve midnight or something?"

"Umm... Yeah. He gets off at twelve. Midnight."

The two hand each other doubtful stares. Dice grabs Joanie's elbow. "Are you sure it's twelve midnight Joanie?"

"Yes I'm sure!" she declares. "Twelve midnight... I know what time he gets off 'cause that's when my living ends."

Both Dice and Spike think unsure thoughts trying to figure the strategy to use for the job. Joanie returns to staring back down at the grass, saying nothing, not even showing signs of belonging with the two. Then like a pop, suddenly, she perks her head up. "He works in the token booth on Washington Street."

Dice and Spike look at each other slightly impressed. Dice gets closer to her to make sure. "The token booth on Washington Street around the way?..."

"Um-hmm," she replies to his correctness.

Spike smiles relieved. "Oh shit. How effortless is that?"

Dice shows the palm of his hand to halt him. "Don't jump to the line yet. Closeness just means we ain't gotta search high and low for his ass to satisfy our duty."

Joanie asks Dice, "Are you gonna hurt him?..."

After a sigh of deep breath Dice looks her squarely in the pupils. "You got some protesting about this now Joanie? Don't tell me your thoughts are jumping ship on this now?..."

"Oh no," she finalizes. "Not at all."

The two friends look at each other. Then Dice says to her, "Awright. You got the money?..."

She immediately reaches in her purse and pulls out two stiff crackling one hundred dollar bills, handing them over to Dice. He takes them, puts them together, then folds them making the crease along Ben Franklin's nose and between his eyes. He sticks the bills in his palm and drops it on his thigh. Spike is waiting for him. Then, Dice hands the other bill to him.

Smiling as he looks down at it, Spike muses to himself, "The new road begins now, huh?..."

Joanie happily looks at the two of them. "Is that, okay?... Should I give you more later?..."

Dice waves his hand no. "That's alright Joanie. Look, we just wanna take care of this now... We wanna get started."

Spike is still smiling looking at his bill. "Yeah. We should begin real soon I guess."

Joanie is coming to life more. "Oh I understand." She sighs relief with an attached smile. "Well... I guess I'll go. Can I go now?"

Dice rises up to his feet. "C'mon, we all better be gettin' outta here..."

As Joanie and Spike now stand, Dice looks over at her with concern. "Joanie," he calls.

    "Hmm?"
    "You alright? You want us to walk you back home?"

Spike cuts in. "We live in the same building, so I'll walk with her."

    "Oh yeah. Forgot about that."

Gradually, everyone walks out of the grass's vastness, with the quiet there around it still silent.

Chapter Five: Easy

The next evening towards eleven thirty, Dice and Spike are walking down a scantily deserted street where the businesses there show only their burglary gates, instead of the coming-and-going customers that existed hours earlier.

The friends carry small paper bags filled with something. (The tops of the bags rolled tight into their fists like bag lunch.)

Dice says, "See, I just wanna get used to what the procedure is. I need to know the professional mechanics of this so I can succeed like a professional. I need as much assignments as I can get so I can have the seriousness of this carved on my face like woodcut art."

They turn a corner which is Washington Street, where more businesses show that their business activity for the day is over. They clutch their paper bags tighter and walk forward with duty guiding them, past a few passers-by here and there. Spike tells Dice, "My focus is hardcore."

"What?" replies Dice, thinking about something.
"My focus is hardcore. It's not penetrable..."

"Well that's cool, but it doesn't have to be all that man. Just go in there, watch that entrance-- the place has only got one entrance anyway, so we shouldn't have any commotions or mishaps like an assassination or anything."

"Right, right."

"We just go in like lightning and do the job like saints. What more can professionalism be?"

"True, True."

They head directly towards the entrance of the subway station, vacant inside with a long corridor leading down to the lone token booth there. They walk inside and the corridor echoes the rustling of their clothes as well as their rubber sole sneaker footsteps.

Dice's hand stops Spike with a shot to the chest. "Right here," he declares as Spike now knows why he stopped him like that, but still feels the force of it. Dice quietly tells him, "Just stand by the entrance. I'ma go up there."

"Right, right."

Dice (eyes direct) proceeds to walk up to the token booth. He steps. No one is near the booth, not the sound of a train pulling out or coming in below it can be heard. He moves on, focused on the target, no other thoughts exist.

He reaches the booth and steps up to it. Inside, a huge dusk-colored male clerk with sculptured muscles is sitting with his head down reading a magazine. His blunt black colored hair is tied neatly into thick cornrow braids that hang just below his earlobes.

Dice stands there gradually opening his paper bag. The clerk inside doesn't look up at him. Dice looks at the man. Then, all of a sudden he reaches in his pocket. "Lemme get a token, man?" he asks the clerk.

The man gradually raises his eyes up and stares angrily at Dice as he watches him place his money on the counter, and slide it underneath the glass to him.

Spike is watching everything from the entrance of the corridor wondering what Dice is doing. Then, a young woman walks past him, entering the corridor. Spike glances at her. He gapes at her now.

The token clerk slides Dice a token with contempt. He takes it saying thank you, and turns around to leave. He sees the young woman approaching him heading for the token booth with Spike's alarmed face staring behind her at the corridor's entrance, watching.

Dice heads back down through the corridor on the way out, passing the woman who passes him, almost reaching the halfway point of exiting. But he slowly comes to a halt.

Spike is looking at him wondering what's happening. Dice looks at Spike with an expression saying nothing, then looks back at the young woman now approaching the token clerk.

Dice turns back around facing the booth from the midway distance. He stands there watching the young woman and listens as he hears her say, "Two tokens please," then sees her following that with the holding up of two of her fingers against the booth's glass, just in case he didn't hear her.

The token booth clerk yells, "I heard you!!... I heard you the FIRST goddamn time, bitch!!!" The young woman jumps back frightened (clink! went the sound of her tokens when they landed on the ground after he slid them to her through the glass).

She cautiously bends carefully down to pick them up as Dice stares at the scene now with anger. Spike is still watching with thoughts of what Dice is actually doing. The young woman nearly runs through the turnstiles after retrieving her token and disappears. Dice glares fire at the token booth now.

He storms back over there, quickly opening up the paper bag, pulling out his Colt 1903 pocket hammerless pistol. He walks even faster, rushing as Spike looks on spreading a smile across his face.

Dice gets up to the booth. The clerk looks up at him. Dice shoves the barrel of his pistol under the glass. Fires it, one, two, three times. (The corridor's echo makes it sound like three explosions.) The clerk's body slams against the back of the booth, slides down at the same pace as the blood on his chest slides. He drops on the floor.

Dice immediately turns around, quickly shoves the gun back in the bag, folds it back up like bag lunch, walks back towards the entrance of the station, casually. Spike is not there.

He walks out of the subway corridor into the street looking for Spike. Suddenly, two gunshots snap out loud beside him. He turns to it. In the street lies a young teenage male lying on his back-- his right cheek resting beside the manhole cover there.

Standing over him is a young beige teenage girl with long pigtails, holding the gun in her hand down beside her thigh. She looks down at the body with satisfaction proudly on her brow. Cars coming close by creep to a halt. The few pedestrians that are around run over to the scene. Dice hears, "Oh shit!-- that was a wild scene!"

He turns around. It's Spike. Dice asks him, "Where the hell did you go?"

"I was right here," Spike says, "checking out this shit. She told the dude she was fed up. The inspiration was impressive. Hey!-- things went okay in there, huh?..."

Dice looks at him. "You got a lot of learning to do about carefulness, man."

"I fucked up??... I was watching the entrance all the way like you said. I saw everything, including the bangs."
"C'mon, let's get outta here."

The two walk fast, not quick but steady, heading down in the vicinity of Dice's place. Spike asks him, "How long d'you think it'll take for word of mouth to create more business for us?..."

"I don't know... But we ain't gonna get nothin' but laughs if we can't handle our business efficiently."
"C'mon Dice, you keep thinkin' I fucked up. You think I fucked up?"
"I'm sayin' you were sloppy man. You wasn't at your post, let's face it."
"But I'm telling you I was just on the other side checking out that shooting."
"But I came out, I'm like, Where the fuck is Spike? and I'm almost panicking not seeing you."
"Sorry man."
"I mean, c'mon, you gotta be efficient with this shit if you wanna be with me in this..."

Spike's look strives to stay positive while Dice continues. "I mean, suppose like later on one day I get so good at this, I'll get asked to take care of some white people... You think we'll be able to maintain sloppiness like this?..."

"Well if that happened they probably wouldn't be asking us to do anything like that..."
"Well I gotta get dough to get my existence outta that destruction called 'my home.' A large sum of it's gotta come from somewhere if I'm gonna move. I'm gonna be homeless if I don't. You realize that?..."
"I won't be slippery again man. I declare it."
"Demand your senses to get the fuck back here then."
"Sorry..."

Turning the corner they reach Dice's building. From a garbage can in front of there, a rat shoots across their path (they stop motionless like a photograph). The rat dashes away like wind, into shrubbery across the street.

Staring shocked, Dice says, "You saw that??... Now, I coulda shot his ass! But an action like that justifies the death penalty for stupidness, after the job I just carried out. Wouldn't you say?"

    "Oh, for real," agrees Spike. "I definitely see your point, with a vengeance."
    "Aww sh--! I forgot! You still wanna pick up some sandwiches at the deli? My stomach's strangling me."
    "That sounds cool."

Later upstairs at Dice's place, the two are sitting on the floor munching hardily on their sandwiches. Both show satisfaction while they quietly enjoy their food.

Spike utters while chewing, "I bet Joanie'll be whistling choruses when she finds out you can bury nightmares, huh."

    "Yeah," Dice says, spilling some of the soda he gulped over his lip. "I just can't see sittin' in the house everyday surviving no shit like that."
    "Listen... when you shot that guy, did the back of him spread open?... You know, because you were shooting at a close range and all?..."

Dice has to think about it as he swallows his turkey and American cheese on rye. "Hmmm... I don't know... Couldn't see..."

    "Oh... It probably did tho," Spike confirms, sucking the mustard off two of his fingertips.

Dice wipes his mouth with the back of his hand. "You know... I wish I had a been in a position... to pee on that mothafucka in the booth... Somehow, I feel my job's not done..."
    "Oh yeah... A guy like that is supposed to be sliced up with paper cuts or somethin', then peed on... But I guess that's kinda too soft huh..."
    "Yeah, really..." Dice feels, shoving a bite of the corner of his sandwich into his mouth. "I really wanted to do something to represent his passion for torture... But not copying him... I'm a man of realistic differences. But that stuff she said he did couldn't even be practiced by Josef Mengele without wincing..."
    "Hey Dice," Spike laughs as he finishes a long gulp of his soda. "What if... what if Joanie, was like, lying?..."

Dice clangs his soda can down on the floor. "Spike... what the fuck you mean, man?... You recommended-- what, you heard something night as opposed to day?"

    "Nah, nah, I'm just sayin'..."

"Well don't think that man. There's no humor in it. There's a sense of duty involved in this. If that were the case, all was done for nothing."
"Nah, nah. I'm not saying that I believe that's the deal... I'm just saying, wouldn't it be kinda funny, if that were the deal. Wouldn't it be kind of, ironic?..."
"Man, that shit would be fucked up! Don't even intimate dilemmas like that, even in Gothic..."

Three knocks boom on the door. The two pop their eyes out, staring fear at each other. Three more knocks come again bearing down harder against the wood. Dice cautiously rises from the floor to answer it. "Who's that!" he yells before opening. The voice at the other end yells, "Landlord." Dice looks at Spike in disbelief, then opens the door.

There at the threshold stands the landlord, looking surprised to see Dice there. "Hey," he begins. "You're still here?... We're gonna be up on this floor soon you know."

"Yeah, I know."
"Well, you ain't got much time... Okay?..."
"Yeah yeah. I got ya..."

As the landlord turns to leave Dice closes the door.

Spike almost whispers, "Oh shit!... What's he doing here so late? What is he, spying?..."

Dice is glaring sharply at the door. "You know what I should do to that mothafucka?..."

"What?..."
"I should kill that mothafucka right now, like a proverbial Caesar..."
Spike warns, "Now now."

Dice immediately goes over to his paper bag on the floor by the window. He pulls the Colt pistol out of it. Goes to peer out the window looking determined. Spike reminds him, "Hey man, it ain't worth it. Ain't no money involved..."

Still looking out the window, Dice points the gun barrel at the pane, tapping it with it. "See?..." he says with certainty. "I can shoot that mothafucka right now."

"And get jail time??... He's a white guy. And, the financial reward for something like that is hiding somewhere in the heads of the Brothers Grimm."
"Grim?... Well now that would be perfect, wouldn't you say?..." Dice taps the windowpane again, two times. "Things are pretty grim for me right now, don't you think?"
"Well, I--"

"Like let's face it... when you leave here, you go back to a constant roof over your head. I mean constant." He looks and spots the landlord opening the car door of a cotton white 1975 BMW 2002. "Me... well..." Dice lifts the half opened window all the way up. "He's not gonna walk around here all calm 'n shit, waking up every day without burdens and headaches... I wake up everyday, and it's like..." He aims his gun at the landlord. Fires. Once. Twice-- hitting him in the neck.

Spike stands up astonished. "Damn, Dice!!..."

The landlord coughs, gags (trying to suck air loudly into his throat).

Spike comes to look out the window at him as Dice smiles peacefully at the landlord.

The landlord staggers on the vacant sidewalk against the car, bumping into its body noisily, gasping, holding his neck-- his pupils roll up into his eyelids. He takes the other hand to lean on the handle of the car door. Drops on his knees smashing an empty wine bottle there, rasping backwards, trying to hulk in air with his knee doused in blood.

He flips on his back against the car door, removing his hand from the door handle, placing it on the back of his neck with the other hand-- the blood now streams out of the bullet hole, running through his fingers. He's choking and makes the sound of it.

Both Dice and Spike grin as they watch the landlord out there loudly gasping. (No one is passing by to help him.) No eyes see him but Dice and Spike's as he loses the strength to hold his torso up, hoarsely gulping. Loudly he coughs up blood now-- it shoots out high from his mouth, some of it landing on his thighs and the concrete.

His elbow hits the asphalt hard with the bone making the sound of it heard. Spike happily exclaims, "Oh shit!" Dice observes, "He's like a wounded beast!... A sacrificial lamb!..."

The landlord's hand grapples at the concrete as if it were soil. He coughs more now, gasping, strangling from the blood coming up inside his throat, gagging from the force of the blood surge and lack of air coming in (horribly loud). He moves his legs in drags going no where, ripping his pants on the roughness of the concrete-- the sound of his shoes scuffing themselves quick, drowns out the gasping he makes louder for a few seconds now.

Dice remembers something and snaps alert quick. "I got a better idea!" he tells Spike, leaving the window and heading for the kitchen-- Spike is wondering what (?) as he looks at his friend. Seconds later, Dice comes out of the kitchen holding up a bottle of Pepsi Cola for Spike to see.

Spike slams, "Oh shit! He'll be cauterized Dice!"

"No," Dice replies, then runs downstairs with the bottle, saying, "He's not feeling my pain! He has to feel something to represent my pain!..." And Spike runs back to the window to see Dice's intention.

The front door downstairs opens with Dice cautiously stepping out of it with the Pepsi. He looks left and right for witnesses, tip toes to the struggling landlord on the ground, unscrewing the cap off the bottle.

He stands over the landlord, who's still holding his blood drenched neck, gasping for air with moaning pain. Dice steps over him, kicks one of his hands away-- the blood drops fling up diagonally. He says to him, "You're not feeling my pain! You're not feeling my inside pain!..."

He looks around again before pouring the Pepsi on the landlord's neck, into the gunshot wound-- his body convulses violently when it splashes on it. His hands flutter to clamp onto his neck. He pants hard, his legs, arms, zigzagging wildly wiggling everywhere.

Spike laughs silently hysterical as Dice sneaks back into the building.

The landlord's limb movements begin to slow down as the gasping sounds he made decreases in intensity, in slow motion, coming to a stop.

Spike says out the window to the dying landlord. "Thank him. A comet can hit this mothafucka any time. Thank him for sparing you terror when seeing your last achievement..."

Dice comes back in and goes over to the window again, looking at the landlord, now sprawled out motionless on the concrete. Spike looks at Dice and chuckles, "Well... maybe it was worth it after all, white man or not."

"Anything for the advancement of mankind," Dice replies, putting his gun back in its paper bag. "At least he won't have to worry about being a food phenom at dinner anymore... Fat mothafucka..."

Spike laughs but shifts to seriousness. "I guess you gonna have to get outta here now. That wasn't exactly any old field or house nigga you know."

"Granted... Well look, there's no problem gettin' the fuck out, leaving everything, 'cause let's face it... life here is over. I'll just go and visit my destiny now, taking the clothes on my back."

"What about our bounty positions?..."

Dice goes over to the closet, reaching in clothes pockets while Spike looks at him waiting for an answer. Dice tells him, "I gotta make sure I ain't leaving no money in here." Then he speeds his actions up further to hurried haste. "We gotta get the fuck outta here. C'-mon!..."

And the both of them immediately grab their paper bags with their guns and walk out of the apartment.

As they quickly head down a street outside the vicinity of Dice's place, they pass a convent where a large forest green dumpster sits in front of it to the right. Dice notices the tub instantly. "Hold it!" he stops Spike's walk with his forearm. "We can drop our removers in here. This is as non-searchable as freedom can get right here."

Spike tosses his paper bagged gun in the dumpster along with Dice. They then proceed walking to their destination with the same hurriedness as before.

Dice, with his breath heard in quickness, asks Spike, "So, you comin' with me, right?"

Spike shows surprise in his face and eyes, but before he answers, Dice continues with, "Because don't even think for a millisecond they won't seek the likes of you along with myself?"

"They will?"
"'Course they will. Continue breathing. Do yourself a favor and don't fuck around on crucial decisions..."
"Well, where you planning on going?"
"Around your way first. That way you can take some stuff you'll need, like dough, and I can explain something to Rosie."
"Well... then where you gonna go?... What you gonna tell her?"
"I dunno. But by time my face hits her home I'll think of something, I'm sure."

Chapter Six: Truth & Consequences

Later at Rosie's place, Dice is sitting solemn in the easy chair in her living room while she stands in the center of the room, donned only in a bra and panties, staring at him hard with her arms folded. The silence reigns over Dice's ability to look at her. She stays in that position with annoyance in tow behind her facial expressions.

A few more seconds like this go by until Dice utters, "Well..." in waiting for silence's end. Rosie still stares at him with relentless disdain. Then Dice says, "I guess I'm fucked up in the final solution, huh?..."

Rosie automatically swipes an empty crystal-like candy bowl off the glass coffee table there, throws it down on the floor in front of Dice-- it smashes (making him jump), scattering sparkling pieces all over the floor. She sharpens her sight at him more, saying, "Yous a real stupid mothafucka, you know that?..."

Dice stays calm and in silence looking no where but down at the shattered bowl.

She continues. "I think I must have real bad karma or something, to keep getting mixed up with jail junkies like you... Ev-ery fuck-in' time I turn around I'm getting drowned by people like you, who just give up all the damn time."

Dice stumbles confusion over that. "Give up on what?" he asks with earnestness.

Rosie is even angrier now, and snatches the other candy bowl off the table, slamming it on the floor, smashing it on top of the other pieces. "Give up on what," she snarls with contempt moving her tone. "I have to tell you?... Same thing with the other one, who's already padlocked by the city's wishes..."

Dice shoots up to his feet to make a point. "Listen Rosie, you don't know nothin' about pain either. Everybody's walkin' around here with roofs over their heads all hoity-toity like nothin' can't end for them abruptly."

"That's your reason??... That's your reason for joining in with all the other good-for-nothings, feigning brilliance with a gun barrel??"
"Hey look!-- it's more complex than that!"

Rosie looks around swiftly left to right, looking for another object. She takes the cigarette lighter (made in the same faux crystal style) right off the same table, throws it down hard on the floor. It doesn't break. She bends down to swipe it up angrily with Dice just standing there looking at her. With the lighter in her hand again, she throws it back down, and it smashes this time, on top of the rest of the broken pieces of faux crystal.

Dice looks at her. "What does this destruction you're doing mean, the relationship's smashed up now?"

"You damn right! The shit is smashed up because you ain't nothin' but a slave, you ghetto politician!!"
"Oh?"
"Damn straight. You ain't nothin' but a politician, smooth talkin' your way up my clothes, promising a whole lot of career moves entrusted to fantasy."
"Hey, I wasn't lying 'bout nothin'. All the things I ever said to you were legit. I don't have to lie. I wouldn't a told you what me and Spike did if I was a liar, would I?"
"Aww you're nothin'. You're my husband all over again. You're not different at all. You're not change."
"I'm not change. But I buy you stuff when you need it. He did that, right?"
"Aww you're nothin'. Yous a jailbird. That's all."
"Yeah awright, so what does that say for you then? Convict... What does that say for you? That's the best you can do for yourself?"
"Fuck you."

"Eh?... That's the best you can do for yourself, I'm so bad, huh?"
"Where's your mind? I thought you were different."
"Different..."
"I thought you were different, or gonna be different, from all these other similar thoughts around here like everybody else's."
"You know you fuckin' act like this mothafucka's end was premeditated or somethin'."
"The landlord didn't do nothin'! And Joanie's husband--"
"I did the right thing."
"You don't even know nothin' 'bout Joanie. Shit, I don't know nothin' 'bout Joanie and I see the bitch everyday. Shit, she acts like--"
"Look, I don't need nobody complaining about how I choose to make my money."
"What money? You ain't got no fuckin' money. You're like a Peruvian sheepdog."
"Yeah, you know so much. Enroll me in your school."
"You ain't nobody."
"Enroll me, enroll me where they manufacture your brains."
"Yeah, you ain't got none. You're everybody else... Every body else."
"Yeah, the grand priestess of wisdom. Why didn't you get yourself out of the projects sooner, bitch."
"You can't do it. What can you do? All you know how to do is fuck! That's all you know."
"Right."
"That's your volume in history-- crime and fuckin'."
"Yeah, that's all I know, right. That's all of my history, right bitch?"
"That's it. You ain't nobody."

Dice takes his forearm and swings it, knocking her on the floor backwards on her back-- Rosie's face contorts to confusion. He bends down and pulls her up by the arms, then pushes her up against the wall there (her eyes wince from the shock of it).

Rosie starts to move but Dice, slams her back against the wall with the palm of his hand on her chest and she winces again.

He then takes his foot, places it behind the heel of hers and, sweeps her feet up-- she slides down the wall and hits the floor hard on her buttocks. She stares furiously at him. "You fuckin' bastard!!"

"That's right," he says, and gets down on his knees, quickly pulling down the zipper of his pants. He takes his hands and spreads her thighs out wide with a push, as she slaps his face, again, and again, with Dice seeming not to feel any of it but absorbing it.

He then looks her straight in the eyes and says "You fuckin' bitch" to her, grabs her underneath her thighs, pushes the both of them way up over his head with force and drops them on his shoulders, then takes the palm of his hand and holds her down by her chest. He then takes out his penis and forces himself inside her. She says nothing, looking at him with pain and confusion.

After a few eternal moments, he orgasms. Stops. Stays there motionless. She looks at him. Then, he pulls himself out of her, flipping himself over on the floor on his back. He looks at the ceiling, resting there. Rosie slides herself up upright, against the wall, looking at him. "Big man on campus," she says.

    "Whatever," Dice replies.
    "Oh boy, what a man. I guessed you showed me."
    "Whatever."
    "Grandiose."
    "Awright, grandiose."
    "Your manhood is grandiose. Everything's settled now."
    "It should be."
    "It is. You're so good. You taught me a thing or two."
    "No one told you to preach."
    "Preach... That's what I was doing, preaching."
    "No one told you to be judgmental."
    "Yeah but you showed me. You showed me who's boss."
    "Whatever."
    "I should've never questioned it. Your cum has negotiation capabilities unheard of."
    "Okay."
    "How could I've been so dumb."
    "How could you?"
    "How could I... Boy, I'm like a new woman now."
    "Good... Long live birth."

Some time later, Spike is standing outside in front of his building. No one else appears outside this evening with the exception of an approaching woman, walking slowly towards him in the dim darkness. In her hand she carries what looks like a 12 inch pipe. She hits herself in the face once with the object. Spike does a double take because he thinks that's what he saw her do.

Suddenly, Dice appears behind him and steps out of the building. He notices Spike standing there not seeing him and says, "Sorry I took so long man." He then stands next to Spike, looking at him watching the approaching woman. "Hey," he announces.

Spike turns around to him quick. "Huh," he answers.

Dice sees the woman getting closer to them, then asks Spike, "What's the deal man?..."

"Huh," Spike says again, as he stares at Dice dumbfounded.

Dice looks at the woman approaching. She hits herself in the face again with the object. Dice's face turns solemn.

The woman is Joanie, who walks past the two (not even seeing them) right into the building.

Dice looks at Spike now with disbelief smashed on his face. Spike turns away from him and looks straight ahead, at nothing. Dice continues looking at him with his features slowly evolving into anger. "Tell me I'm on hallucinogenics mothafucka. Tell me somebody snuck some mystery in me today when I wasn't looking..."

 "I can't claim nothin'," Spike says, still looking in the same direction. "My notion is that you're normal."
 "Mothafucka, you better tell me I'm not normal!... Do you realize what we just saw?..."
 "I witnessed it," Spike replies, beginning to shed tears now.
 "Aww man!!" Dice hurls, turning around and away from Spike, throwing his hands up.

Spike still stands there motionless except for the streaming down tears from his eyes. Dice has his back to him, his stance and his posture in anger. Spike continues standing there, heaving in his tears, sniffling his nose and not wiping it.

Dice swiftly turns back around to him. "I took your recommendation man!"

 "I know," Spike sobs back.
 "You said, this would be a good one to start with!... like you knew her more than hello and how are you!..."
 "I know man, I know."

Dice shakes his head and turns back around with disgust. Spike finally turns his head to him. "So what d'you think my penalty should be for fuckin' up?..."

 "I didn't design no constitution for that... You said, she would be a good one to start with, 'cause you knew her well!"
 "I know, I know."
 "Well... if you knew her so well like she was flesh 'n blood or some other blood tie... why this fuck up?... Why this malfunction, if this was so precise?"

"That's why I asked what your penalty is?"
"I ain't got no penalty, man. I told you, I'm not a legislator..."
Spike stands there thinking, looking up at the sky. "I fucked up real bad..." Dice turns back to him. "Look man, do you know this bitch real good for real?..." Spike speaks painfully with great effort. "Awright man... I've seen her just comin' and goin' back and forth in the building and around the way like you. Later I've seen her with all the extra non-human attachments on her face... I'm tellin' ya man, I didn't know the bitch was wacky."

"But in the projects everybody talks... I don't see how--"
"But I don't hang out around here. I'm never out around here lingering..."

Dice turns back around with disgust. "Aww man, this is so fucked up... How do we know he was really bruising her?..."

Suddenly and brisk he snaps up vertically and slowly turns back to Spike with the appearance of something found. "But you know what?" he says to him with a certain mark of glee on his face. "That mothafucka was intensely rude..."

Spike looks at him to understand his point more clearly.

Dice continues, walking towards him. "Look... when I left the token booth before and that girl came, remember that?"

"Yeah, I remember."
"Yeah, well, did you hear the way he yelled at her when she came up there asking for tokens?..."

Spike takes a few seconds to retrieve memory on what Dice is talking about. "Okay," he says. "I got you."

"Awright. Well, if you had heard him, you'll know that talking to a young lady like that should be a punishable offense. There was no reason for it."
"Oh yeah. Yeah, I remember that. You're right, there was no reason for it."
"Exactly. And for that Neanderthal to lunge at her like that... I'd say he deserved some kind of retribution, wouldn't you say?..."
"Yeah," Spike replies, appearing to cheer up a bit. "I'll agree with that."
"Any reasonable man with their thoughts in order would say that." Dice claps his hands once with satisfaction. "So it's settled. We were right after all..."

Spike ponders his conclusion and finally agrees. "Yeah... Okay. That's a good point... Now I don't feel so uncommitted to the betterment of personkind."

"Fuck that. I'd say we were almost doing God's work. Lettin' somebody walk around like that jumping on defenseless women, abusing them 'n shit... I'd say we're ridding the Earth of evil in the form of bipeds."
"Yeah... He was probably beating her anyway. We just didn't know about it."
"Exactly. How wrong could we have been?... Not very."
"Not very. I agree with that."

They both stand there motionless, satisfied now. Their silence makes them relaxed from any thought for a few seconds, then Dice resumes talk with, "Awright man. So let's get started."

"Right."

They immediately walk with haste away from the building.

Later that evening in another neighborhood, bearing rows of three-story walk-up buildings, Dice and Spike stand against a parked car facing one of the building's stoops, waiting there.

Coming out of that building is Lube, wearing the same black shoe polish on his face and white grease paint around and on mouth. His dog bone remains securely through his nose, but this time, he has on a white tee shirt instead of his message-filled black sweatshirt, and carries a banjo in his hand, as he heads down the stoop to greet Dice and Spike.

The two see him approaching and immediately remove themselves off the car to great him. Dice says to Lube, "I haven't even checked the time man. I hope we ain't too late."

Lube happily greets him with, "Your timing is splendid my good man... I see you are accompanied by Spike as planned."

Spike says, "What's happenin' Lube?... Long time no see."

"Yes," Lube replies, going straight to the windshield of the car the two were leaning on. He looks for his reflection in the glass to check his makeup. Finding some of it, he pats his face, firmly positions his bone to make sure everything is in place. "Dice, as far as the time that you suggested..."

"Yeah."

"...well... it seems that you two buddies have arrived in a forthwith manner. I am pleased by your fortitude in time checking."

Dice looks around. "So where's your car, Lube?"

Placing his banjo under his arm, he plucks the strings, checking to see if it's in tune. Then he replies, "I have borrowed a 1969 Chevy Impala, for my own remains in the shop in shambles."

Spike points down the block. "It's down that way?..."

Lube happily agrees and they all begin to walk down that way, with Lube still fiddling with the tuning pegs on his banjo.

Some time later, a maroon 1969 Chevrolet Impala is riding down a highway with moderate traffic rolling to and fro.

Inside the car behind the wheel, Lube keeps pace with the speed limit, keeping his voice silent as he concentrates on the road.

Seconds later, a gray state trooper's patrol car is cruising up behind them-- pale blue light on the hood of it, flashing and flashing as Lube pulls the car over to the side of the road, both coming to a stop.

Lube waits patiently behind the wheel while Dice and Spike sit in the back seat trying to undo their look of fear. The state trooper gets out of the car and walks up to Lube's side, and stops in his tracks, looking at him. Lube says nothing, looking straight ahead at the road.

The state trooper stares hard at Lube, holding his ticket book in suspended animation. He then looks in the back seat at Dice and Spike, who say nothing. The state trooper looks back at Lube. "You all happen to be going to a show or something?..."

Lube calmly answers, "No sir, officer."

"No?" the state trooper answers in disbelief, staring a bit harder at Lube. "Well... you in charge of some kind of magic shop or something?..."
"No sir officer," Lube says again, with politeness sincere in tone.

The state trooper looks back at Dice and Spike, who keep the same motionlessness in their expressions. He addresses Lube again. "I'm gonna have to search this car. Where's your license and registration?"

Lube robotically immediate, reaches for the glove compartment, opens it, and dutifully hands it to the state trooper, who right away looks at it assuming a something-is-wrong reality. He studies the license up and down, then, hands it back over to Lube.

"Listen to me," the trooper begins, leaning his forearm on Lube's car door to address his face. "My advice to you is to get somewhere where you can get that makeup off. You're not going to a show?..."

Lube looks at him like he's crazy. "Absolutely not!" he replies insulted.

The trooper raises his torso to leave. "Well... I suggest you get that makeup off," he says finally, and walks back to his patrol car.

Dice and Spike both breathe in and out hard, with Dice asking Lube, "You feeling okay, man? Did he make you--"

"Never better," Lube replies quick and brusque with pleasantness. "Let us proceed."

And Lube starts the engine of the car and heads down the highway again, minding the rules of a proper speed limit.

The Chevy Impala continues with ease down the highway comfortably, along with scant traffic moving with them for twenty minutes or so, until a state trooper patrol car pulls up behind them again, lights flashing. Lube once again pulls the car over to the side. Dice and Spike brace themselves in their insides while Lube pleasantly awaits the state trooper's appearance.

The patrol car door opens and a different state trooper gets out and walks over to Lube's car. When he gets there, he stares at Lube almost startled. "What the hell's on your face??" the trooper says, expecting an adverse response.

Dice and Spike sort of tremble watching Lube as he appears to be offended. "My face, sir, is intact, and ready to answer your questions."

The trooper stares stunned at him, then looks in the back seat at Dice and Spike. "What's your friend's story here?"

Dice begins to answer but Lube stops it before coming out. "My story," Lube says to the trooper, "is one of mundane usualness, as usual..."

The trooper stares confused at him and his answer. "Where's your license and registration?..."

Lube looks straight ahead pleasantly, staying motionless for a second that seems much longer. Then, he reaches in the glove compartment for the license again and dutifully hands it to the trooper. The trooper takes his time studying it as Lube patiently waits behind the wheel. Dice and Spike wait with apprehension all over their bodies.

Lube still waits and the trooper still studies his license. Lube then, extra slowly, pulls his banjo up from the floor and the trooper's eyes shift to the side to watch his move. Dice and Spike's faces start looking nervous.

Lube looks in his windshield mirror, patting his makeup softly with one hand to make sure it's still on (holding the banjo's neck with the other), positioning his bone with his first two fingers and wiggling his nose.

The trooper's eyes shift back to the license. Lube then takes the banjo and places it on his lap as Dice and Spike watch in horror. He begins to pluck the strings like an amateur playing.

The state trooper drops Lube's license down to his side. "Put that shit down!" he orders. Lube, graciously returns the banjo back down to the floor as Dice and Spike become relieved. The trooper, still staring at him, asks, "You a fuckin' wise guy??"

"Absolutely not, if you are suggesting defiance sir," Lube replies with confidence of being understood. Dice and Spike start together to get jittery again as the trooper hands the license back to Lube.

Now he looks at the two in the back and addresses them. "If I search this fuckin' car am I gonna find drugs and guns?..."

Lube says, "Sir, I can assure you, we are not purveyors of the criminal element of life..."

The trooper stares with uncertainty at Lube. Then, he bends down aiming his ear at him. "You called me a what?..."

Lube answers, "Sir, I have been fair and accurate with my statements and words. No pun is intended at your series of work."

The trooper looks back at Dice and Spike. "So... you boys refuse to tell me what show you're appearing in today?..."

Dice quickly responds. "We're not in a show officer."

Lube adds, "But we do have an important engagement to meet, and it is a fact."

The state trooper postures himself unsure as he looks down the highway. Then he looks back at Lube. "I'm a let you boys go ahead, but you... you better get that shit off your face before I nail you for trouble..."

The trooper turns and walks back to his patrol car with Dice and Spike becoming a bit more relaxed. As Lube prepares to pull off while the patrol car backs up and drives away, Spike says, "See?... Even with an old car, it doesn't matter. Black folks're still gonna get stopped..."

Lube happily says, "Well gentlemen... let's resume our cause to unknown destiny..."

And he drives the car, pulling back over on the road again.

Down the highway they resume riding moderately down the lane, passing the rural hotels and motels with restaurants overwhelmed in neon below the sky's darkness. The diesel trucks hum motorized wails passing the Impala by, blowing up grit and dust pinging the windows lightly like fingernail taps against thick hard glass.

Candy green signs indicating rest areas swoosh by stiffly on the islands dividing the lanes on the highway, half-lighting quick the faces of Lube, Dice and Spike like candles.

The ride is smooth and the inside of Lube's car is quiet from talk, as the flow of the car's wheels makes them relax their eyes. They are soundless, hearing nothing but the car's engine and other cars cruising by straight as they pass them.

Buildings and homes pass their view-- some are lit, others with activity inside them are not seen for the evening's lateness. The sound of Spike now snoring begins to creep into the atmosphere inside the car, mixing along with the siren behind them.

A siren! Another state trooper's patrol car is behind them! This time its siren yells out round and round with the light on its roof flashing the same way in rhythm. Spike's eyes explode wide open, awake. "Shit!" he pierces. "These mothafuckas're gettin' on my nerves now!"

Lube smiles. "Patiently now, my partners... We'll reach our destination untainted from harm. My confidence for this is practically straddling my neck..."

Lube obediently pulls the car over to the side of the road with precision, coming to a stop. The patrol car stops behind them along with the siren's yelling. The flashing light remains, lighting the surrounding areas of bushes and trees in swoops. Two state troopers this time, swing their doors open and climb out of the car in haste.

Dice sees them quickly approaching the car through the back windshield. "This is fucked up, man" he says. "We might as well had a took a bike..."

Lube pleasantly responds, saying, "A bike would be preposterous friends. I am confident that our needs will be met by law."

The state troopers put their hands on their gun handles, walking up to the Chevy now. The first trooper says, "Out the fuckin' ca--" but stops when he sees Lube's face behind the wheel. He looks at the second trooper to make sure he sees Lube, and his facial gestures move to indicate that he does.

The first trooper checks the back seat and sees Dice and Spike sitting there motionless, then looks back at Lube who calmly sits behind the wheel, waiting for the troopers' orders.

The first trooper glares at him. "You a fuckin' clown, sir niggruh boy?..."

"Sir," Lube begins, "I assure you that we are not members."

The trooper looks at the second trooper with puzzlement. The second one holds the giggle that almost came out.

The first trooper looks back at Lube. "Let me see your license and registration motherfucka..." Then he immediately reaches for his ticket book without hesitation.

Lube keeps his smile on his face, breathes in and out with his hands on the wheel. "FUCKo!!..." he yells with no anger, and the troopers instantly stop what they're doing, and stare at him in disbelief. Dice and Spike's faces droop down sullen.

The first trooper goes back up to Lube and speaks directly to the side of his face. "Niggruh clown boy, are you upset sho nuff?..."

"Sir," Lube replies politely. "May I get out of my vehicle willingly?..."

Both troopers stand back, folding their arms watching Lube with direct vision attached to his movements. The first one tells him, "Go ahead. Let's see you get out..." Dice and Spike sink down a bit lower in the back seat, looking at the car floor.

Lube slowly opens the door. The second trooper shouts, "And put your fuckin' hands up when you get out here!..."

The first trooper tells the second, "I got these other two covered," gesturing to Dice and Spike in the back, who appear to be mourning statues.

Lube's feet come out of the car first, then half of his body emerges, while the other half, banjo in hand, eases out and, SWINGS-- knocking the first trooper in the head with it (he stumbles backwards, falling to the ground).

The second trooper (shocked) draws his gun. Lube yells to Dice and Spike, "Run my partners! Flee the land!" The second trooper turns his head. The car door opens and the two friends dive out the back. The second trooper now aims his gun at them.

Then bam!-- his head is lammed with Lube's banjo. Lube slams him again in the head and the second trooper drops to his knees unconscious while the first one lies on the ground with his motions gone.

Dice and Spike go through bushes in darkness down a hill, away from the area, huffing and puffing.

Lube stands with a hand on his hip and the banjo in the other, looking down at the fallen state troopers. He pushes himself up with his toes ballet style, and twirls around full circle one time (with the banjo leading him). He then raises the banjo up and swings it down like an ax, smashing the first trooper's head again. He raises the banjo up, brings it down again and smashes the second trooper's head.

Cars on the highway (in all lanes) practically come to a halt now to view Lube assaulting the state troopers.

Lube still has one hand on his hip, staring down at the troopers, holding the banjo down low enough to graze the grass tops as he moves it back and forth in a pendulum manner. He addresses the trooper's unconscious ears. "I am GROWING, very WEARY, of always having to REMIND everyone... ALWAYS!!!..."

Dice and Spike continue running into the blackness, down the dark hill of branches that scrape their arms like brushes as they run. Far apart now is the distance between them as they keep galloping, running down the hill. Dice yells out, "Spike!... Separate!... Call Rosie!... We link up thru Rosie!..."

"Right!..."

Still running, the two friends now separate, heading in different directions in the deep night's darkness. Soon only one person is huffing and puffing, and footsteps in the soil can be heard, cracking branches with every hard step down into it, running.

Dice, alone now, sees a break through the bushes and tree trunks via lights twinkling in the distance away. He runs towards them. Coming out of the dark foliage he enters the calmness of one narrow street the width of a car, that's black from the tar that covers it. It weaves like a snake to the entrance of a motel called Landy's, according to the sign's basement-deep orange neon hue.

Spectacularly clean are the grounds of the motel, where various parked cars sit in the area out front, with the rural landscape still prevalent around it and in back, where a cadre of trees stand behind it military-style still, aiming down looking at the motel with protection appearance.

The motel itself bares witness to average family clientele by the two families that now enter it-- one set entering with bags, the other set leaving with bags.

Dice is standing there on the curb of the street, surveying the place, then patting his clothes for his own appearance for presentability. He reaches in his pocket to make sure he has the one hundred dollars that he made, pulling out the one hundred dollar bill to give it a quick look, then shoving it back in.

He then walks over to the motel.

Once inside, he approaches the counter where various clerks scurry about helping the customers that are inside. One of the girls sees him and asks if he can be helped. Dice says, "How much is it a night?..."

"Forty dollars for one room sir." She answers back. Dice immediately reaches in his pocket to hand her the one hundred dollar bill.

He later walks down a corridor, key in hand, searching for his assigned room number. Finding it, he immediately slides the key in the hole and enters it.

Some time later inside the room, Dice is on the phone. Rosie's voice answers "Hello" on the other end. Dice says, "Hey. Listen, Spike didn't call you yet, did he?..."

Rosie says nothing. Then Dice demands, "Rosie!..."

"What!..."
"What's happenin'? How come you didn't answer me?..."
"Answer you like, Oh! Everything's cool now???..."

"C'mon Rosie. What's the matter with you?"
"What's the matter with me. Like I like a swashbuckler."
"You're always jerking around."
"Like I like criminal activity... I hate criminal activity, of all kinds!"
"What, we gonna take this landlord thing to the ends of the Earth?"
"It ain't just about that no more... You think it's cool to vandalize me?"
"What chu talkin' 'bout, vandalize you?"
"You fuckin' made mockery of my body!..."

Dice thinks about what she's saying for a moment, then replies, "Oh! Since when you don't like it like that no more?"

"You know what I'm talking about. It was much different than relationship sex."
"Oh yeah?... Well what was different about it?... What was different about it?"
"I have to tell you? Forget about it."
"Nah, I don't wanna forget about it."
"You might as well. This is elementary. You need to be here. I got a blackboard and chalk. I'd have to start that way with you, right?"
"All of a sudden everything's different now..."
"You're right... Everything's different... I don't understand how you can think that it's okay to injure me for pleasure."
"Injure you??... Awright. You're just still mad about the landlord, right?"
"Wrong."
"Wrong... Well I think that's the deal."
"It's not the deal."
"Look, did Spike call you yet?"
"No Spike didn't call me. Why, someone else is dearly departed?"
"No. He's supposed to call you. Just tell him I'm at the Landy Motel, just outside of town."
"Tell him yourself."
"Tell him yourself... Everything's comedy with you today, right?"
"Hey, I'm not laughing. Hear any sniffles from the roar of it? I think not."
"This is serious Rosie. Tell Spike where I am. He's gonna call you..."

No words from Rosie come out on the other end for a moment. Dice calls her name once and gets nothing. Then he calls it again.

"What," she replies.
"What about what I said? You gonna tell Spike?..."
"I'm gonna bring you up on charges for sexual assault."
"Rosie... Just tell Spike, okay? He's gonna wanna know where I am, and tell him to leave a number where he's gonna be at, or where he thinks he gonna be at... Okay?..."
"Bye!"

"Rosie!..."

And the dial tone he hears is quite loud. Dice hangs up the receiver with a bang. His expression wonders if she will do what he asked or not.

He stands looking around trying to figure his next move. Then, he grabs his keys and leaves the room.

As he locks the door out in the hall, he hears another door being locked. He turns to that direction and sees a short young toffee colored shapely woman (thirtiesh in age), with braided hair touching her shoulders. She stares at Dice with doe-eyed fright with her key in the door, not moving like a still life painting.

He immediately turns away and heads down the hall for the stairs to the lobby.

When he gets down there he starts to go back to the sales counter. Then changes his mind. He turns back around and heads back upstairs.

Walking down the hall to his room, he reaches it and unlocks the door, going inside.

He heads for the phone on the nightstand in there until two knocks on the door stop him. He stares at it a moment before going over to answer it.

When he opens the door, he sees it's the very same young woman with the braids who was at her door earlier. She stares up at him with the same doe-eyed expression and addresses him. "Um... I was wondering, if you could help me with something?..."

"Well," Dice responds, admiring her good looks and not trusting her. "Depends on what the something is."

She has no expression on her face. "Um, do you mind if I come in?..."

Dice says "Yeah" while gesturing her to do so with his hand, doubtfully.

The young woman walks over to Dice's bed while he notices how tight her black miniskirt fits. She immediately sits on his bed and crosses her legs slow enough for him to see.

Dice looks at her with desire and concern, cautiously. "So what's happenin'?" he asks.

"Well... My father... I think he's dead?... and, I don't know what to do about it?..."
"Your father?..."

She points to the direction of her room, where she was locking the door.

Dice is slightly stunned. "He's in there? He's here with you?..."

She nods up and down with shy solemnity. "He's in my room..." she says. "I thought he was sleep, but..."

Dice looks at her with disbelief at her calmness. "Well damn," he replies, "did you go downstairs and tell anybody about it?"

"Oh no," she says, "I can't do that... I think I did it... By mistake..."

Dice frowns at her. "What?..."

"I think I killed him..." She uncrosses her legs and opens her thighs a bit.
"Well... damn, that's kinda... How'd you do that? You said by mistake?..."
"Yeah, well, I was scrubbing him. That sounds weird, right? I mean, he was practically disabled."
"Practically disabled?"
"Um hmm..."
"So, what d'you mean, he's in the bathtub or something?..."

She nods up and down.

Dice turns away from her in contemplative fashion. "Look... when I go in there with you, I'm gonna take a look at him, check his pulse and see if he's gone, then we deal with the downstairs people, okay?..."

"Alright."
"So what're you saying, like he drowned in the tub?..."

She nods up and down.

Dice is in thought for an abrupt second, then he heads for his door, leaving her on the bed. He turns and tells her to come on with another hand gesture, and she gets up and walks over to him, leaving the room.

Reaching her door she opens it with Dice standing behind her. She enters the room. Dice carefully steps in with caution, looking here and there.

She heads for the bathroom, looking behind her waiting for Dice to come closer. He comes up to the bathroom door as she slowly pushes it open more.

Dice sees an olive tinged, slightly heavy set, sixtiesh bald man lying in the bathtub with his eyes closed asleep style. He carefully walks over to the tub, extends his hand gradually to the man and touches his arm with his fingertips. He jerks them away. "He's real cold," Dice tells her, deciding not to examine him anymore by moving back.

He says to her, "You said you made a mistake... What did you do? Did he drown or somethin'? Did he slip and hit his head?..."

The woman walks out of the bathroom and goes over to her purse on the dresser. She pulls out a cigarette from the pack that she has in there. Dice immediately lights it with the book of matches he pulled out. She releases, "The mistake I made... was that I didn't blow his fuckin' brains out with my gun..."

Dice looks at her like she's a ghost.

"You look shocked," the woman says, drawing on her cigarette. "Don't be... The mothafucka's been molesting me since I was six years old... I finally got up enough nerve to send him where that fuckin' bastard ass pet dog of his went a year ago..."

Dice looks at the shape of her legs and asks, "So how'd you get rid of him?..."

"Well... I got kinda chicken and did it with poison... Anyway, using a gun in here would be obvious, right?..."
"Oh yeah, of course." Dice now stares at her directly in the eyes. "So now, what kind of cards you got here for me now? What's the deal? You need me for what?..."
"To get his fuckin' ass outta here... I got money..." And she immediately reaches in her purse and pulls out a rubber band stack of twenty dollar bills and holds it up to him.

Dice looks at it. "How much is there?..."

"A thousand... I'll give it to you if you help me move the body outta here..." She slips the rubber band off the stack. "I'll give you half now..." And she begins to divide the stack in half to count out five hundred dollars."
"Wait a minute," Dice says, going over to look at the bills more closely.
"I'm strictly business-- what's your name?"
"Dice..."
"I'm strictly business Dice. I don't have time to play games of masquerade when it comes to the money. But you can check it out," she puts the stack in his hand. "I don't have a problem with that..."

She watches him looking at the money. "You good at counterfeit tracking?" she asks.

He says nothing as he looks at the dollar bills from front to back.

The woman still watches him as she smokes her cigarette. "My name is Wanda..."

Dice looks up from his counting and sticks his hand out to shake hers. Wanda takes his hand and says, "Glad to meet you, Dice..."

"Listen..." he replies handing her back the money, "why do you need to get him outta here in the first place? Why don't you just leave him here?..."
"Look," begins Wanda, "his mother's still alive-- my grandmother. I gotta bring him back to his mommy's."

Dice glances a look over at the corpse in the tub, then back at Wanda. "What kind of poison did you use on him? You just gonna send him to his mother's with poison in him?..."

She shrugs. "Well... I gotta get him outta here..."

"What're you gonna do about the poison?... They're gonna know that you poisoned him?..."
"Yes, but they're not gonna think I did it."
"Why not?"
"Because, why would they think I poisoned him?... I'm gonna bring his everloving ass back and put him in his house, that's what I'm gonna do."

Dice looks like he's trying to believe her.

Wanda continues, "I have no problem driving with a corpse... It only means that I don't have to listen to his crap anymore."

Dice looks back over at the corpse. "Well how you plan on gettin' him outta here?..."

She shrugs. "That's why I'm hiring you... 'cause I don't know..."

Dice turns away to think. He looks around Wanda's room surveying the area with his hand on his chin. She continues to watch him, calmly smoking her cigarette, keeping stationary with her arms folded.

Dice walks over to her unslept bed and examines the covers. He pulls the top one off and examines it, pulling it onto the floor. "You didn't come in here with any bags, the two of you?..."

"Not really," she replies. "Just a normal regular suitcase that everyone carries."

He looks around again, then notices the window in a sudden manner. He immediately goes over to it and looks out of it.

He sees that the window looks out onto an empty lot, filled with huge garbage tubs and debris. They are on the second floor.

Dice sticks his head back in and quickly walks back to the bathroom to look at the corpse in the tub. When he gets there, he measures the size of him with his eyes from side to side, then walks out and over to Wanda. "You drove here, right?"

    "Yes."
    "Okay... This is what I'm gonna do..."

Wanda immediately starts counting out the five hundred dollars. "A promise should always be like stone," she tells him.

His thought was interrupted when she said that. Looking at her hands counting, he resumes, "I'm gonna wrap your father in those covers, and dump him out the window. You seen what's back there?"

    "There's like an empty lot?"
    "Right. I'm gonna dump him out there. You're gonna pull your car out back there so I can put him in the back seat."
    "The front seat... I don't mind having his corpse ass beside me."
    "If that's fitting to you..."

She hands him the five hundred dollars without hesitation and he takes it, folding it in half and shoving it in his pants pocket.

Dice then heads over to the bed, pulling off the rest of the covers there. Wanda looks at him. "You need some help?" she asks.

    "Nah. Not right now at least..." He goes over to the bathroom and prepares to pull the body out of the tub. Dice's facial features start wrinkling. He breathes in deep, closes his eyes. Then, he stoops down a bit to be able to pull the corpse up by its arm pits. Before starting he remembers the covers. "Could you push those bed covers over to me please Wanda?..."

She immediately slides the covers over to him slowly with her foot. He notices how shapely her leg is.

Dice then begins to pull the corpse out of the tub, pulling with his strength and lacking enough of it to drag him up in one full swoop. He pulls and pulls, walking backwards on his heels step by step as Wanda watches him to see if he needs any help.

The back of the corpse slides slowly up over the top of the tub, then its buttocks thud drops on the bathroom floor-- Dice almost loses his balance. He immediately goes to the sink and washes his hands with the soap there.

Then, Dice tries to lift the corpse up and onto the top bed cover on the floor (again by the arm pits). He drops its back on the cover (the thud happens again). Then he positions the body's torso on there, stands straight, and heads back over to the sink to wash his hands again.

Wanda looks at him wondering what with her eyebrows.

Dice now takes the corpse's legs and positions them in the center of the cover, carefully shifting the hands neatly, crossing the legs, then the arms. He raises himself back up, and, heads back over to the sink to wash his hands.

Wanda looks at him with exasperation.

Dice now takes the long end of the cover and flips it over on top of the body. He then rolls the corpse into the cover, pushing it by the ribs until it's fully covered.

He stands and brushes his hands together, and, starts to go back over to the sink.

Wanda looks at him sternly.

He changes his mind. "Uh, I'm gonna need some help getting your father over to the window," he says.

"Oh sure," Wanda answers dutifully, and comes over to where he's standing. "Yeah, just take his feet, that's all."

The two of them take the bottom of the cover with the corpse inside and drag it over to the window. Dice tells her, "Now you go downstairs and drive your car to the back out there. Don't park it directly underneath the window, but almost near it."

"Okay."

And Wanda instantly leaves her room, taking her purse. Dice goes right into the bathroom again and washes his hands, then, returns to the window, sticking his head out of it.

After a few seconds of nothing seen, he sees the grayish blue shimmer of a 1972 Honda Civic, slowly backing up towards the window but to the left of it.

Dice now prepares to heave the body up to the windowsill, and he does so with difficult strength, stopping to do deep breathing before he drops the body out.

He sticks his head out of the window again to measure the drop with his eyes.

Now, he lifts the covered corpse up with his arms underneath the bottom of its buttocks. He catches his breath, then, hauls the body out of the window.

Dice watches as the cover sails off the body going down, with the naked corpse smacking the ground first with a thump on the concrete. Dice gapes "Oh shit!!" and runs not fast enough out of Wanda's room to get downstairs.

Wanda is out there getting the bed cover as it falls from the sky. She desperately covers the corpse with it, looking in every direction. Dice is running towards her now as she says to him, "I gotta get his clothes, and the suitcase!"

"Go 'head! go 'head!..."

And she tippy-toe runs back to the front of the motel, but before she gets there, she stops, tugs the bottom of her skirt down, and walks, casually.

Dice opens the passenger side door of the Honda and struggles to get the corpse in, but does so.

A couple of minutes later, Wanda is heading back towards the car with a suitcase in her hand. She gradually walks faster with each step as she gets closer to it, until she's just about running. Then she runs full blast to the car, her braids bouncing rapid fire up and down like continuous automatic weapon shots.

She reaches the car and sees that Dice is sitting behind the wheel. She asks him, "You driving?"

"Halfway," Dice tells her, sticking his hand out. "Give me the keys..."

Dropping them in his hand, she opens the door, throws the suitcase in the back seat and climbs in. "Okay, but I can't pay you extra for it. I don't have that much money."

"It's awright. Which way ya headed?..."
"South, that way."

Dice sticks the key in the ignition and starts the engine, soon pulling off and heading in the direction she gave him.

As the Honda heads down the highway at normal speed, Dice tells Wanda, "You know what?... At some point I gotta let you get behind the wheel... The state troopers're sacred in their harassment tonight. Believe me, I got enough wisdom on this subject for the century..."

"We gotta pull off somewhere anyway, in the woods or something, so we can get these clothes on him."

Dice gestures agreement with his hand and he continues down the highway a couple of extra miles before pulling off the road, rolling down into a wooded area.

Dice lets Wanda dress the corpse at her request and he watches her as she does it. His eyes examine the roundness of her buttocks in her tight skirt, and the back of her thighs opening and closing with her movements in dressing the corpse, force Dice to emit words not relating to the current situation.

With his vision moving up to her breasts he says, "You're about the finest girl I seen in a long time, you know that?..."

Wanda smiles not looking at him while putting the arms of the corpse in the sleeves of a jacket. "Oh yeah?..."

"Yeah. I don't write novels and shit like that, you know?... If I say something like that, I'm meaning it, crucial..."

She continues with the corpse while Dice moves closer to her. "You been showing me a lot of your shit tonight too, you know?..."

"Oh yeah?... Wanda replies, fixing the clothes on the corpse now.

"Yep," responds Dice, who then takes his hand and places it squarely on Wanda's buttocks. He gently squeezes it, letting his middle finger rub up into the outline of the crack between her buttocks, as he slurps desire with his teeth shut.

Wanda's feels him but her motions reveal nothing as she finishes dressing the corpse. She then turns around smiling, looking from down to up at him as she leans her back against the car, shifting her thighs open and semi-shut from side to side, back and forth. "You wanna fuck me Dice?" she says, then leans over towards him and feels his penis with a cupped hand grab.

Dice gives a knowing smile to her as she raises her skirt all the way up to her buttocks and leans back more against the car. "Alright Dice, you wanna fuck me?"

"What do you think? Either you give it up or I'll just fuckin' take it, pronto."
"Yeah?... 'Cause if you gonna fuck me, you better fuck me hard, and for a long time... You better not wham bam me! You gotta fuck me for hours goddamnit! You're gonna have to fuck me for a real long time! You got that?... I like my shit hard and for a long time! No rest periods, none of that shit! And if you start disappointing me, wanting to rest and smoke cigarettes 'n shit?... I swear to God, I'm gonna run out there on that highway, and scream that you're trying to rape me, my hand to God!... So let's see what you got. You wanna fuck me?... C'mon, you gotta turn me on first. Let's go! Turn me on..." And Wanda lifts the front of her skirt now. "Let's see what you got baby..."

Dice stands there wilted looking at her. The energy he had welled up now drips down slow like thick malted as he watches her.

"I'm waitin', Dice," Wanda says, looking a bit serious now.

Dice feels that he has stood there for hours just looking at her. Then, he abruptly turns around and storms back over to the diver's side of the car. "C'mon!" he slams. "I don't have time for games. You finished with your father?..."

Wanda lowers her skirt back down, smiling to herself, and climbs back into the back seat of the car with a few chuckles under her breath.

Dice glares at her. "I said, are you done with your father?"

She smiles at him. "Yes, I'm done."

"Well which way you headed, you still going in the same direction?"
"Yes."

Dice starts the engine up again, then remembers, "That's right-- you gotta drive. C'mon..." And he gets out of the car and opens the door for Wanda to change over to the front seat. She gets out and climbs into the seat behind the wheel still smiling at him, as he now sits in the back seat. Wanda starts the car and they pull off again.

As Wanda heads down the highway, she continues to smile while looking at Dice's grim expression in the rearview mirror. After a few moments of deafening silence, she asks him, "You want me to drive you back somewhere?..."

"You can take me, right back the fuck where I came from! And give me the rest of my money, please!..."

Wanda obediently pulls off to the side of the road and stops the car. Reaching in her purse, she gently hands the rest of the money over to Dice, looking at him with a smile. He takes it with a "Thank you," and shoves it in his pocket. "Matter of fact..." he says, getting out of the car now, slamming the door.

Wanda turns to stare at him, waiting in disbelief. "Where're you going?..."

"Fuck it, I'll walk back!"
"You're crazy."
"Nah, you got something, and I got something. So let's leave it at that. You just go ahead and take your father back to where you came from, okay?..."

Wanda frowns at him. "You asshole. That's not my father. It's my husband. What daughter you know bathes their father in the tub? You need two hands to count the number?..."

Dice looks slightly shocked with more anger smashed on his face. He starts to walk away but turns back around. He then takes his pinky, and shoves it into his left nostril, digging around in there before pulling it out.

There, on the tip of his pinky, is a pale green booger of exceptional size. He takes it, puts it in the palm of his other hand, takes that, and smashes Wanda in the face with it, wiping the booger real hard on her cheek.

She violently grabs her face with both hands, tapping it, trying to find out what and where it is by way of touch. Her finger finally finds it as it sticks to her index finger. She looks at it, chuckles, then looks at Dice and laughs out loud.

Dice looks at her with puzzlement.

She then takes her finger with the booger, and shoves it into her mouth, eating it with guffaws as accompaniment.

Dice stares at her amazed.

She prepares to leave now by racing the car engine, laughing at him. "Get over it loverboy!... Thanks for your service, and, the fingerprints!..."

Dice's face now explodes with alarm.

She then screeches the car tires pulling off, with the wind from it flapping his clothes every which way as he stands in the darkness-- his head turned towards the direction she left.

Seconds later, she screeches back backwards to Dice, stopping along side him running the motor, aiming her mouth at him. "Just kidding!...Maybe!" she yells, with a loud laugh following it. Then she jets off and away again in the same manner (wheels screeching, Dice's clothes flapping). The dust from the road flies in his face, hitting it. The only lights around are the to-and-fro headlights from cars as he begins to walk down the highway somewhere.

Chapter Seven: Marcus Garvey

The next morning Spike is sitting down at a kitchen table. His head is inclined before a plate of scrambled eggs, shining yolk yellow, sparkling in their fried appearance. The bacon is crimson on the plate with no toast yet that's on the way.

Over at the stove preparing the food is a round caramel woman with the height of about five two and an age of sixty. The silver framed circular glasses on the tip of her nose displays a grandmotherly status as she struggles with the food in frying pans and percolations of the coffee pot.

Spike's face beams embarrassment which is helped by the fact that he is not touching his food. The woman at the stove addresses him. "I 'clare 'fo God," she says, "I ain't never seen nobody like you..."

Spike's eyes never roll up to glance at her. She continues to handle the food on the stove like combat maneuvers (elbows pointing upwards) while her hands switch places with each other on the handles of pans-- smoke rising from them. "And you ain't got no money?..."

Spike takes a deep breath. "Right now I got a hundred dollars, ma," and he shoves a forkful of eggs in his mouth.

"A hundred dollars?" lifts his mother's voice. "You mean to say that's all you got to your name?..."

Spike breathes in deep and breathes out slow. "That's all I got right now, ma..."

And she flip slams the eggs over in the frying pan with a smack of no acceptance. "Well how you gonna make it in this world boy?... How you gon' make it?..."

Chewing his food with slow motions, he breathes in deep again and lets it out gradual.

Getting toast out the toaster with her fingertips, his mother drops them on a plate with finished satisfaction. "This ain't no joke out here boy," she says, grabbing plates of breakfast and walking over to the table with them to sit.

Spike responds sluggish. "I know ma, I know..."

"What chu gonna do when you get my age?... You're not gonna be able to survive, you know that?"
"I know. I know."
"Well you sure as hell better start thinkin' about your future... How you gonna keep walkin' around here with damn near nary a dime, day in and day out?"
"But I been workin' on it ma, I told you."
"Well what kind of plans you got?... What kinda job you planning on gettin'?..."
"I--"
"Why don't you look into sanitation?... You tried sanitation?"
"When--"
"You gotta take a test for that, you know that?"
"I--"
"And you got the post office... You need to go around and take tests for a good job."
"It's--"
"You got tests for that... You got tests for city jobs you can take..."
"I know that ma. I know all a that, believe me."
"Well you better start thinking about the future boy... How long you think I got on this Earth, forever?... You think the Lord's just gonna leave me here to pay taxes for the length of eternity??..."

Spike sighs and shoves another forkful of eggs in his mouth. "No ma..."

"Well you sure as hell don't act like you know..." She pours herself a cup of coffee, then clangs the pot down. "I 'clare, you act like you ain't got a bit a sense..."

They both eat silent with Spike's mother putting more force into her forkful shoves and coffee sips. "Where have you looked lately?..."

Spike slowly inhales. "I told you before, Dice had something he knew about that he was gonna turn me on to..."

"Dice..." she says with a punch. "What does he know about finding a job? I heard he don't have one himself?"
"That's what I said. We both are supposed to look into this thing."
"Doing what?..."

Spike takes a sip of the orange juice that's there. "Doing some truck loading..." He lets his mouth grab another forkful of eggs.

"What kind of trucks?..."
"Diesel trucks. You know, the long trucks that deliver stuff to stores?..."

She lets her fork bang on her plate. "I know what it is Spike..."

And the two go back to silent eating for a few moments-- Spike never looking up, only eating with caution. Then his mother says, "All I know is--" The phone cuts her off, ringing. She gets up to answer it (which is on the wall next to the stove). Then she holds up the receiver to Spike. "Speak of the devil..." she intones, as he gets up to take it from her.

Spike says hello into the receiver and hears Dice's voice on the other end, asking "Why did I know all you was gonna do was go back home?..."

Spike answers with a phone manner wiped clean of alarm. "Hey what's happenin' Dice! You hear anything more about that job?..."

"What, your mother's standing around you or something?..."
"Yeah, I could probably do that."
"Awright, cut the scenarios for a bit. You didn't see or talk to Rosie or nothin'?..."
"Nah."
"She didn't ask about me either?-- but if you didn't see her you don't know I guess. Right?..."
"Nah... So where ya callin' from?"
"Ehh I'm at a gas station not too far from the city. I ran into this real bitch-- I gotta tell you about her when I see you."
"Yeah?"
"Yeah, and I made money from her too."
"Yeah??"

"Yeah, like a thousand dollars."
"What??"
"Yeah, but check it out, I gotta get off this phone. You should've never went back home tho man, what'd you do that for? Freedom's boring?..."
"Awright. So get with me later... And thanks for the job."
"?"

And Spike hangs up the phone with jubilance-- sitting back down at the kitchen table. He finishes his breakfast with optimistic intakes. His mother's is looking at him. "So..." she inches verbally, "did Dice get chu somethin'?..."

"Oh yeah ma. I told you... But I'm not gonna say nothin' 'bout it yet, until it's definite. You know..."

She says nothing as she continues with her breakfast. Him, continuing with his faster than her now.

Some time later Spike is walking towards a supermarket, passing an empty playground vacant of sound. He walks, and as he does, a 1973 black ash colored Buick Electra 225 pulls up gradually behind him.

Now along side him, the Buick rides slowly with the passenger window rolling down and Spike not noticing or hearing anything. Out the window of the car, as it still moves, an automatic gun barrel comes out, resting on the top of the door's downed window. A familiar voice renders out "Hey!" from there.

Spike twists his head around to the direction of it and sees the gun pointing at him (the hole of the barrel staring into his eyes). The shock on his face keeps him moving without realizing it. The same voice yells out "Come here Spike" as the car now rolls to an abrupt stop.

Spike stops now, staring stunned at the weapon. He sees that four men are inside the car. The driver (who's not holding the gun) is leaning over the other passenger and makes his face visible. It's the dust brown colored man, his smile appearing to be pasted on. He tells Spike, "Get over here for a second while this thing's pointed at ya..."

Spike looks around seeing no one, and carefully walks over to the car. The dust brown man reveals to him, "Nah nah nah, you have to get in. You have to get in the car. Let's go..."

Reaching the rear door, the passenger beside it automatically opens it, sliding to the side so Spike can get in.

Inside the car Spike notices that two of the men are looking straight ahead with solemn facial expressions, not giving a hint of knowledge about Spike's attendance. The man with the gun on the passenger side has turned around, and is aiming his gun directly at Spike. His ears are pushed all the way out. He smiles with a mouth full of teeth busting through.

The dust brown man's torso is twisted around as he looks at Spike to make sure he's in the seat. "Okay," he says satisfied. "We drive."

The car pulls off casually down the street.

Spike asks the dust brown man, "What's our destination? Where you takin' me?..."

The dust brown man screeches to a halt! He turns around and looks at Spike. Then reaches over and snatches his collar, nodding once to the man with his ears pushed out and the gun. That man takes his gun, and, whacks Spike across the face with it in a smack. The dust brown man yells, "Questions??... No!!..."

He releases Spike's collar and turns back around to resume the driving. The side of Spike's face is peeled in spots to reveal the glazed covering underneath the skin, red inside. He appears to be holding something in his mouth, and lets out a large gulp of blood down to the car floor (a corroded tooth sticks on the corner of his bottom lip after doing that). The men in the back scoot their feet backwards to avoid the blood.

The one nearest Spike wallops, "What the fuck you doin', asshole!!" and raises his fist to pound him in the ear (Spike flinches back) when the dust brown man shouts, "Hold it!..."

The man stops-- holding his fist up in the air-- waiting for an explanation with his eyes. The dust brown man explains, "I have something more effective, so hold yourself..."

The man lowers his fist and Spike moves himself forward unflinching.

The car rides on with the dust brown man carefully steering the wheel pleasantly. All is quiet inside with Spike trying not to appear frightened. The other men remain stoic, looking straight ahead through the windshield like statues.

The vehicle rolls moderately through a ghost town factory district with occasional tar-stained stray dogs moping across streets. The dust brown man continues driving through the area until he approaches an abandoned post office building. The car gradually comes to a stop. The dust brown man turns to everyone. "Okay. Everybody out. You first, Spike..."

The man next to Spike opens the door with a fling while the other man with the gun aims it at him. Spike carefully climbs out of the car with the others climbing out following.

The man with the gun grabs hold of Spike's upper arm, pointing the gun barrel three inches away from his head. The dust brown man comes from around the trunk of the car with his hands in his pockets. He steps up to Spike's face. "Where's your boy Dice at?..."

"Dice?" Spike's face postures surprise at his question. "Dice ain't here man. I ain't seen him since--"
"I know you ain't seen him. What I want to know is, where he's at?..."

Spike shrugs earnestly. "I'm tellin' ya man, I really don't know... I don't have a clue where his image is projecting..."

The dust brown man throws his hands up and lets them drop to his sides hard, twirling around one time, exasperated. "Do you know..." he begins, pointing his index finger at Spike's nose. "Did he tell you what he did to me?..."

"I don't even know who you are, man."
"LIAR!..." The dust brown man twirls around again. "I don't think you realize... what your boy has done..."

Spike watches him and soon starts to frown. "Nah man, I don't know shit about your anger."

The dust brown man gets up closer to Spike's face and speaks in confidential tone. "You know what?... Your friend has altered me. You know that?... He made a little girl outta me, did he tell you that?..."

"Nah man. I don't know what you're talking about.
"OH!... You never HEARD of me, huh?... HUH?!"
"Nah man! I don't know your ass!"

The man with the gun asks the dust brown man, "Now?... Should I do it now?"

"No!" the dust brown man replies. He paces the ground in front of Spike for two seconds. Then says, "You know what?... He thinks I'm a little girl now, your friend Dice thinks... Sí?... Well I'm gonna show him, startin' with you..."

And he backs up to address everyone. "Awright... How many homosexuals we got here?..."

The three men look at each other with perplexity on their faces.

The dust brown man is more exasperated, waiting for an answer. "There ain't nobody homosexual here?..."

The men hand him innocent stares. Finally the one holding the gun with the pushed out ears says, "We're all into women here..."

The dust brown man looks at them all with incredulity overtaking him. Then, he walks back up to Spike, aiming his index finger and shaking it. "You know... I wish to God I was homosexual... so I can remove your manhood through the anal passage, the way your friend did."

"Hey, wait a minute. I've known Dice a lifetime of moons, and he ain't never been no homosexual, screwing no men 'n shit."
"He kissed my girl in front of my vision man!... That's the same thing, sí?..."
"Oh."
"That was down right detrimental to my relationship, my mellow!..." The dust brown man's knees start shaking. "You're his friend and I'm seeking some kind of restitution thru you mothafucka!..."

Spike begins to let his anger look at the dust brown man. "Well, I didn't do anything to you, and if your girl's unfaithful... what's that expression, about the fishes in the sea?..."

The dust brown man knowingly waves his hand. "This ain't no lecture scum bucket, or, a history class in June, understand? This is about, restiTUTion!... for violatin' my substantial status. Sí?..."

"Yeah... Sí..." meanders Spike's words.

Turning his back to Spike the dust brown man clamps his hands on his hips in fired up contemplation, while the three men watch him with awaiting eyes.

Spike moves his pupils to the corners to glance at the man holding the gun at his head.

The dust brown man swiftly turns back to him. "You a religious man?..."

Spike shrugs. "I dunno... depends on what kind of day I'm having I guess..."

"Because, if you're a religious man, then we could crucify your ass..." And he turns around to look at his men for approval. "Whada y'all think of a crucifixion?... Would that be good for him?..."

The men all look at each other for guidance in their answers. One nods his head up and down in approval, then the others follow suit in chain reaction fashion, agreeing.

The dust brown man turns back to Spike. "Ya see?... They're all pretty much down to crucify your ass... Oh wait-- I have more..." And he runs over to the trunk of the car toddler style.

Spike's face forms a worried expression as he watches the dust brown man, opening the trunk of his car almost diving his torso in. He finally comes up, happily holding up a hammer.

Then he joyfully runs back over to Spike, showing him the hammer. "See?... See what I have?... I have the hammer... but... I don't got no fuckin' nails..."

He turns back around to address the men. "You guys don't have no nails, do you?..."

The men all look at each other. One of them shakes his head and says no, and the others follow that reaction.

The dust brown man turns back to Spike. "See? No nails. But wait a minute! YOU got nails! Why not let us use YOUR nails, sí?... Wait a minute..." He runs back over to the trunk of the car.

Spike stares hard at his rummaging in the trunk, wondering what to expect. The dust brown man's torso pops back up again, then he runs back over to Spike. He happily holds up a pair of pliers. "See?..." he says with anger underneath his smile. "We'll pull out YOUR nails," and he grabs one of Spike's hands with a snatch and points at his fingernails with the pliers. His hyena style laugh slips out.

The insides of Spike holler low and hollow as they melt down below his heart and underneath his stomach. His eyes bulge out but he thinks they appear normal. He knows it's time to think of what to do but ideas and thoughts do not come.

Suddenly, the sounds of sobbing in the distance is heard by everyone-- the dust brown man turns to the direction from where it comes. Spike looks that way with the others.

Walking from around the corner of the post office building is Dice, weeping loud and profusely with the strength of an ocean liner horn.

Spike's happiness rays out with the sameness of his surprise as he watches Dice slowly approaching them, dragging his feet gradually with the trudging sound of it being outstanding.

The dust brown man looks astonished, then satisfied seeing Dice approaching. With a Georgian Appalachian accent, he calls out, "Mister Dice, is that you?..."

Dice continues approaching in dragging manner, wailing loud enough to be deafening now. Spike yells out with concern. "Dice man, what happened?"

The dust brown man turns swiftly to him. "Basta!" he commands. "No peanut gallerying please..." Then he turns back to Dice coming. "What's the matter little enfant? Boo hoo boo hoo?... Sí?..."

Dice suddenly stops and drops to his knees on the ground-- his torso is partly doubled over, him, crying intensely inside his hands.

Wondering shows on the faces of the dust brown man and the others now, as a bit of concern starts to prevail the entire atmosphere. Spike displays more concern than the others who stare. "Hey Dice man, what the hell's the matter man?... What happened?..."

Still on his knees, Dice weeps in drowned, wallowing-in-tears fashion. The dust brown man turns to the man with the pushed out ears who's holding the gun at Spike. "Bring the creature along with us..." He begins to walk towards Dice, with the man with the gun, hauling Spike along by his upper arm. The other two men stay behind.

The dust brown man steps up to the knees of the kneeling Dice. "Get your little sissified ass up, crying like an enfant!..."

Dice remains down there crying while Spike relays, "Dice... It's me man. What happened?..."

Dice slowly raises his head to show the pools of genuine tears welled up in his eyes. He tries desperately to form words but the trembling quivers his pronunciations away.

The dust brown man lances, "What, little scum bag?... What chu talkin' 'bout?..." Then he addresses the man with the gun. "Pull up that little girl-- weeping 'n shit..."

The man with the pushed out ears and gun lowers his torso a tad and brings his arm down to pull Dice up off the ground. Dice stands up quick! Kicks the man with the gun in the eye-- the man drops, the gun flies up in the air, he scream shrieks, holding his eyes.

The dust brown man is astonished gaping. (Spike catches the gun as it drops from the sky.) The two men in back start forward, alarmed. Dice laughs now. The dust brown man stares shocked at him. The man who had the gun still screams in shrieks-- bent down holding his eyes, through his fingers a waterfall stream of blood runs rampant.

Spike tosses the gun to Dice, who catches it. The two men are running towards Dice. Dice fires three times, hitting the two men. They fall dead to the ground.

The dust brown man stands alone now, wilderness helpless— eyes wide open. The man with the pushed out ears holding his eyes is on the ground, yelling "My EYE!!... My EYE!!..."

The dust brown man screams at him as he backs away from Dice. "Get up you fuckin' period rag!!... You fuckin' shit pail!..."

The man holding his eyes screams in a shriek one long time.

Dice grabs the dust brown man by the shirt, takes the butt of the gun he has, and, whacks him in the neck, and, whacks him, and whacks him, whacks him again, and whacks him.

Spike giggles exuberantly, jumping up and down clapping his hands with electric fan speed.

Dice continues whacking the dust brown man in the neck (who falls down now, hard on the concrete half-conscious). Dice pounds him again down there on the neck, and pounds him, and pounds him. The man holding his eyes shrieks out again.

Spike, still giggling, calms his jumping and clapping down, pulling away Dice's arm with the gun. "Hold it Dice! Wait a minute wait a minute!..." Dice stops his hand holding the gun from pounding.

The dust brown man, on all fours now, cranes his head upwards, looking at the man holding his eyes. "Fight you dirt bag!... Fight you piece of snot!..."

The man holding his eyes (bent over on the ground), real slow and gradual, moves his hands away from his eyes. From his right eye socket, a long seven inch blood strand drops down hanging, with the eye ball on the end of it, swinging low.

He tries to swing a punch at who he feels is next to him, but no one is close by, so the air is only struck.

The dust brown man stares at him in shock shared by Dice and Spike, looking as the man slowly swings again clumsily on the ground, with the eye ball touching the asphalt softly, pushing the blood strand up in folds.

Spike goes over to him, stooping down to look in his face.

The dust brown man yells to Dice, "Why don't you just kill us, pussy!... Just shoot us!..."

Spike busts out giggling at his suggestion, looking at Dice, who looks at the dust brown man as he holds the gun barrel down at him. He glances over at the other man on the ground and gives a careful aim at him with the gun, closing one eye for perfection. (Spike stands back to allow him perfect clearance.)

Dice fires the gun, hitting the man in the head-- he stretches out on the concrete with sudden stiffness in his motion. His last breath is breathed.

The dust brown man now looks up at the two with expectation shadowing his eyes. Spike sees him looking and tells Dice giggling. "Look, he thinks he's gonna be saved..."

Dice twists his head back to the dust brown man. "You think you gonna be saved mothafucka?..."

The dust brown man doesn't answer.

Dice continues. "I really don't see the logic in you thinking like that..."

The dust brown man's lip starts quivering looking at Dice. Then the anger hollers in his insides and comes out through his mouth sharp. "You fuckin' little toilet brain! You don't have the guts to pull the trigger on me, and that's what I thought. Ya fuckin' toilet... I shit on you everyday, you know that?... I piss on you... piss in your mouth, ya know that?..."

Spike chuckles as he looks over to Dice. "Please Dice, don't be a barrister... Do not end our fun while it is just beginning..." And he laughs jolly with anger inside it.

Dice is just staring at the dust brown man who remains on the ground on his knees. Spike's look salivates at what he thinks Dice is thinking. Busting with enthusiasm Spike's voice leaps out, "Let me think of something for his soul Dice."

    "You wanna injure his spirit, man?" Dice asks, handing him the gun by the handle.

Spike snatches it immediately and points the barrel at the dust brown man. Then he snaps his fingers like he has an idea. "Wait a minute..." He hands the gun back over to Dice and runs back to the car where the fuel filler is.

Dice has the gun aimed at the dust brown man. The dust brown man is looking up at him.

Spike says (looking at the fuel filler), "Hey man, there's no way to get some of this gas up outta here?..."

"Nah," Dice replies. The dust brown man quick!— tackles Dice down backwards. The gun flies out of his hand.

Spike runs to get the gun with his arm outstretched. Dice jumps up and gives the dust brown man a right cross with his fist, stunning him, throwing his chin up in the air. The gun hits the ground.

The dust brown man-- seeing Spike blurry now out the corner of his eyes, heading for the gun on the ground-- throws his arm out falling forward to snatch the gun up from there.

Spike beats him, grabbing it first, swiping it off the ground. Dice, head butts the dust brown man and he falls backwards sideways, hitting the concrete that way.

Dice standing immediately sticks his hand out to Spike, opening and closing it. Spike instantly hands him the gun and Dice takes it, as soon as the dust brown man tries raising himself.

Dice steps over to him, grabs the top of his hair, cranks his head back so the Adam's apple shows, takes the gun barrel, slides it in his mouth like intercourse, pulls the trigger-- one, two, three times.

A yarmulke sized piece of the back of the dust brown man's head slaps out, blood drenched against the car door after the first shot. It slides down it now, hesitantly unperturbed.

Spike looks at the corpse with disdain. "Do you believe the audacity of his nerve?..."

Dice is out of breath staring at the corpse, holding the gun barrel downwards, with his anger boiling. "This mothafucka... made me minister justice to him... early."

"I know," Spike agrees with disgust.
"I mean... he's got tons of just medicine to receive... Just look at him now..."

"I know... He cheated us, and, his lawfully wedded destination with new Chinese water torture..."

"Shit!..." Dice turns around and throws his hands up frustrated.

Slowly coming towards him down the street is the 1953 white Buick Skylark.

Dice and Spike both stare at it dumbfounded and motionless.

The car coasts gradually forward, slowing down without drama in its stop.

Spike's facial features have drooped. "I think we're busted..."

Dice just stands there with no expression now, waiting to see what awaits from the car.

The door on the driver's side opens and out comes a six foot five, two hundred and eighty-five pound wide cocoa-colored man, topped with a shaved head and aviator sunglasses, midnight in color. He wears a tarnished gray silk suit with matching gray alligator loafers. His shirt is a tee shirt, and the whiteness of it would be called dingy.

Dice and Spike's eyes are astonished looking at him. Words without sound fall from their mouths quietly.

The six foot five, two hundred and eighty-five pound wide man is just standing there facing the two, standing stiffly there, still, with his head mimicking the exactness of his body in not moving. Because the eyes are shaded in movie star darkness, they reveal nothing about who he's looking at or where.

Dice and Spike just stand there waiting and the white Buick is like a block of ice standing, not melting.

The wide six foot five man suddenly bends his knees (lowering himself, quick) one time-- his right hand bent at the wrist, fingers straight, pointing out away from his shoulder's side, he strangely says, "Shoe?..." then unbends his knees, re-standing himself straight up again, as if he did nothing.

Dice and Spike glance at each other concealing their worry.

Both doors of the Buick simultaneously open now. Climbing out of the car are the two African brothers, who had earlier offered the two a chance to work with them. They both display great smiles as they walk towards Dice and Spike, almost outstretching their arms in a welcoming manner, while the wide six foot five man continues to stand placid in monument fashion.

Spike says to Dice, "Look at the deja vu scene..."

The second African announces, "Ahhhh!-- it is our friends from our past acquaintance!..."

Dice summons a "Hey, what's happenin' baby?..." as the second African jubilantly shakes his hand, while the first African calmly shakes Spike's, showing his teeth as usual. (Spike manages to smile back with the strength of it lacking in sincerity.)

The two Africans continue greeting the friends by hand, exchanging them as they're shaking, while the second African still smiles as he notices the corpses on the ground. "Ahhhh!" he says with pleased poise. "I see that business is going good for you, yes?..."

Spike's face tries not to announce alarm as Dice replies, "Um... well..."

The second African throws his palm up. "It is not necessary to show concern about what we are viewing my friend."

The first African concurs with his brother. "Absolutely," he remarks, showing his teeth. "We are like-minded in ideas and thoughts, yes?..."

Dice tries to stay focussed on not panicking from being witnessed. "So what brings you guys around this area? It's coincidental like a mothafucka, huh?..."

The second African's smile dips a tad. "Coincidental?..."

Spike is watching both Africans.

Dice answers, repeating, "Yeah, coincidental... Like, guys of our calibre and make, meeting again? under work environment circumstances?... A coincidence..."

The second African's smile dips down some more as he looks over at his brother, whose toothy smile becomes closed by his lips.

Repelling a slight frown, the second African says, "It is really not a coincidence..." He points to the dust brown man's corpse on the ground as he walks over to it. (Dice's hand is still married to the gun, with his finger wedded on and off to the trigger.) The second African speaks while looking at the corpse. "It seems to be ostensible that you have done our work for us."

Dice asks, "What kind of revelation you bringing man?"

"Why, this man was supposed to enter the spiritual side-- this is true. But I must tell you, that my brother and I were commissioned to pronounce him dead ourselves. It is quite astonishing to us that you have, beat us to the punch as you say?..."

The first African's lips crack a thin smile of teeth. "Yes... to the punch..."

Dice and Spike look at each other with some astonishment. Then Dice formulates, "You mean to tell me you were suppose to kill the same guy?..."

The second African returns himself to smiling broadly. "By all means!... We have worked together after all, my brother! You see?... It is our ancestors at work, trying to bring us together, yes?..."

"Damn," Dice claims with stark wonder. "That is some wild authentic shit." He looks over at Spike, who shrugs with unsure amazement. The first African's teeth blares at everyone happily.

The second one walks back over to Dice. "You have done us a great service... And your work is very efficient... Just like I knew it would be when we spoke some time ago, yes?"

"Yeah, well, I'm glad your impression is influencing your heart over this."
"Oh, it is a wonderful piece of work, your execution."
"Mmm."
"Yes. Now, my brother and I must set about taking care of the debt..."
"Debt?... What debt?"

The wide six foot five man just stands there, still without flinches.

The second African presses his words down harder as they come out. "When my brother and I accept a job, we believe all agreements made, should be carried out... You see, it is credibility that reigns in this profession, in order to receive excellent opportunities, on a consistent basis."

Dice is looking into the man's mouth for clarity to come out. "I'm on another continent, lost. Help me understand what nature this is I should know about."

"Why my brother, being that you have already carried out our assignment, we therefore have to pay you for the job!..."

Dice looks over to Spike for confirmation on what he just heard. Spike has ecstasy on his face with a serious posture.

Dice says, "So you're tellin' me that we get paid for killing this scum bag for you?..."

"Because my brother and I are supposed to deliver this man in an expired state to our client, and we have been partially paid for our services, we must in fact pay you, for helping with our assignment." Then he snaps a serious expression on his face as he gestures the first African to come forth.

The first one heads over to his brother immediately in motion, with his facial features now matching the second one's.

The wide six foot five man still moves not from head to toe.

The first African reaches in his pocket and pulls out a rolled knot of dollar bills and hands it over to the second one dutifully, as Dice and Spike look on with expectation grabbing their breath.

The second African unwraps the roll and immediately counts out one, two, three thousand dollar bills and hands them over to Dice. Taking them, Dice says to him, "I hope you know what you're doing muh man..."

The second African now stands back, watching Dice count the money. The first African's eyes and his brother's eyes meet in agreement.

Dice tells him, "Hey, there's three thousand bucks here..."

The second African seriously stares at him. "Precisely... Do you consider that to be substantial payment for an assignment?..."

Counting the bills over again, Dice says, "Spike... I think I know what you think, but what chu think, three thousand's enough?..."

Spike chuckles excited. "Sí" he says, spreading the tone out Mexican style. Everyone laughs as they recollect the dust brown man. (The wide six foot five man shows no quivering.)

The second African relaxes his laughter and looks at Dice's amazement at the bills closely. "So my brother... you will consider this a payment?..."

"Yeah man, of course it's a payment!..."

Then the second African snatches the money back from Dice's hands. Dice stares at him stunned. The second one then twists his head angrily to the wide six foot five man. "Debbie!..."

The wide six foot five man moves!-- swiping his sunglasses off to show his eyes gnawing the atmosphere. He storms over to Dice and Spike like lightening.

The second African backs back some more as Debbie (the wide six foot five man) heaves his knee into Dice's stomach-- Dice doubles over grabbing it, dropping the gun on the ground.

Spike's mouth snaps wide open in shock as the first African steps up to him, malicious in expression. He takes his hands and pushes Spike hard over to Debbie and the injured Dice (who's still doubled over).

Debbie snatches Spike's arms, pulls them backwards, clamping them there with his own arm. The second African (rolling his sleeves up) slams Dice's back against the car door. Debbie follows that action, slamming Spike's back against the same door, pulling him off it by the shirt, slamming him back on it, pulling him off by the shirt, slamming him back, pulling him off, slamming him back on.

The second African is perspiring rage, still raising his sleeves up by pushing them in that direction. Addressing Dice, he says, "Fucking American black boy!... We give you opportunity to make money, and you turn us down??..."

The first African comes towards Dice with his face etched in anger. He motions his brother with his index finger and the second African grabs Dice's arms and holds them behind his back. The first one then takes his hand and slaps Dice across the face. "Fucking black American boy!... You American Negroes amuse me!..." And he slaps Dice again across the face.

Debbie takes his elbow and pile drives Spike in the side of his ribs and Spike grunts pain after he does it.

The first African now smacks Dice on top of his head. "You do not want to make money, black American!..." He slaps his head again. "You should make money when any opportunity to come! You are bottom of garbage barrel here!" And he punches Dice sharply on the chin (Dice looks semi-conscious).

The second African gets his brother's attention with his eyes and the two of them switch positions, with the first one now holding Dice's arms behind his back. He positions Dice's face for a punch from behind. "Did you hear my brother, Negro American boy?" he asks.

Dice's eyelids open halfway, heavily weighed down from the stress of staying up. The second one returns, "Did you hear my brother, black American?... You turn us down like your financial status is the same as white man's. You do not have luxury to turn us down!..." And he punches Dice hard in the face-- the first African lets him drop on the ground hitting his ear on it, half-conscious.

The brothers both go over to Debbie and Spike, who's also half-conscious now. The second African raises Spike's chin with his fingertips. "You are nothing. Therefore, we shall leave you that way..." And he gestures to Debbie, who then lifts Spike up high over his head, holding him there for a few seconds, then letting him drop, landing right on top of Dice on his stomach with an empty thud.

The second African gestures again to Debbie, for him to pick the gun up off the ground. He does so. Then, all three of the men head back to the white Buick, with Debbie, opening the driver's side door and pulling the seat back so the African brothers can climb in the back seat, which they do. Debbie then climbs in behind the wheel. He starts the engine and slowly, inches the car forward towards the two grounded friends, preparing to run them over.

Dice sees the car's front wheels approaching his face but is unable to muster up movement to raise himself.

Suddenly the car stops, two inches away from their heads. Then swiftly, it backs up. Now it makes a U-turn, and drives away in casual cruising speed.

Dice and Spike lay there on the ground breathing steady with their eyes half-opened. Their limbs rest limply as they both make attempts to apply movements to them. Spike calls out to Dice with raspiness. "Dice... You alright?..."

Dice winces trying to open his mouth. "Yeah..." he answers in a whisper.

"Can you move?..."
"I dunno..."
"You... you think they're coming back?..."
"I dunno..."

They lay there still and motionless as the wind's calm passes over them. Spike becomes able to move his arms a little more, saying, "Dice... I think I can roll myself over."

"Good..."

Spike then rolls himself off Dice, landing flat on his back. He stays laying there, trying to catch his breath while Dice now struggles to tilt himself over. His face shows the pain from the movement of his arms as he pushes himself up, and over, on his back with a heavy weighed thump. He turns his head to Spike and says, "Listen..."

"Huh..."
"Listen... we gotta get ourselves outta here... We got... dead men over here..."
"That big dude... took the gun tho..."
"Don't matter... We probably... got prints on them... or somethin'... We, gotta get outta here...We gotta get, to that empty building over there... so we can hide ourselves, at least..."

"Can you make it," Spike asks, gradually climbing to his feet slow, contorting his features from the pain that makes him do so.

"I dunno... I might have to crawl..."
"C'mon... I can help you..."

Spike labors on over to Dice and slowly bends down, pulling up Dice by the arms. He then begins tugging Dice along, slowly stepping backwards in small increments-- the sound of it like boots dragging across dry dirt.

A few feet away from the empty post office building, Spike continues to drag Dice over towards it-- Spike, moving forward without the earlier difficulty (gone, since the movement of his limbs began exercising the pain away there).

They get to the corner of the building and go around it to the other side, which faces a waterfront river-- overlooked by city office buildings across from it. Spike drags Dice along the base of the building. Dice tells him "Look... see if one of those doors're open over there. All we need to do is just get enough inside to recuperate, that's all."

Spike goes over to one of the four doors that were long ago active entrances to the building. He takes his hand and pushes one of the doors. Locked. He takes his hand and pushes the adjacent one. It squeaks difficulty opening up, with sounds of rust on it.

Spike then goes back with quickness to Dice, lifting him back up under the armpits, dragging him stepping backwards inside the building.

The cold musk smell inside overwhelms them secretly with the darkness there disrupted by slivers of light peaking through cracks. The wintry tranquil feel of the atmosphere there helps Dice and Spike's bodies, as Dice now, slowly begins to stand up on his own, still holding his stomach.

Spike starts doing jumping jacks with determination cast on his face. He then begins to touch his toes, widely swinging his arms windmill style when doing the touching. Dice, standing up (one hand still remaining attached to his stomach), now jumps up and down to get loose.

Spike glances at him as he continues his exercise. "Hey... You look better man."

"Yeah," says Dice, as he gradually begins to remove his hand away from his stomach. He jumps up and down a few more times before stopping himself, climbing back down on the floor to rest, leaning against a splintered wooden plank.

Spike stops his exercising. "What happened?"

Dice waves his hand. "I'm awright man... Damn, that big automaton really took the wind outta me... I almost feel paraplegic..."

Spike also decides to sit on the damp dry rot floor. He begins to look around himself with apprehension. "Dice..."

"What..."
"We gotta get the fuck up outta here..."
"Granted... Safety's the last thing with its legs open around here..."

Spike rolls his eyes up and turns his head this way and that. "Damn," he grieves, "it's real quiet around here..."

Dice tips his head up to get a better listen. "Yeah," he wonders. "But we gotta try to get going tho, before our heads're crushed..."

"Hey, what the fuck was you crying about when you came up?..."

Dice smiles proudly. "What, you thought my heart was broken?"

"I was like, 'mother of mercy' in my head... I thought you were amputated inside or out or somethin'. I didn't know what the hell was iron clad as far as my guessing went. How'd you do that?..."
"Nah, I was just acting."
"Damn, but how'd you do that? You had real tears coming out tho."
"I know. I just thought of the most fucked up thing I could think of."
"What was that?..."
"Easy... I just thought of how much of a nightmare it would be, for me to stop breathing here and now, without ever having reached, a status a centimeter or more higher than the sorry status I'm in now..."

Spike shifts his head back and thinks about Dice's comment in full. "Yeah..." he agrees, musing. "Yeah, I can relate to that... That's regular Edgar Allan Poe right there.

"Alive in a coffin!... Buried alive in a coffin!"

"Nah, I don't think I'd wish that on my worst enemy... A quick shot to the temple is much more conciliatory."

"Almost saintly."

"But how'd you get back here? I didn't think you was planning on returning in any near future?..."

"Well, to tell you the truth... I walked back... I wasn't that far away from town anyway. How far away was I?..."

Spike tries to think of the accuracy of his question. "I dunno. I don't know too much about mileage calculations 'n shit."

"Don't matter. I was just outside of town, you know that."

"True, true..."

"I didn't know where the fuck to go anyway... Hey, you seen Lube when you got back?..."

"Nah, I didn't see him. I wonder what happened to him-- you think the police caught up with him?..."

They both look each other in the eyes at the same time, then bust out laughing, knowing the answer. Dice says, "What law can hold Lube? What institution?..."

Spike adds, "What state trooper? What system of reason?..."

They laugh with comfort in their sounds at the thought. Suddenly Dice's face morphs into serious thought. "Hey, we gotta get outta this building, pronto."

"I know I know... Wait a minute..." And Spike gets up on his feet, standing up looking through the cracks in there at the outside. "Which way should we head when we get outta here?..."

"Hell if I know," Dice returns, slowly raising himself up, off balance.

Spike is looking at him with concern inside his staring. "Damn man, you sure the signs you're giving me ain't dangerous?..."

Dice steadies himself, waving his hand again which replies to Spike, nonsense. "I'll be concrete in a few minutes. Trust me..." He walks slow and careful to one of the wider slivered cracks that reveal the outside's light. Looking through it he says "I wonder if my grandmother has disowned me..."

"When was the last time you seen her?" Spike asks while moving closer to the door they entered through.

"I dunno... My memory holds up nothing but pictures of cemeteries..."

"What?? You think she's dead??..."

"Nah nah... I see that 'cause that's what I'm gonna get for not checking up on her enough..."

"Oh. Neglecting responsibilities."

"Listen... I'm lookin' at our position out here, and we might as well walk along the waterfront, and go down those side streets until we get out of this area..."

Spike looks out the same crack, then turns back to Dice. "So rather than stepping over sí and this dude's dead bodies, we cross over, 'cause that's the only other direction we can go in!"

"Whatever. You don't have a better idea, do you?..."

"Nah, I guess not," Spike says, preparing to leave the place. "After all, these dead bodies ain't prime or presidential... They're just dead bodies, like dead walruses, and dead squirrels on park rocks..."

"C'mon," Dice summons as he moves towards the door they entered. "Let's get started before we won't be able to do anything..."

And they both start leaving the building with Dice leading-- him, carefully opening the door with gradual motion in his movement of it. The door squeaks the same rust-screamed sound in its opening.

Out they come from the building with a sense of caution about them. Dice's walk is improving from slow to moderate as he leads, looking in every direction without alarm. Spike (behind him) is looking behind himself, walking.

Along the waterfront they continue next to the empty factory buildings which are adjacent to each other. Both Dice and Spike's walking gets better with each step that they take along the waterfront lined structures.

No cars nor trucks approach in sound or visuals as the two friends edge their way out of the area via large degrees of here-and-there watching in their stride.

They finally approach a wide four-lane street leading out of the area. They start walking along the curbs of the sidewalks along the street. Then Spike asks "You think this idea's decent?... with all the cars coming and going here?..."

"There's no other way to get across to get outta here," Dice says, checking the amount of cars heading down the street. "We should try to get on the other side when we get some spacing in the cars..."

When the moving cars on the street lessen in number, Dice and Spike both shift themselves abruptly to face it, and quickly head for the crossing of it which they do efficiently enough to succeed.

On the other side of their accomplishment, Dice and Spike now walk more casually, somewhere. Spike inquires, "So what kind of wavelength's gonna be reasonable for us now, you think?..."

"I dunno," Dice returns, "but we gotta get off the street. We need to be holed up together somewhere for a while. Maybe in a hotel room or somethin'."
"Why don't we go to the Sand's Hotel then?... It's in a white neighborhood and everything."
"That sounds decent. But we gotta get two rooms tho. I don't want no images of us, like we float, dance and smile together in anybody's guess work."
"Of course."
"I don't think the police is gonna be lookin' for us in a white neighborhood. The smell of that idea is far fetched."
"It's a certainty..."

Some time later, the two walk into a neighborhood filled with three family homes dressed in copper red brick fronts, with stoops armed with black cast iron banisters. In the middle of the block of these houses, standing twelve stories taller than the others, the Sand's Hotel shows its rust-stained rectangular sign, sticking out like a hand jutted right turn signal.

As the two approach the hotel, Spike wonders, "Hey Dice..."

"Yeah..."
"We still gonna pursue this bounty huntin' enterprise?..."
"We'll make money. The dye is set."
"Cool... Check it out, I swear, right? No more clients from the neighborhood."
"It don't matter no more..."
"It don't matter?"
"Nah."
"How come?"
"'Cause, like I told you, the dye is set. Our course has been drawn! Once incidents come into being you can't go back and change `em. They map out the course of the road, man. We gotta keep going down it and see where it leads. And besides... the money you get dictates the course of your life. It don't matter where it comes from, and it don't matter how much..."

Spike stays silent for a few seconds, then says "Yeah..." as he keeps on staring at the hotel's sign. Anxiousness soon coats his face as he starts to walk a bit faster than Dice.

Dice, noticing knowingly, reminds him, "We're in a white neighborhood brother man, remember? What schedule is scolding you for lateness?..."

Spike looks at him. "What?... Nah I'm cool I'm cool..."

And they both head into the hotel where the outside is ornamented with three Scandinavian-looking males standing in the front without aim, but with four to five day old beards. Various varying colors of tweed jackets hang on their shoulders as they stand around smoking cigarettes together, with one standing alone doing that.

Inside the hotel's lobby, the sparseness of articles for lounge convenience displays an interior hailing from the 1960s. A once clean long ago, now worn, orange gold vinyl couch sits in the floor's center. The rug there is a shag with the color of it struggling to imitate the color of the couch. The grease-filmed beige wallpaper on the wall reveals outlines of flowers all over it.

Nearly no folks stand around at the front desk which is manned by another Nordic looking gentleman, slim in built but short of height. An elderly couple has just left the desk as Dice and Spike approach and step up to it.

Dice addresses the man. "Yeah, we need a couple of rooms..."

The man smiles. "One room?"

"No, two. Two rooms. Separate."

The man smiles again. "Okay. Whatever you say."

Spike frowns and launches, "Hey, whadaya mean by that?"

Dice turns quick to him. "C'mon Spike. Take it easy..."

The man smiles again.

Spike fires, "Well what the hell kinda implication was that?..."

The man's face now drips downward, perturbed. "Sir. I merely thought that you and your friend might consider a one room suite."

Dice cuts in with, "No, we just need two separate rooms please."

"Sure," the man replies with intentional politeness. "The rates here are forty a night."
"That's fine."

Dice proceeds to reach in his pocket while Spike fumes to the side, giving Dice his forty. The desk man stares at him with his own anger searing in a calm sales manner. The man receives the eighty dollars from Dice and proceeds to log the two in. He gives a focused laser look at Dice with deliberate pleasantness. "Your rooms are twelve-eighteen and twelve-nineteen," he says, and hands him the keys.

Dice says "Thanks," as he takes the keys and hands Spike's his. He proceeds to head for the elevator. Spike follows Dice and stares hard and mean at the desk man, who stares back with intent to intimidate.

Getting to the elevator Spike releases, "Aww man! Did you see him, trying me??..."

Dice replies relaxed, "Aww you were just jumping on assumption man."

"The mothafucka was smirking at us, like we were gonna do some clandestine act to his liking!"
"Yeah, but he sensed that you were gonna freak out, so he did it, and you freaked, then he gets mad. How disputable..."
"Fuckin' zoo man! An unbelievable nuisance that's living..."

The elevator opens its doors and the two enter.

When the elevator reaches the twelfth floor, the two step out and immediately find their rooms to be close to the elevator and adjacent to each other. Dice goes over and unlocks his door, telling Spike, "I'll be in there to check you out in a few man..."

Spike says "Right" with a remaining attitude from the downstairs desk man as he unlocks his door and enters his room.

Inside he sees a furnished room that echoes the 1950s, as opposed to the lobby's 1960s decor. The bed is small and rounded at the edges with a checkered print bed spread that matches the drapes on the windows, the color of which is dull turquoise. A black and white sixteen inch tv sits in the corner of the room.

He walks over to the window where an old fashioned chip-peeled gold pole lamp with three dull lamp shades pointed in different directions still exists in the other corner. Pulling the drapes back a bit, Spike glances out the window, looking across the street at the same type of houses that occupied the hotel's block. There's a young girl about twelve years old dressed in jeans and sneakers walking by.

Spike moves his face closer to the glass to get a better look.

He realizes that the girl is the same one he attacked earlier in the empty lot.

His face stays there, smashed with astonishment as he watches her across the street, walking past the houses in front of the hotel.

Dice walks into the room. "So," he states, looking around the place. "The joint's identical in every way, including the smell..."

Spike swings around to face Dice, with apprehension trying to bust out of his casualness. "Yeah," he replies with a mundane drive in his volume. "It's all the same shit anyway..."

"What kinda view you got?..."

Spike walks away with his head forced down. "You know... Same shit..."

Dice looks out the window. "Yeah... Everything's always the same shit..."

"You see that weird guy out there?... staring at the front of the building?..."

Dice sticks his face closer to the glass, looking in both directions. "What guy?" he asks, still looking everywhere. "I don't see nobody out there..."

Spike's face freezes surprised, then he walks back over to the window, quickly sticking his head forward to look out it.

He sees the same sidewalk with no one on it. "Oh shit," he says with wonderment. "He's not there..."

Dice steps away, asking "Why? What'd he look like?..."

"Nah, he was just weird `n shit," replies Spike, stepping away from the window, not looking at Dice. He drops himself down on the bed with his back staring at his friend. "You got any cigarettes on you man?..."

Dice goes in his pocket for his cigarettes. When pulling them out, he tosses the pack over to Spike. "This is cool enough for hiding out at least."

"Yeah... Can't be in the projects, that's for sure," Spike muses, taking out a cigarettes and lighting it with the matches embedded under the pack's cellophane. "Hey, you got a pretty nice bundle from that girl at least, huh?..."

"Yeah, but she's giving me the creeps in my slumber... I keep thinking she's gonna walk in this room, or somewhere else like it again..."

"Eh... Maybe she got busted wherever she went or somethin'..."

"Maybe..."

"So... boredom's gonna massacre our balls off here." Spike gets up and goes over to the window, reaching it, pulling back the drapes there slightly wider. "How we gonna find more clients? Shouldn't we be moving around or something?..." He glances at the empty street out there, seeing no one.

"I dunno... That kinda reminds me of The Fugitive for some reason... like I'm on the run from some crime or somethin'..."

Spike laughs out loud at the irony of that, while Dice just gets it moments after. "Remember?..." Spike says, after chuckling. "Think back..."

"Yeah, I know. Well, that's different... We've got a sense of justice about ourselves, don't we?..."

Dice sees Spike widely looking here and there up and down out the window. He says to him, "Just how weird was that mothafucka out there, Gothic weird?..."

"Nah. You know..." And he re-closes the drapes with embarrassment over opening them in the first place.

Dice wonders. "Well..." he comments, "There's gotta be a better way to obtain clients than the way we have."

"I know."

Dice begins to head for the door. "Let's go see what's happenin' around here outside."

"Nah, wait…"

Dice turns to him. "What's the hold up? There's no kind of drama breathing 'round here."

"I know... It's just, I dunno... I don't feel like having my eyes venture across that guy at the desk's vision right now just yet."

Dice contorts a frown on his face. "Fuuuck that guy's behavior! He's just mad 'cause nobody ain't ripped his panties off. C'mon..." And Dice leaves Spike's room right away not looking behind to see if his friend is coming.

Spike's body bares reluctance the way he walks behind him.

As they wait for the elevator, Spike's face wears worriment with the prolonged buzz of the approaching elevator drowning his thoughts out thoroughly.

Dice, suddenly. "You know what tho?..." he hurls, "there's a lot of absolute fine females existing in this neighborhood. I stand as a witness to that..."

"Yeah," drones Spike, forcing the appearance of casualness. "I heard the testimonials on that."

The elevator rises and settle-jump stops to its spot with its doors opening. The two enter it and the doors close.

When the elevator doors open up down at the lobby, Spike sort of storms out-- his facial expression, soiled with angst from his expectation of what to expect.

On he walks (with Dice behind him) passing the desk man, whose back is facing Spike's passing. When he realizes he's passed the man, Spike, slows his stepping a bit, then remembers he has no ache to go outside. He stops abrupt at the lobby's glass entrance-- looking through it across the street.

Dice stops just as abruptly from being behind him. "Hey!..."

"Sorry man. Thought I saw somebody comin' in..."
"Well let's go," Dice says, opening the door to leave, befuddled.
"Right," Spike replies, letting Dice lead the way.

Outside Spike's head turns here and there, swiftly left and right.

Dice queries, "What the hell you lookin' for, man?..."

"Huh?..."
"You still lookin' for that weird guy?"
"Guy??... Oh!... Nah, I'm not lookin' for him..."
"Listen Spike... You're fuckin' driving me to drink something... `Cause you're like freakin' out... severely."
"Me?... C'mon, you act like I'm hemorrhaging in my noggin up there."
"Nah it's not like that. But I mean..." And Dice can't think of any words to follow.

As they walk down the block Spike's eyes roll left and right and shift the same way, instead of his head moving that way. He sees the girl no where and starts to relax a bit inside as he approaches the corner with Dice.

Dice says, "The quiet here is deafening enough to be abusive almost."

"Yeah... It is quiet around here..."
"But that's cool I guess. Better quiet than diabolically noisy I guess..."

When they reach the corner, a short sixtiesh man immediately jumps out of the driver's side of a parked 1970 pea-green Saab Sonett III. The two friends notice him. Spike also sees the twelve year old girl at the other corner of the block they just turned. She's standing there, looking searchingly down another block.

As the two remain walking, the man calls out to them. "Hey buddy!" Dice's head turns to him while walking, Spike (staring scared at the girl) stops in his tracks, turns his back to her direction to answer "What's happenin'?" to the man.

Dice stops now, and stares at Spike in disbelief as the man says to them, "Listen... I was wonderin' if yous can do me a favor?..."

Spike emits a "What's the deal?" moving closer to the man as he tries to glance from his eye's corner at the girl's whereabouts.

Dice still has disbelief on his face as he waits for the man's words to come out to Spike.

The man begins, "Listen... yous guys wanna make fifty dollars apiece?"

"Sure," accepts Spike, keeping his back to the girl's direction before Dice's mouth releases a sound.

The man graciously reaches in his inside jacket pocket. "Here... twenty five for each of yous till I get back..." He hands them each a twenty dollar bill and a five dollar bill. "Just stand by my car and watch it... I gotta run across the street for a couple a seconds... Yous get the rest when I come back, okay?..."

"Sure," Spike says again, taking the dollar bills and gloating over their appearance.

Dice takes his and says nothing. His look-- dumbfounded and confused.

The man instantly runs across the street now, his arm and leg movements go up and down like pistons, with the action of it resembling a sixteen year old boy unleashed. He runs all the way down the block near the corner and goes into the deli that's there. Directly opposite that, across the street, is the twelve year old, who is now walking towards Dice and Spike.

Spike turns his back to her direction quick. Dice fires to his friend, "Tell me you know that mothafucka I'm standin' here holding dollars from, and why am I standin' here suddenly holding dollars from someone who's reeking Cosa Nostra like he is..."

Desperately trying to not let the approaching young girl see him, Spike positions his back to her by shifting it the closer she gets. To Dice he says, "How can we turn down opportunities to make money if we're enterprising gents now?"

"Fuck that. Who the hell was that? What are we doing standing here like this? You navigating this ship now man?..."

"C'mon Dice, that ain't it... Wrong on all counts," Spike tells him, shifting and shifting as the young girl comes by (not seeing him), then passes him, turning the corner, heading back down the block where the hotel is.

Dice now frowns at him. "What the hell is your energy making you do, short circuit?"

"Huh?"

"What the fuck are you doing man?-- shifting around 'n shit like a stuck duck at a rifle range..."

"Oh... Listen, be patient. We're twenty five dollars ahead in the poles for existing right now. Ain't that important?..." He sneaks a look away from Dice at the young girl, who continues to head down the block towards the hotel.

"Are you kiddin' me or what?... Look at us standing here like cops ticketing the homeless... You ain't acquired no wisdom from dealing with those maniacs from Africa?... Our heads might be off in another few minutes... Maybe even worse..."

Spike shrugs, with Dice's thought appearing to slowly sink into Spike's head. "I dunno man... We just gotta make money... Don't we?..."

"Yeah yeah we gotta do that. But bounty huntin's what we're supposed to be doing, right?... I mean, look at us standing out here-- and where'd that guy go?"

"He went in the deli across the street."

"Great... Well he's been in there a long time. Who says he's comin' out?... Aww shit man!-- this was a bad move Spike. I'm tellin' ya, we're in the unknown here..."

"Awright, so I fucked up the word carvings on my headstone, mon-u-men-tal-ly..." The enthusiasm on his face dwindles below him.

Dice glances at Spike with a pinch of anguish in him. "Look," he says, "accidents are accidents. But stupidity can be avoided, like any other bad advertisement..."

Just then, the short sixtiesh man runs out of the deli, heading back over to the friends in the same piston driven manner. Spike says, excitedly, "Here he comes now..."

The man reaches the car. "Good boys!..."

Dice frowns at him, holding it a few seconds, then straightens his eyebrows with the speed of a blink.

The man continues, reaching inside his jacket pocket. "Yous two guys'll go places in the world." He pulls out more dollars from his pocket, then counts out two twenty dollar bills and two five dollar bills, again. He hands twenty five dollars to both of them. "Okay?" he asks, now opening the Saab's door, climbing behind the wheel. He grins at them.

Spike hides his jubilance unsuccessfully. "Hey, thanks a lot man."

The man starts the car's engine and roars it one time, turning the steering wheel to swing out of the parking space, while Dice stands there watching him, holding the money at his side.

The man sees where Dice is holding the money. "Hey," he calls to him with disturbed force.

Dice answers "Huh?" to hear the man's comment.

"Put that money in your pocket-- don't be a wise guy, eh?" the man orders.

Before Dice gives any kind of word or visual response, the man shoots his car out of the parking space-- Dice and Spike step back from it quick. The man then pulls off like a leapt cheetah. The car screeches away from them up the block in jackrabbit fashion.

The two friends just stand there looking at him, peering through the exhaust. Dice wears a stupefied look of acceptance. "Wait a minute," he says to Spike, trying to catch his senses. "Did we just make money here?..."

Spike happily taps his shoulder. "I told you to have patience in your pocket."

"Yeah, but why do we have money in our hands? What labor did we produce to get this?..."
"You gotta stop living in the past on this, man."
"Look, Spike..." And Dice looks around himself and across the street. "C'mon. Let's get out of this spot..." And the two walk away opposite the hotel.

As they continue walking, Dice says, "Look... I ain't turning ancient or weak on methods Spike, but I got fifty dollars inside my pocket and I don't have answers as to how I got it. That's a problem in my book."

"How we got it?... We did a guy a favor."
"Yeah, but who?... A question mark enters my head."
"I thought it was law that if opportunity's hollering at us we should snatch it?"
"You just can't snatch anything that knocks you in the head tho man."
"But we don't have the luxury to stand around and be choicey."
"Yeah but... Why am I getting deja vu?... Did we just go thru this already?..."
"I guess it's very hard for me to turn down money, especially when I'm not making it."

Dice's face looks confused as he ponders his own spoken thoughts for a few seconds. He thinks deep now as they walk on in silence for a bit. Then he says to Spike, "You know what?"

"Nah, what's up?"

And Dice suddenly stops in his tracks. (Spike follows the stop with his own.) "I think I'm gonna try to check grandma out..."

"Yeah?..."
"Yeah... I mean, I got some money... I can take a cab over there."
"Yeah, but ain't risk yelling your head off, here?"
"Yeah I know. But as long as I'm not on the street--"
"But what if she wants you to take her shopping or something, and you gotta walk with her on the streets and stuff?..."

Dice thinks for a moment. "Well... it's just that I haven't seen her or called her or anything. She probably thinks hard of me for that. Plus, I got a couple a dollars-- I'm sure she can use that, ya know?"

"Of course."

Dice thinks some more on it as they both stand there. Suddenly Dice says, "You know what? I'm gonna go check her out man."

"Awright."
"They still got that cab service place around here don't they?"
"Probably. Down the street where we were standing and around the corner," Spike says, facing the hotel's direction now, looking down that way with concerned anxiety.

"Well I'm a head down there. What're you gonna do? Why don't chu come?..."
"Nah..." Spike muses, still keeping his eyes facing the direction of the hotel. "I'm a go upstairs there and check out the tv. Knock on the door when you get back."
"Awright man." And Dice gives Spike a quick pound handshake. "So I'll see you when I get back." He walks on, heading back in the direction they were standing earlier. Spike now hesitantly begins to head back to the hotel.

He walks looking grim to the left and right with his eyes only moving. No one appears on the street of note except a few elderly passersby, passing both his sides. In the distance is Dice's voice, yelling "Spike," fuzzy in the air over to his ears. He stops sudden and turns around, seeing Dice far away from him on the block they were on. Dice says "Don't harass that guy in there!..."

Spike laughs to himself and throws his hand up "okay," then turns back around and heads back towards the hotel.

Onward he goes, getting closer to the hotel and its entrance. His eyes still check around, circling and scanning the street and its bareness as he walks.

Coming up to the entrance and going in he takes a deep breath, and keeps heading forward inside, as the man at the desk (now fully facing forward) looks right through the eye sockets of the approaching Spike.

Spike, sensing him seeing him (then seeing him), starts steaming inside as he walks onward. The desk man fixes his mouth to form a stern straight line of rebuke as he watches Spike getting closer.

Spike comes and passes the desk man while trying to look at him with the eyes in the back of his head he thinks he has. The desk man watches him hard, heading for the elevator. His face is flashing rage.

Spike enters the elevator when it comes and heads up to his floor. When it gets there and the doors open, he steps out and finds the twelve year old girl there, standing in the hall leaning against the staircase banister there that's off to the side. Eating a chocolate bar, she sees him when he gets out.

Spike's face is frozen. The elevator doors close. He stands there like granite as the girl takes the chocolate bar out of her mouth and walks towards him, solemn.

She stops in front of him and looks up at him as he stays there frozen. "What took you so long?..." she says.

Spike can't make his mouth open up. Stuck in action for a moment, he finally opens his lips wide enough to utter, "Ww, what?..."

The girl still looks up at him with her emotions canceled. "You heard me," she says, and takes a bite off her candy bar. "What took you so long?..."

With fear still drenching him he tries to gush a bit of anger up. "You better get away from me little girl..." And he gets up enough force to immediately push her out the way to walk to his room door and unlock it. Instantly the girl steps in front of him, blocking the door.

Spike just stands there holding the key in his hand as he stares in disbelief at the girl blocking the door. She continues looking up at him. "I'm not going anywhere," she says to Spike, "and if you say anything, I'm gonna say you raped me, again!..." And she slides herself down against the door and drops her bottom down on the floor, pulling her knees up to her chest, biting her candy bar again.

With exasperation settling inside him, Spike looks around quickly to see if anyone else is approaching or peering. "Look little girl," he says with his tone a bit lower. "If you don't move away from my door, I'm gonna snatch you up and do the same thing I did to you in that lot."

"Big deal!..." she fires, taking another bite off her candy bar. "Everybody does that to me anyway. You got my money?..."
"Money?... You better be quick about gettin' away from my door or I'll--"
"You'll do nothin' 'cause you don't wanna go to jail!..." And she bites a bite off her candy bar once again.

Spike stands there looking at her without recourse. Inside his head he searches for another method to use to move her away from the door. He looks around again, checking for sounds or bodies from hotel residents who might be viewing this.

The girl just sits there on the floor (not looking at him now) eating her candy bar with no trace of concern.

Spike makes his calmness ironclad. "Look little girl... How much money's in your vision to let me breathe alone, five dollars?..."

She stops in mid bite to look up at him. She rolls her eyes, stereotypically insulted, and completes her bite, not looking at him.

Spike stands there, trying to find another idea again. "You're nothing but a little blackmailer, huh?"

She fires back, "I'm a little girl! and that's what people like you always wanna forget!..." She takes another bite off her candy bar while Spike still stays there with confusion in his thinking. The girl says (again looking at him), "I bet you wanna do it to me again too, don't cha? Just like everybody else..."

"What I want you to do," Spike explains, deliberately pounding his words, "is get away from my door, like, quicker than an eye blink..."

The girl sticks her hand out (not looking at him), opening and closing it, opening and closing it.

"How much?" Spike asks with the insult intelligible in his tone.

"Right now? Fifty dollars... They might even could give you that amount of years in jail, for rapin' me." And she goes back to eating her candy with the other hand, opening and closing the other hand out to Spike.

"What makes you think I'm decorated with fifty dollars?..."

"You better hurry up and decide before people come..."

Spike stands there, staring down at her. Then, he reaches in his pocket, pulls out three twenty dollar bills, then shoves them out to her. "Here," he declares. "Now get outta here!..."

The girl immediately stops eating and looks at the bills. "Hey," she says with disappointment. "I said only fifty..."

"I ain't got no change on me. Take the sixty and be happy. What's the problem?..."

The girl rises up and confronts his face. "Suppose I only want fifty dollars..."

Spike glares at her but is exasperated.

She then says, "Never mind," snatching the bills from him with a quick forced smile. Then she moves out of his way and heads over to the stairs there.

Spike still watches her as he slips his key in the door's keyhole. The girl slowly, step by step, walks down the stairs still looking at him. "I should come back here," she tells him, "everyday!..."

"Look kid," Spike says, camouflaging his snarl. "You got your money, so git! Or I'll get murderous next time and slash your fuckin' ears off... fuck you in your ear sockets... Both of `em!..." He turns his key and his eyes back over to the door, opening it.

"Big, deal!" the girl replies and trots down some of the steps, then stops. "Just for that, I'm comin' back here tomorrow!" She continues, trotting on down the stairs.

Spike watches her leaving and tries to sigh out his overwhelmed state. Then he enters the room and closes the door, with concern latched strongly around him.

He walks around inside wondering the extent of his next move. He heads for the window but stops short of looking out of that. Now he stands in the center of the floor. The sweat beads that proceed from his brow rolls calmly, but his hand wipes a row of them off when he raises it to scratch his head. He sits himself down on the edge of the bed.

"Shit" he says, as he feels himself getting hotter searching for a thought on what to do next. A knock is heard on the door-- Spike jumps. Three more knocks hit the door and Spike gets up like a flipped on switch.

Staring at the door now motionless, he generates enough urge to move himself over to it. He gradually extends his hand to turn the knob on the door and opens it.

Three police officers stand on the other side. Spike's heart jumps up inside him as the cops stare at him head on like deers. He stands there stiff looking the same way, until one of the officers breaks the ice. "Sorry," he says calmly. "Wrong door..."

Spike hums out a sedative "Sure..." as the officers turn like soldiers and casually walk away. He carefully closes the door so it doesn't slam. He stands there now, thinking about wondering if the cops might have been called on him. He moves his ear over to the door to seize a sound worth listening to. He hears nothing.

Not hearing the sounds of the officers' footsteps walking away causes disturbance in his insides. He drops his head down and rubs his eyes with his hands.

Chapter Eighth: Pussy Has No Face

Dice is in his grandmother's house, sitting at the kitchen table. Grandma is calmly sipping a cup of tea, looking in one direction away from her grandson. He looks at her as she takes another sip of tea, then carefully places the cup back on the saucer. She takes a deep breath and says, "The white supremacists were here looking for you today..."

Dice frowns a stare at her to clarify what he just heard. "What'd you say ma?..."

She takes another sip of tea, still patiently looking one way, and sets the cup on the saucer. She takes in a deep breath, exhales, and repeats, "I said, the white supremacists were here looking for you... Today..." She sips another sip of her tea once again.

Dice is staring at her with a face of waiting. "What white supremacists ma?..."

Grandma takes another deep breath looking in the same one way direction. She patiently lifts up her cup of tea, takes a sip, then sets the cup back down in a gentle manner. "The ones who wear blue uniforms..." she points out.

Dice feels the smack of that shock on his forehead. "Cops were looking for me, ma??..."

Keeping her head one way, she stares passively in that direction while reaching for her cup of tea. Gradually raising the brim of it to her mouth, she sips, then says, "Same thing..." She sips her tea again, then lowers the cup and sets it back down on the saucer. "Cops, Klansmen, I don't see a clothes line dividing the laundry..."

"What, what'd they want ma? What'd they say?..."
"Say?..." Grandma asks while reaching for the cup. "Do they have to say anything? They don't have to say anything..." She slowly brings the cup of tea back up to her mouth and takes a sip. "They're politicians too you know..." And she brings the cup back down like the drip of a drop of molasses in motion.
"Ma, you don't remember what they said? What they come here for?"

She stares straight in the same direction, with no movement reaching for anything now. "I don't remember. What difference does it make. They only come to arrest. They were probably going to arrest you."

"That's what I'm sayin' ma, what were they saying they were gonna arrest me for?"
"Pooh!-- what difference does it make? We're all gonna be arrested before long anyway."
"Did they say they were coming back?..."
"Coming back? They always come back. Unlike some people I know..."

Dice thinks quick to realize the implication of that. "C'mon ma. I always come back. That's why I'm here now. Why you say stuff like that? I always check on you, you know that. It's just that I had a lot of things I had to take care of. You know how sometimes I got a lot of stuff to keep up with..."

Lifting her cup back up (bringing it to her lips but not drinking yet) she replies, "Who cares..." and takes a sip of her tea again, gradually taking the cup back down to the saucer and setting it down there gently. She takes in a deep breath and lets it out slow.

Dice moves his head closer to hers and stamps a kiss on her cheek. "I love you, ma. You act like I'm alien or somethin'..."

"No. Like a politician? Yes. Alien? No..."
"Ma, you don't remember any thing the cops were talking to you about?... Can't cha just think of somethin' they asked you?..."

Grandma takes a deep breath in, still looking in the same one-way direction, and lets it out. "Think, he asks... like I'm some backwoods drifter," she says. "I was born in the north, not in some slave state where you wasn't allowed to think, only pick cotton. Thinking, I can do..."

Dice tries to keep his patience awake as he waits for her to remember something.

His grandmother gradually reaches for the cup again, bringing it almost up to her lips and holding it there in mid-air. "Let's see..." she muses, her head remaining faced in the same direction. "They come here and they said, `Ehh, old lady...'--"

"Aww c'mon ma, they didn't call you an old lady, did they?..."
"Hey!... Who's tellin' this story here, you or me?..."

Dice throws his hand up in submission. "My mistake ma. Go ahead."

"Oh thank you Mr. Lee Harvey Oswald," she says with vindication. "Now, where was I?"
"You said they called you an old lady."
"That's right, believe it or not... Sometimes cops say things to be crucified for, right?"
"Right ma."
"Thank you for the opportunity to be right... Now..." And she goes back to thinking with the brim of her cup going up to her lips. She sips her tea from it, then says, "They said `Ehh, old lady... Where's your son at?'..."

Dice is looking at her, waiting. "And what'd ya say ma?"

"I said, `Hey! Where do you get off comin' in here harassing a senior citizen like myself?'... Then I told them you don't live here anyway..." She sips her tea again, then carefully puts the cup on the saucer.

"Ma, when you told the cops all that, what'd they say to you?"
"What'd they say??... Pooh!-- they stood there like emasculated little boys is what they said..." She reaches for the tea cup again and slowly takes a sip from it. "I wish they were right here now, so I can throw this damn tea at `em... The idea..." She drops the cup back on the saucer.

"Did they search the place or anything like that ma," Dice asks, looking around as he does that.
"No."
"No?..." he again inquires, still looking around the apartment, seeing nothing out of place. "They didn't go to the bedroom back there or nothing?..."

"They just looked back there..." She takes a sip of tea from the cup. "I didn't see `em throwing my bloomers out on the floor from back there or nothin'..."

Dice walks towards the back to check the bedroom. He sees her neatly made up oak master bed standing tall without articles of clothes strewn about it or disheveled on the floor. He walks back to the kitchen table. "Well ma, I don't see that they did anything back there."

"Well," Grandma asks, slowly setting her tea cup down. "What'd you do anyway, become a Bolshevik?"

"Nah ma. I didn't do nothin'."

"Fat chance!... What're you, your brother now?"

"Nah ma, I ain't changed my visuals or my mentals."

"Hurrah!..." She lifts the cup up to take another sip of tea but stops, realizing she's finished it (she actually looks in the cup with one eye to make sure). "Don't tell me my torturer has ceased to abuse me," she says, aiming her words at the tea cup's bottom inside.

"Umm... Listen ma, did they say I was wanted for somethin'?... Like, did they have a charge or somethin'?..."

Grandma clangs down the cup on the saucer. "Whadaya want a sign language revival?"

"Huh?"

"I told you what I said I told them!..."

"Oh."

"Don't get me all bothered up like a Republican newscast!"

"I'm sorry ma. It's just weird that they didn't get more domineering and demanding with you. I'm surprised."

"Don't be!... Help me up..." And she slowly rises from her chair with great ability, while Dice holds her elbow anyway for good measure. She verbally continues with, "You better be innocent boy, I'll tell ya that. I'm going to the sofa!" she declares, leaving his assistance seconds ago-- his hand suspended in mid air when her elbow leaves it.

"Why you look so weak today ma, you don't feel so hot?..." Dice asks, joining her on the couch.

"Things like that are determined by the day I'm having in the first place. I don't take kindly to right-wing terrorists gestapoing their way into my home, elbowing me in my neck with questions, of any kind."

He takes his hand and feels her forehead. "Well, you ain't hot or nothin'."

"That, I know," Grandma replies while pushing his hand away. "Stop making a Mayday alert out of this... And are you inside some kind of trouble?..."

"Huh? What trouble?"

"Do I have to get a lexicon and an interpreter to shed light on my new language for you?... Did you call these bastards here with your actions?"

"Nah ma, I didn't do nothin'!"

"Or did Angie call `em here to bust what's left of my ass?..."

"Yeah, that's right!... Maybe it was Angie who called them!... Ma, you been messin' with that little woman again?..."

"She's no woman. She's a sickness that still comes in the bingo hall... I'm sure she has ties to some kind of Slavic Mafia."

"Yeah, that's probably who called them. Angie... So ma do me a favor and stop making her hemorrhage."

She cranes her head to give him an admonishing look. She follows that with, "You better not be in no trouble boy... How pedestrian would it be for me to give you the back of my hand now?..."

"I know ma. Very pedestrian, I guess."

Back later at the hotel, Dice gets out of the elevator and walks on the floor where his room is, but before stopping there, he stops and knocks with knuckle taps on Spike's room door. Opening it, he finds him sitting stretched out on the bed, watching tv with blankness as his expression.

Dice comes in sullen. "What the fuck is the tragedy man?..." he says to him.

Spike's look almost appears as if he heard nothing. His stare stays blank at the tv screen.

Dice asks, "Hey Spike, what's the deal, man?..."

Spike now hears him-- turning his head to his friend, keeping the same blank look. "What's happenin' man?"

"Yeah," Dice replies, "like can you tell me quick? I'm starving for answers here..."

Spike turns back to the screen, looking one way with his eyes not shifting. "Hey man," Spike begins, "how many times in your life would you say you made a bona fide mistake?..."

Dice thinks about the question but tries to think behind it. "I dunno... Mistakes come and go like the life and death of human beings... Who can keep track even with funerals... Why, you made a mistake?"

"Aww I raped some little girl... somewheres..."

Dice stares hard at his friend for a few seconds. Then he asks, "How little?..."

"I dunno... Eleven?... Twelve?... I dunno..."

"When was that, just now?"
"Nah, nah... It was a while ago..."

Dice starts to walk around, trying to contemplate something. He looks at Spike with solemn disbelief, then snaps out of it. "But wait a minute!" he says. "Don't tell me she's dearly departed?"

"Nah, she's on Earth walking with the flesh. She breathes."
"Oh," replies Dice, relieved, starting to pace the floor now, disturbed. "What would make you make a choice like that man?..."

Spike's dazed look at the tv screen gives way to a chuckle. "Choose?... It's not like I was planning it like a business investment or somethin'."

"Yeah, I know that," Dice returns with wrinkles on his brow as he looks away distant.
"She's been following me."
"Get the fuck outta here! She's been following us??"

Spike nods his head up and down, then adds, "Well, I mean she's really following me."

Dice's alarm has stopped him enough to make him move himself closer to his friend's face for clarity. "I'm saying, if she was following you she was following us."

Spike plays with a small ashtray that's on the nightstand there, twirling it around on his index finger. "Yeah well, she knows where we are tho."

"She knows where we are??"
"Yeah... You know, remember when I was looking out the window before?..."

Dice quickly remembers Spike's looking out the window. "Aww man! This is highly problematic Spike. I feel... I feel my BLOOD beginning to boil!..."

"I know I know--"
"You KNOW... that THIS... is a big problem man!..."
"Yeah..."

They let silence set in for a few moments, then Dice surmises out loud. "My guess, is that-- how long do you think she's been eyeing us really?..."

Spike stops twirling the ashtray to dig into his thoughts. "Well, I didn't start seeing her in my vision until we got to this hotel."

Dice drops his hands at his sides then behind the back of his head in deep thought. Spike adds, "She's been up here, harassing me too."

"She black or white?"
"Black I think... Probably mixed with something... But she's quite the little blackmailer tho, as in Columbo and Agatha Christie characters. She even got sixty dollars out of me..."
"Fine. Then she has to be killed."

Spike looks over at him with a bit of surprise. "Oh..." he moans out, with nothing else to follow it for a few moments. Then afterwards, "Where d'you think is a good place to do it?..."

Dice remains in the contemplative stance he took before uttering his decision. "You know... that should be your decision really... I, didn't fuck her. I'm more traditional than you..." Then he turns and looks him in the eyes directly. "I can't believe your sense of morals man..."

Spike pushes himself up off the bed. "Look man, I'm sorry okay, but I was mad when I did it. In fact, I was mad over that thing we had when we were arguing over those Africans who made us the offer. I needed for somethin' to make me feel good, so I took some pleasure."

"It don't matter man!... What'd you wanna go make inroads for some kind of trouble like that for?... Professionals-- analyze this picture. That's what you see?..."

Spike's arms drop downwards like embarrassment settled in them. "Awright man, you want me to kill her?"

"Yes. It should be your duty to kill her. Fairness. Spell, fairness."
"That's all right, I don't have to."

Spike flops himself back down on the bed with a look based in disappointment. Dice is looking at him with an aftertaste of malice, trying to think of additional points to make. He then says, "I mean, this does not smell like professionalism by any stretch of the imagination..."

"You're right man," Spike replies in nolo contendere style.

Dice now turns away with a guilt-ridden posture when he turns. Silence comes out again, filling the room and surrounding the two friends, engulfing them. Spike goes back to staring at the tv screen with blankness.

After some moments pass, Dice turns back to Spike. "Awright man, I'll help you get rid of her..."

Spike still stares at the screen not saying anything. Dice is standing there waiting for him to answer. Then Spike replies with "Nah man, you're right! I should do it. You're right about--"

"We'll do it together Spike."
"Nah, I don't wanna impose. I firmly believe that this hell should only be mine, not my friend's."
"It's no problem man, we'll do it together. `Cause the sooner we can do this and get her out of our plans, the quicker we can get back to pursuing what we're supposed to be pursuing career-wise..."

Spike sits with helplessness expressed in his posture. "I just want you to know that my thoughts on this are your thoughts, so I ain't statin' that you're wrong or nothin'..."

"Well... we won't get into the deepness of this. Let's just get back to where we're supposed to be as professionals..."

The two say nothing for a while as they become self-absorbed in their activities-- Spike, playing with the ashtray in slow twirling motions, Dice, staring out the window with a contemplative stance and hands behind his back.

Spike finally says, "You want me to think of a place?..."

Dice throws up his hand not looking at him with no care in the gesture.

Spike drops his head down with shards of embarrassment still encroaching around him. His facial look shows him trying to come up with a place to kill the girl in his head. Then he says, "What about that empty post office building where we were with those African guys?..."

Dice slowly turns to him. "I don't think that's a spot where we should wanna go venturing back to, do you?... Think of the bodies we left over there..."

With his look at Dice expressing agreement, Spike gets up and puts his head in a thinking position, starting to pace the floor now a bit, showing work in his thoughts for a decision on a good location spot.

Moving away from the window, Dice says, "I think the best place for killing any kind of black people is in a black community, don't you?..."

Stopping, Spike thinks about that. "Yeah, I guess you can say that."

"I mean after all, who's gonna heave up sweat over any kind of black people dying any ol' where except black folks?" Dice asks, appearing to be certain from his expression.

"Yeah, nobody, authority-wise anyway, is gonna be breakin' no doors down pronto, shouting `Awright! Awright!--"

"Exactly."

"...everybody get against the wall...' Nah. I can see your reasoning in my eye with that one."

"Alright."

"But what neighborhood?... How we gonna get her to be sucker enough to go into a situation where no siege'll take place?..."

Dice begins to pace to try and find a solution to Spike's question.

Spike suddenly walks over to the door as Dice swings around to look at him. Carefully placing his hand on the doorknob, Spike turns it slowly and opens it up, looking out in the hall.

Dice is staring at him. "What, you hear warnings out there?..." he asks.

"Yeah," replies Spike, closing the door back. "At least I thought I did."

Dice sparks, "Wait a minute!... She followed you you said, right?"

"Definitely."

"Awright! It's all settled then. To classify this as a problem now is bullshit." You got a spot? you got a spot?" Spike shouts relieved.

Dice cracks a smile on his face and quickly heads over to the bed, where he drops his bottom down on the edge of it-- a piece of excitement drives his expression as he begins to speak. "Listen... She follows you..."

"Right."

"Ureeka!... This is how the story will go..."

The next day is midday when Spike is moderately walking on the outskirts of a neighborhood of five story housing project buildings. The streets are barely populated, and he walks without ever looking behind him at the twelve year old girl, who is following him, and keeping her distance one full block behind him.

Within a few yards distance, he leaves the housing project area when he crosses the street, walking towards a line of stores-- cleaners, Chinese take-out and grocery. He passes them, walking up that block that they're on, which is a hill. The girl still follows.

At the end of that block across the street at the top of the hill, is a burnt-red apple colored brick church, with a white cream-green painted steeple touching the bottom of the clouds. A tiny tiny gold cross is on the tip of it.

As Spike gets closer walking towards the church, the girl stays behind him, keeping a steady pace in her steps. Spike approaches the front of the church, which is abandoned-- signs indicating that hang on the outside of it, with various wooden boards nailed on it lopsided here and there.

Spike opens the rusted black cast iron gate that stands in front of it, being pronounced when he doesn't shut the gate back behind him. He climbs through the weeds and shrubbery there, nearly losing his balance doing so, but accomplishing it. Then he disappears.

The girl soon comes up to the church, slowly looking and peeking around the area where the shrubbery is. She bends her torso forward with her hands extended out, tiptoeing step, by step, by step, peeking behind the bushes, stretching her neck upwards to look over them. Hands grab her face!

Spike has his hand over her mouth as she complains loudly in moans while he drags her into an opening in the church, with the heels of her shoes leaving wiggly train track markings.

Inside the church is damp darkness with slivers of outside light from the openings here and there. At the end of the space that they're in is Dice, standing with his back facing a wall. On the floor in front of him is a large black trash bag, appearing to be filled to capacity. He reaches down into it.

Spike brings the girl to the center of the floor, releasing her head and mouth. She stands there and looks at the two. Spike tells Dice, "The infant is here."

The girl glares at him. "Infant?... I ain't no fuckin' infant, and if you're trying to scare me, I'm not scared!... What're you gonna do, rape me? Both of you are gonna rape me? So what!" She turns to Spike. "You better up fifty dollars again or I'll scream, mothafuckka!..."

Dice lets his voice be heard by raising it a bit. "You're not gonna do anything young lady," he says, still reaching in the trash bag.

The girl squinches her eyes, trying to make out who he is standing all the way back there. "Oh, that's supposed to scare me?... Well, you're gonna have to give me money too if you're gonna fuck me! You're gonna be in big trouble, scumbag! Big trouble!..."

Dice shouts back, "You better shut your goddamn mouth little bitch!... Little bitchy!..."

The girl replies loud, "You shut up! You think I'm scared of you?? Just for that, I don't even want your fuckin' money now! I'm gonna tell the cops!..."

Dice calmly tells Spike, "Grab her."

Spike grabs her arms and she tries to get away, wildly swinging and kicking her limbs. She cranes her head around to Spike with, "Oh, you guys are into kinky shit like my parents! Well I don't want your fuckin' money now, and I'm gonna scream!"

Spike slaps his hand over her mouth.

Dice runs like a diesel to her, holding a white handkerchief and a yarn of rope.

When he gets to the two he swings the handkerchief around her head and yanks it around her mouth, pulling it tighter when he ties it. Dice shouts to Spike, "Hold her down so I can hog-tie her fuckin' loud ass!..."

Spike pushes her face-down on the floor and lands on top of her-- "Hmph!" she exclaims from the pain of the fall with her mouth closed. He grapples to keep her down there while Dice takes the rope and begins wrapping her wrists, then her legs in hog-tie fashion (Spike jumps off her when Dice completes the tying.)

There she wobbles on the cold floor, screaming through her nose-- she flips over on her side, struggling to free her limbs.

Dice and Spike stand over her, staring down at her struggle. Dice tells Spike, "Keep an eye on her."

    "Right."

And he runs back over to the trash bag full blast, rather clumsily. Spike keeps an eye on her and watches him reaching in the bag. Dice finally pulls out a small ax, holding it up to Spike to show that he has it. He sees Spike seeing him, and runs back over in the same clumsy freight train manner.

Out of breath when he gets back, he tells Spike, "I'll do the first half, you do the second. Bet?"

"Right."

Spike starts standing back as he watches Dice taking a stance on the side of the girl-- she sees this and moan-screams louder in short spurts, frantic in emission through the air. Dice positions himself, holds the ax up, brings it down into the girl's neck, leaving an open gash showing the whiteness of flesh and the red pinkness of it. The girl convulses, jerking herself impossibly backwards.

Dice hacks again at her neck in the same gash, hacking as blood splashes out-- the girl's movements have ceased, as the only ones she makes now, comes from the movement of Dice's hacking.

Spike waits as Dice continues hacking at the girl, hacking her neck until the head snaps off in a quick crack sound, with the blood pumping out from the torso's neck stump. Dice begins to hack at one of her arms now, as Spike patiently waits his turn, watching Dice's precision as he pummels the arm with the ax.

Minutes pass and Dice is almost finished chopping off the other arm, as he hacks and hacks one more time-- the arm tumbles off, and nearly lands next to the other arm on the ground in a wide blood puddle.

Dice hands the blood dripping ax handle to Spike with a bit of exhaustion showing. "Here," he breathes out. "Go ahead, you get the legs..."

Spike grabs the ax business-like as his friend steps back from the corpse to give him room. He positions himself over the remainder of the body, lifts the ax up and brings it down on the corpse's thigh (he grunts when he chops at it, emptying all his strength in it.)

Minutes go by after which the two friends are standing there looking down at all the body parts, partially out of breath. Spike exhales, "Awright... What we do now?..."

Dice says "Wait there," and runs all the way back locomotive style to where the trash bag is. He looks inside it, spreading the top of the opened bag wider with both his hands, dunking his head inside, looking more in there.

Spike is waiting, looking at him, wondering what the wait is.

Dice brings his head back up with a bit of confusion showing. He surveys the area with his eyes, then looks back at the bag. "You know what?..." he begins. "I tell you what, you toss me the parts and I'll dump `em in the bag..."

"Awright."

And Spike goes over and begins picking up the body parts and tossing them over to Dice, with the blood slinging off each one of them-- droplets, flight scattering up and all over the place. After they complete the bagging of all the parts, Dice goes over to the bundle of clothes that's in the corner away from the trash bag. "The clothes are here man," he says, placing a set down next to him, then beginning to unfasten his pants, which are tie-dyed with blood. Spike comes over to where the clothes pile is and begins to remove his shirt.

A few minutes later, Dice steps out of the church with a new set of clothes on. He carefully and slowly looks around, rotating his head from the left to the right before inching the whole body outside nice and slow. Seconds later, Spike follows the same action behind him, also with a new set of clothes on.

Both friends soon walk out of the church's front yard which is littered with garbage bags. Their knees rise high up, stepping over what's there as they carefully walk, continuing to look around as they do. They both soon touch the sidewalk, and, head down the block towards an electrical power plant.

That evening, the two are calmly sitting on the edge of the bed in Dice's hotel room with containers of Chinese takeout food. The tv is on and both have their eyes on the screen.

On it, is a show called "The Most Wanted Criminals." The show's host is introducing a story about an attempted murder on a young woman.

He stands in front of a stilled screen shot of the young lady, an attractive beige twentiesh woman with well wept eyes on the screen.

The host says, "Mrs. Eternal Jones was stabbed repeatedly, seventeen times by her husband, and lived to tell the tale."

Dice and Spike both open their mouths wide in the astonishment that she lives.

The host continues, "It was the morning of January twelfth-- a typical rush hour morning for most people-- when Mrs. Jones was hurrying to ready her twin sons for kindergarten."

On the screen a reenactment appears, with actors portraying the principals: a twentyish looking woman in a darker complexion is seen, rushing to put jackets on twin boys in a kitchen.

The host goes on, "She herself was late for work, and had minutes to go before missing the designated bus that took her to her job minutes away in Urdsville."

The woman quickly slides into her jacket fumbling with it, and says to her boys, "Okay soldiers! To the car!..."

The host relates, "But her husband, thirty-five year old Eric Jones, had other plans for her."

Sitting at the kitchen table is a bald dark brown muscular man with a traditional thick mustache, watching the woman angrily as he gulps a quick gulp from a can of beer.

The host reveals, "An unemployed construction worker, who had just recently been laid off a temporary stock clerk position, Eric had been suspecting that his wife was having an affair, charges that were widely known to be unfounded by all those who knew the two."

Eric takes another gulp from his beer can, looking down at his wife's black mini skirt. As she opens the kitchen back door to leave, ushering her boys out through there, Eric slams the beer can down on the table "Where the hell you think you goin'?!!..."

She stops in her tracks (as does the kids, staring terrified). She turns to him. "I'm going to work, Eric," she says with innocence. "You know that."

He sledges his fist down hard, clanging the drinking glasses. "Who the hell you talkin' to??" He pushes his chair back getting up, slamming it against the wall. "Ya-- slut! You ain't goin' no where with that dress on! Take it off!!"

"No! No!"

He lunges at her, grabbing her by the back of her jacket collar, pulling her down backwards on the floor. The kids scream shaking-- standing with their backs against the door.

She scrambles to get up. He slaps her back down. "Shut up I said!!" And he slaps her again for good measure, then goes over to the kitchen cabinet, pulling open a drawer and snatching up a five inch knife from it. "Gon' see now!... Gon' see now!..."

The host continues, "Eric Jones then went on to stab his wife a total of seventeen times as her two boys watched in horror."

With the knife in his hand, he brings it down and up, down and up, as the twin boys cry with their mouths wide open, and the woman shows the frenzy on her face-- her arms moving up and down up and down, the same way the knife does, trying to fight off the stabbing, with no success.

Says the host, "When it was all over, Eternal Jones laid unconscious in a pool of blood, with her children desperately trying to wake her."

The little boys are pushing and tugging their mother's upper arm, rocking her body back and forth, not waking her.

The host says, "Eric Jones, just walked away, leaving his wife and kids behind in their home, as if nothing happened."

The kids now cower beside their mother's now semi-conscious body as the man walks towards them, aiming his eyebrows down angrily at all three of them, then stepping over her and leaving, opening the back door and walking out.

The host shakes his head with disgust and continues. "That was the last time anyone has seen Eric Jones." He turns and faces another camera, with the stilled shot of the real Eternal Jones behind him. "Eternal Jones however," he continues, "miraculously recovered from her wounds with the help of doctors, neighbors and friends."

The stilled shot changes into motion, with the real Eternal Jones receiving hugs and kisses from her children and other apparent family members on a hospital bed.

Spike still casually eats his Chinese food on the bed while Dice is staring at the screen minus movements. He is silent. Spike looks at him. "Damn, that's some wild shit, huh?..." Spike says, taking a forkful of Chinese food and shoving it in his mouth.

Dice says nothing, still staring at the screen in a trance state, while Eternal Jones' solemn happy face shows pleasure accepting the hugs and kisses.

Spike concentrates on looking at him now. "Dice... What's happenin' man, you hear signals?..."

"Nah," Dice replies, never taking his eyes off the screen. "She's unbelievable..."
"Who, that chick?" Spike answers, shoving more Chinese food into his mouth. "Yeah, she's fine."
"I mean... I mean she's special... I mean, like, everything about her..."

Spike takes his time to look at him even closer. "Wait a minute exactly... What is your mental state really saying?..."

"Hey listen... This girl... I can't believe anybody would do something like that to somebody like her..."

Spike still studies his friend. "Why not tho? She's just as different as everybody else. What makes her so unordinary?"

Dice is still staring at the screen as he stands up to make his point. "I know she's part of the population like everybody else. But did you look at her eyes?... Did you check behind her eyes for a millisecond when she was on the screen?..." He waits for an answer from Spike, who only shrugs and shoves in more forkfuls of Chinese food.

Dice walks away from the bed in deep thought and begins to pace the floor. Spike looks up at him and comments, "Sorry man... I just missed the boat on the paradise of this..." He scoops another forkful of food on his fork.

With his head down Dice begins to pace a bit in contemplation. "That guy," he begins, "the guy that stabbed her up like that?... That guy is evil man..."

Still eating, Spike asks innocently, "Then what are we?"

"Hey! We're not evil man! What're we, we're just trying to make a living man... We're just trying to get ours!... I mean, something happens, like somebody makes a mistake or something, and of course, we gotta take care of it, unfortunately."
  "Awright awright. The picture's all the way up to my ears, man," Spike replies, waving the fork in sing-song motions.
  "But him tho..." Dice shakes his head with disgust and halfway paces. "Now, that guy is the scum of the earth. And, he's still walking around somewhere free like, like some sort of armistice casualty..." He shakes his head with disgust again.

Spike looks up at him still munching. "You act like you wanna take action or somethin' about it..."

Dice stops and looks at him head on from the side. "Well... would that be a bad idea if I did?..."

"I dunno... She didn't look like she had too much money to me..."
  "Listen... I see a girl like that... Shit like that shouldn't happen to a girl, like that..."

Spike continues eating. "Yeah... I guess you're right about that..."

Dice looks at him with a mist of hesitation in front of him. Then he gradually walks over to the window there. "Where'd they say she was living at, that girl?"

  "Urdsville..."

"Yeah that's pretty close by," he says almost to himself, looking out the window.
"Take the train there 'n shit..."
"You thinkin' about going there for real? You think it'd be worth it?..."
"I'm thinking about going there and look for the girl."
"You mean look for the guy..."

Dice swings a look at him in 'of course' fashion. "Yeah, the guy..."

The next day, the Amtrak railway train at the station is motionless as the passengers move out of it dutifully, with Dice and Spike marching out right along with them.

The sun yells bright gushes of nonstop sunshine in bucketfuls on the Urdsville station. This day the weather has a part of itself in August, and most people wear shirts and blouses only of formal wear, with some casual wear showing its taste in the form of tee or sweat shirts. Dice and Spike look around and about themselves as they walk casually out of the station.

Later they enter a shopping district, filled sardine tight with passersby on both sides of a snail's pace traffic street. Both sides are oceans of cotton blouses and shirt fabrics, walking in up-and-down-the-block directions only. The sun rays off car hoods and fenders, blinding the sight of those who may view this. Dice and Spike walk through this.

Dice soon stops a man and says words to him, which makes the man point his finger in a direction away from the street where they stand. Dice and Spike both gesture a thanks to him, and the two proceed in that direction.

They walk and pass through a block looking similar to the district they just left, only narrower in passerby width and space. The stores are not linked together as the other district, but spaced with rectangle slits wide enough for cars to park in.

The two walk and look on both sides of the street, with Spike struggling with confusion marked on his face. Dice stops and looks around at the stores. He also shrugs, and the two then turn and head back in the direction they came.

They walk and look at stores and buildings as they do, with perplexity fixed on their faces. Moments later, another man approaches them, and Spike this time stops the man and exchanges words with him along with Dice. The man then quickly points his finger across the street, and the two gesture thanks to him and quickly head that way. A bus immediately pulls up there and stops with the two getting on it.

Ten minutes later the bus enters a shantytown neighborhood of two family wood-framed houses. Pulling into its route stop, Dice and Spike get out of it. The bus now pulls off and away from them in a cruise speed manner.

As the two begin walking they carefully survey the numbers on each house. A few seconds later they stop in front of one that's apple green. Spike comments, "The number calls itself out. This is it."

Dice sort of tugs at his shirt for the preparation of proper appearance. Spike sees him and says, "You act like this is the celebrity ball, man."

"Cut the crap, Amos. You don't want her to think charlatan before we even etch out our words..."

Spike chuckles with an "awright" gesture, and the two proceed in walking up the porch steps.

Knocking on the door a couple of times it finally opens, revealing Eternal Jones herself, wearing the same solemn face that was broadcast over the air.

Dice's stare tries to melt down a bit of its shock from seeing the actual Eternal Jones. "Umm... Yes, are you Eternal Jones?..."

"Yes..."
"Yes. Well, my name is Dice Jackson, and I uh saw the thing they did on you on `Most Wanted Criminals'..."
"Uh huh..."
"And I can't begin to tell you, how much it moved me... It moved me so much, that I came down here to help get this... man... and serve him with a permanent comeuppance..."
"Um, are you with the police?"
"Not exactly. You see, me and my friend here, Spike..."

Spike smiles and says "Glad to meet you," and she smiles and nods the same.

Dice continues, "...we take care of things like this for people..."

"Oh, you do?"
"That's right we do. And it ruins my soul that someone like you had to go thru something like that..."

Eternal's head bows slightly at the thought of her injuries. Dice says, "I hope I didn't rattle your sense of peace right now."

"No," Eternal replies with a distance. "You didn't rattle anything."

"Oh... Okay... Well, I hope you won't mind if me and my friend come in, so we can get some information on this... guy..."

She looks at Dice with hushed acceptance in her eyes. "You said you're not with the police?"

"Nah. We're--"

Spike shoots out, "Like bounty hunters..."

Dice glances at him like he's lost his mind with her not seeing him. Then he corrects for her with a smile, "Sorta like bounty hunters..."

She moves back to open the door slowly with hesitation in her motion of doing that. Dice asks, "Is it alright to come in?..."

"Oh, yes,," she replies with a piece of hesitation still remaining. "I just still have some pain in my joints when I move sometimes."
"Oh yeah," Dice remembers. "I forgot about that."
"Come in, please..." And she opens the door all the way wide with full grace now. Dice and Spike politely walk in.

Eternal's place inside is drape-ridden dark, with flickering illumination coming from a floor model television set only. It is the living room they have walked into, and the evidence of children inside is shown by the articles of toy trains and trucks strewn about, along with candy purple volley balls, and kid socks and jeans with small pairs of sneakers.

The couch is undetectable, except for its outline underneath adult coats and blouses and shirts.

Dice and Spike come inside real careful as they walk, with Eternal gracefully showing them the couch for them to take seats on. She comments, "You'll have to excuse my place. I haven't had the energy to really clean anything or nothing... since--"

Dice jumps in. "That's alright. Really, you shouldn't worry about something like that. We're fine."

And the two friends stiffly take seats on the end of the couch.

They both fold their hands between their knees as Eternal takes a seat on the couch's other end. She smiles another gracious smile at the two friends, who smile back at her in the quietness that lingers there for a while. Dice keeps cautiousness on his conscious before he begins

Eternal and Dice together say, "How long--" They laugh at the same time too. Then Dice says, "You go first."

Eternal smiles and says, "How long have you been doing this type of work?..."

"Not that long really," Dice reveals to her, glancing quick at the outline of her legs in her pants. "We kinda started this year, when the need yelled at me for it..."

"Oh... You don't kill people or nothing like that right? You just bring them to the police and stuff, right?"

"We--"

Spike cuts. "Nah we don't venture into Vincent Price territory or stuff like that." He chuckles nervously, trying to show the unlikelihood of her idea.

She smiles back at him cordial while Dice breathes in and breathes out. Then she utters, "Well... I just asked, because I think that killing is such a crime."

Dice's eyebrows go up. "You do?" he asks.

"Yes... Sometimes it can be just as horrible as beating someone..."

Spike turns his head to look at the draped window. Dice braces himself before speaking. "Yeah... I guess you can say that as fact..."

"Yes," she jerks alive a bit more. "I think everyone deserves the right to live once they're here..."

Dice looks into her eyes and notices that they glisten. "So... I want you to tell me some things about this... uh... You know, sometimes it's hard for me to address this guy as a human being, ya know that?..."

"I know," she says, bringing her head down to a sad hang. Then she perks up. "Sometimes it's hard for me too." She chuckles.

Dice smiles at her without showing contradiction. A few more seconds pass before Dice and Eternal say together, "Are tell you me--"

They both laugh together again while Dice shakes his head in disbelief. Spike looks at the two of them involuntarily as Dice says to Eternal, "Houston, we've got a problem... huh?" and she laughs silently harder. Then he begins again. "Listen..."

"Uh huh," she replies, perking up more relaxed.
"Tell me when you last saw him, was it after the incident?..."

She buckles down her thoughts on this and goes over them. "Yes," she says with a drawl of sadness.

Dice goes on with, "Have you like, heard anything lately maybe, about... something like, maybe you heard someone say they saw him somewhere?..."

"I know he's in the neighborhood tho..."

Spike's eyes light up. "You're kidding?..."

Dice turns his head to him, then sets his eyes back on Eternal. "You said, you know he's in the neighborhood??..."

"Uh huh..."

Dice gathers more thoughts to ask as questions. "Um... Who seen him? Someone told you they saw him?"

"Yes. A girl I know."
"Where'd she see him?..."
"Well, there's like a strip area not too far away where they have a bar and grill... She said she thinks she saw him at Rudybell's. That's the bar and grill."
"She thinks she saw him?"
"Yes, but she said she was pretty sure it was him tho..."
"What was he doing tho? She just saw him go in or something?"
"Uh huh. I guess. She just saw him go in, or saw him in there..."

Dice and Spike look at each other on the same beat, as if they know something. Then Spike asks her, "How far is that bar and grill away from here? Can we walk from here, or do we have to take a bus?..."

She shrugs and replies "You could do either really."

Spike's face reads difficulty understanding. "I still have disbelief hollering in my ears. I mean, they have a crime show on about this guy and they're looking for him and stuff, and he's walking around vibrant as a whistle, like everything is neutral and forgiven?..."

163

He shakes his head like a death in someone's family. "I can't believe my understanding is working right on this..."

Dice stares at Eternal's nipples pouting through her white tee shirt. "He hasn't come back here or nothing, has he?..."

"No," she sounds out with relief. "He hasn't come back..." Then she drops her head down and shift her eyes up to his face.

Spike says, "But he's so close by... Aren't you scared `n stuff, with him being so close by?..."

Eternal sighs and thinks about the reality of the question for a few moments. Then she almost whispers, "I always sort of thought the police would protect me... I mean... I did get on `Most Wanted Criminals'... so I guess they're here to help me in some kind of way..."

Spike hoots "Ta!" with Dice and Eternal looking at him simultaneously after that. He follows that with "Lube should be here to school her on the realities of crime fighting, huh?"

Dice glances at him with hesitant caution, then looks at Eternal. "Well... I promise you we won't be an ordinary solution..."

She smiles nervously as she notices his posture. Then Dice and her both say, "Are where are your pri--" They laugh again, precisely at the same time, while Spike lets exasperation show when he exhales.

Dice tells Eternal, "We're freakin' my friend out with this," and they both chuckle while he immediately gets serious. "Where are your kids tho? I know you had a couple."

"Oh, they're at my sister's house... for a while..."
"Cool..."

Dice stands up now, contemplating something. "Do you have some pictures lying around of, you know who?..."

"Oh, of course."

And she raises herself and goes over to a bureau in the corner of the room, colored by the shade of the darkness that's there. Dice gets the chance to notice her figure in full, which is modelesque, and desirable. He watches her as she gently reaches for the top of the bureau, taking off a framed photo of herself, her children and her husband, who looks exactly like the man in the reenactment of Eternal's story.

She comes back over to Dice with it and shows it to him, with Spike standing up now to get a look at it. "Hey," Spike replies with surprise. "He's almost the spittin' image of the guy that was playing him on tv, right?..."

Dice gives another glance at Spike that spells uneasiness. Then he looks back into Eternal's eyes. "Listen-- I'm gonna be like a cactus on this, `cause the injustice is protruding in a skyscraper sorta way... We're gonna go huntin' for this animal, and I want you to know, we're not expecting no money from you on this."

Spike's face frowns up quick like a twitch.

He continues, speaking to her lips. "I know you don't know me from nothin' or nobody, but I want you to get a grasp of what I'm saying... so I look into your eyes..."

Eternal stares into his eyes straight, while Spike's look shows his thoughts wandering in and out of attention. Dice continues with Eternal, telling her, "I swear on my soul, I'm gonna take care of this guy for you, the way guys are supposed to be taken care of who do things like that..."

Eternal shyly bows her head with her smile aiming toward the floor. She shows that words are trying to leave her mouth to express her feelings on Dice's feelings, then finally utters, "Well... I, do believe you'll do what you'll say... But..." and she shyly chuckles to herself. "I just don't know why you would wanna do something like that for me, being that you don't know me and all..."

Dice gets a bit closer to her while Spike's impatience gives hints of itself on his face. Dice addresses Eternal even softer. "Listen... the beauty of your eyes told me through the tv, and here right now, that a man beside your presence should always worship you, because of your willingness to share yourself with him."

Spike rolls his eyeballs up to his eyebrows.

Still going on, Dice tells her, "I want you to know, that yes, it is your kindness and your beauty that's made me throw away thoughts on money from you for all this, but more than that, I wanna see justice in a real party mood when I help it slay the evil that would make a guy do a thing like that to you..."

Eternal is nearly melting, keeping her head bowed but smiling. She takes a deep breath and slowly lifts her head up. "Well... Dice... I do thank you for being concerned..."

He extends his hand to hers to shake it. She casts her sight on it and tries not to look up at him, but does anyway. Dice takes it, gently, looking into her eyes. He says to her,

"Thank you, Eternal," and he softly shifts her hand up and down closely simulating a shake.

Eternal replies in her usual shy tone, saying "Thanks for being concerned, Dice..."

"It's more than a concern..."

She looks at him with pleasantness in her surprise. "Well..." she says more bashful than before, then she chuckles to herself. Suddenly she looks up with a remembrance. "Oh, but you're not going to go looking for anyone now... Are you?..."

Dice and Spike look at each other with the intention to shrug, they don't know.

Eternal goes on. "Because I thought maybe you and your friend might want to stay a while before you go looking for him. I have so much food here now... Do you like steak?... I have steak..."

Dice looks at Spike again, who this time takes it upon himself to shrug "I don't know." Dice looks back at Eternal, saying, "Well, we didn't come here to put you out of your way or nothin'..."

"I have potatoes-- do y'all like baked potatoes?..." she asks. "I can make y'all some steak and potatoes?"

Dice and Spike look at each other again, with Dice replying to her, "Well... Again Eternal, I don't want you to go through a whole lot of trouble for us..."

Spike says, "Wow... I can't remember the feeling of a steak, quite frankly..."

Eternal slowly gestures for them to return to their sitting. "Why don't you guys sit back down," she says, looking only to Dice with a smile suggesting that the meal is only for him. "I'll just go into the kitchen and fix something for you... It won't take long, really..."

Spike looks at Dice and giggles kind of goofily. Then Spike shrugs. "Tell the queen I'll be staying the night?" he says, then giggles the same goofy way. Dice says to her, "Awright Eternal. Umm... we'll... take a seat..."

And they both sit almost immediately while Eternal shows more happiness with her smile than seen since they been there. Off she goes with spirit into the kitchen, saying, "I'll be right out. Just let me put the food on and I'll be right out..."

Dice and Spike sit quiet for a few moments, then Dice speaks in a middle whisper, "Listen.. I think I'm making an impression on her. She goes beyond gorgeous-- that's a lame adjective. I'm up to my ears in hope here."

Spike uses the same whispering tone. "Listen..."

"Hmm."
"What was that about no dough? What kind of sermon is that?"
"C'mon man. We'll make dough. We know how to make dough."
"Yeah, but I didn't think we were coming all the way down here because your dick is all smitten."

Dice gives him a look of sheer surprise. "How could you state that man?... You think all I wanna do is bed this girl?..."

"You saw her on tv and got lumpy inside."
"Didn't her story mean anything to you at all?..."

Spike looks at him with a look of not knowing who he is. "Confusion is trying to strangle me to death or something. I thought you cared an iota about our enterprise man, really..."

"Listen. What I'm sayin' is, this girl?... I'm caring about this girl, right?... Okay. Now... it just may so happen, that we'll get money for this, ya know? Eventho I'm tellin' her precisely that dough's not a significant thing. Now listen..." and he moves himself a bit closer to his friend to be heard, "...if my calculations are math correct, I think she may donate a little somethin' to free enterprise..."

Spike still stares straight into him like he's witnessing a new life form. "I dunno man. I just didn't lay my needs down just to dive into someone else's trouble..."

"Look at it this way... We could do somebody some good for a change..."

Spike is unimpressed thinking about it. "I dunno man... I feel like the math on this is missing a decimal..." Dice is staring at a photograph of Eternal and her kids on the coffee table and sighs inside, not hearing him.

From the back of the kitchen Eternal shouts, "Hey, how come you guys got so quiet?..."

A few hours pass since Eternal's making of steak and potatoes with garden string beans, which the two hurried down with great ease and delight. Now Spike is reared back on the couch, appearing stuffed and satisfied with his eyes half-opened. The tv there still flickers off light which is lightening blue from the speed boat chase on the ocean that's on the screen. Spike's eyelids gradually drop shut as Dice and Eternal remain seated at the kitchen table.

The quiet is dense and their eyes are before each other. The two are talking in semblances of whispers in a chic table-for-two style closeness.

Dice is telling Eternal, "When I saw you on tv, something inside myself told me I was never gonna be able to think again, without seeing your image inside my head over and over, and with me enjoying every second of it." He releases a pleasure chuckle, enjoying the thought of that.

Eternal smiles back at him with the same pleased pleasure on her face. "I can't..." she begins in her usual shy manner, then giggling to herself in bowed motion. "I can't believe... I met someone like you... in such a short time... I mean..." and she chuckles to herself with more shyness. "I guess it's true, that sometimes, out of the most horror, something beautiful can come through..."

Dice smiles back at her with a look of agreement. Then he turns his head to take a look at Spike, who's slumped body on the couch indicates his slumber.

He turns back to her noticing that she sees Spike's napping as well. She looks at Dice. "He looks really tired," she says, as she looks at his lips quick, hoping he doesn't see.

"Yeah," Dice drones out, thinking about something else. "I guess he's really satisfied in his stomach. You know, he really wanted that steak you know."
"I know... I'm glad he enjoyed it so much."
"It was an excellent dinner... And just you having me here with you eating it made it even more enjoyable. I would've laid my life on the line for that one..."

Eternal winces a bit of surprise when he says that. "You have such a unique way of saying things..."

He looks out the corner of his eye at Spike, who's still sleeping. Then to Eternal he says, "A unique way, of saying things?..."

"Mm hmph," she replies in a cheerful gesture of the head.

Dice looks down at the table. "Well... I dunno... Do you think this is unique?..." He slowly stands up from his chair and she looks up at him as he's rising. He gently reaches over the table and takes her by the hand, pulling her up as her eyes stay on him while she comes up to him. He pulls her towards him, embraces and kisses her softly, sliding the tip of his tongue in her mouth. After a few moments, he releases her.

She looks at him with intense want for a second, then kisses him herself with full impact on his lips, sticking her tongue inside his mouth the same way, until stopping after a few moments' end.

The two look at each other, holding hands in a military face to face West Point manner. Eternal bows her head down. "Well..." she says, with no words following. Dice fully embraces her body and kisses her again with no sounds heard inside but the night sounds heard outside. They stop and move back, looking at each other.

Dice smiles broadly at her, while she begins with embarrassment. "You know... I think..." and she bows her head which shows her embarrassment more. "I'm feeling like you might misunderstand me..."

"I don't follow," Dice replies, gently rubbing the sides of her waist, inclining his head down to kiss her again. She turns her head away. He looks at her surprised. "What's the matter?" he asks with concern.

She looks at him with tears beginning to break out. "I... You're gonna misunderstand me, I know it..."

"I doubt I could ever misunderstand anything you say, but I don't know what you're saying. You gotta tell me first..."

Eternal gradually takes his hand, and places it on a spot beside her crotch. He looks deep into her eyes as she moves his hand slowly in that area, staring into his eyes with her tears beginning to spill over her lower eyelids.

Dice takes both his hands and drops them on her shoulders. "Listen... If you're embarrassed for wanting me, I'm sharing the embarrassment 'cause I'm wanting you. I think that you're so special and could never think of you as less than that, no matter what..."

Her features tremble as she tries to smile. Then she moves closer to him and drops her head on his chest. "You don't understand," she says, looking off to the side at an antique sewing machine closed up in the corner of the kitchen.

Dice holds her but frowns a bit as he runs her words around in his head for a few moments. Abruptly, she pushes herself away from him, but takes his hand while sobbing, with Dice standing there waiting and wondering what's next. She then leads him out of the kitchen as he looks back at Spike, who still slumbers on the couch not knowing what takes place.

Eternal leads Dice through a narrow hallway, dark and filled with cardboard boxes lined against both walls, stacked from floor to ceiling. She says nothing as she continues leading him to the bedroom ahead of them (the bed sticks halfway out, seen beyond the opened door over the threshold). The tightness of the made-up bed sheets rebel yells neatness as Dice sees it when he gets closer.

Eternal is weeping as she leads him into the bedroom, and Dice's concern prevents him from realizing that he's in her bedroom. He takes her by her arm and carefully turns her around to him. "Hey," he says with an understanding tone. "We don't have to do this you know..."

Her weeping settles back down to sobbing again. "I know I don't have to do it..." And she looks right up into his eyes with hers filling up again. "But I want to do it," she replies, almost beginning to break down again.

"But why are you crying?" he asks, with concern weighing his voice more.

Eternal lets go of his hand and slowly walks over to the bedroom door to close it. A grapefruit pink light from a lamppost outside her window is the only light that illuminates the room, shining as a ray through the white linen drapes that are there. It makes itself known directly on the bed, as it seems to be shining on it more than the room.

Eternal walks over to it as Dice watches her, not knowing what to expect as she begins to cry now.

Dice says, "Eternal... I don't understand..."

She starts to remove her clothes as Dice just stands there watching her. Her crying increases a bit when she fully disrobes, standing nude in the darkness with her back to Dice. She turns around to face him, stepping into the light.

Dice's eyes hinge unblinking at what he thinks he sees on her body-- they look like little horizontal slits in the skin from his distance, so he steps closer to her. Her weeping has changed back to sobbing.

The horizontal slits are in fact slits, like a female clitoris in appearance, covering most of her torso under and above her breasts. Some of them extend over to her upper arms, with the width of them being one inch wide, and the clitoral lips on them appearing thick, pulled out and over, smooth and swollen looking.

Dice can't believe his eyes, so he steps even closer to the still sobbing Eternal, who looks at him as his sight examines her body.

The slits are salmon in color and bear evidence of all being once stitched, for the remains of thick black suture stay caught up and x'd in some of the skin of the lips-- some going right over the slit itself. Some of the slits go in vertical directions. Some are lopsided. Others are diagonal or border on that.

The longer Dice stares at them, the more they seem to be opening and closing individually to him. The ones still stitched, strain, trying to open up, appearing to try to break their stitches, pulling the skin above and below it into many little vertical wrinkles, all scattered in motion. Dice closes his eyes real tight to relinquish the sight of them, and Eternal sobs a bit harder watching him. He opens his eyes and only sees the slits' clitoral appearance, not moving.

Dice steps even closer now, close enough to touch them as Eternal's look bears more of an answer than a reaction. He raises his fingertips as he stares with hard shock at the slits on her body, and starts to extend his hand to gently touch one of them, then decides against doing it by dropping the hand.

He finally gets his eyes to look into hers for a second, then losing the battle, they go right back to looking at the slits. He sees that a couple of them have iodine colored circles around them, while the others show no stains around them or coloring.

Dice nearly has his mouth open in shock, as he is finally able to look away. Eternal watches him through her sobs as he slowly takes a seat on the edge of the bed, staring away from her into space. She begins to look at him with concern now, as she gradually sits beside him on the bed.

Dice keeps his stare into space but now his eyes well-up with tears. Eternal shows more concern and moves closer to him, taking her arm and putting it around his shoulders. Dice then starts to cry, slowly at first. Eternal comforts him with the caring motion of rubbing his shoulders.

Dice now loudly starts to cry with all his might, while Eternal pats him on the back now consolingly. "Oh shit!!" he screams with much pain, as he wails and wails now-- the tears stream down his cheeks to his chin, and drips off from it like a running faucet. "Oh shit!!" he hollers again, dropping his forehead into his hands and dropping that between his knees, wailing intensely, loud like a stuck car horn. Eternal still sobs herself, but consoles him with both her hands on his shoulders.

Chapter Nine: Good Samaritanism 101

Footsteps heard walking towards him get Spike up quick from the couch the next morning, seeing Dice heading his way looking serious, dazed and groggy.

Spike swiftly swings his face from left to right, realizing it is morning, then realizing that he has spent the night on the couch. Dice approaches him, keeping the seriousness on his face. "What's happenin' man," he says, not really looking at him.

Spike looks at him and grins. "Hmm-- I guess the king has stayed the night, huh?..."

Dice stares at nothing. "Yeah..." he replies with somberness dictating.

"Damn man, you look like a funeral parlor," Spike comments.
"Oh yeah?... Nah, I'm cool," Dice assures him, keeping the same expression on his face.
"Understood," Spike replies, turning away from him, then walking to the other side to the window. Dice is looking at him, waiting for more words to follow, that don't.

Dice then prepares himself to say more words. "Umm..." he begins, fixing his shirt by way of tucking down the bottom of it. "We better get ready to get up outta here I guess..."

"Hey man, is everything cool?..."
"Yeah... She just filled me in on some other stuff..."

"Oh..."

Dice continues to look down at himself, to make sure his clothes wear no slept-in wrinkles. Spike looks over at him and asks, "So... You gonna come back and see her when it's done?..."

Dice looks at him with surprise inside him at the question. "Yeah?" he says in a tone of challenge.

"Hey man, I was just asking for my curiosity's own health. You don't think I'm protestin', do ya?..."

Dice stares at him realizing it's his friend. "Nah Spike... I'm just freakin' out a little bit man, that's all..."

"I understand. No problem."
"Look..." and Dice gets closer to his friend, "we gotta give this beast a bath in blood, understand?"
"Yeah, no question... Listen, did she say a syllable at all about money?..."
"Nah," Dice replies, turning his back to him to unzip his pants to fix them, then zip them back up again. "Believe me tho, once you do a good job for someone like that, they're willing to pay you dough if it's well done... They feel guilty if they don't..."
"Hmm... So when do we do the hunting?..."
"I figure we go down to that bar and grill area and take a look at it at least... even tho it's morning..."
"What's next after that? It'll be a long time before the night time comes. Where're we gonna hang out till then? Unless... you're gonna hang out back here?..."
"C'mon, we can both come back here... I just wanna get a look at the place now... You know... We need to be as professional about this as possible..."

Spike starts to slowly head over to the front door, but stops. "Hey... I guess I better use the bathroom, huh?..." Then he turns back around and heads in the direction of the bedroom while Dice continues to fix his clothes looking down at them. When Spike gets to the bathroom he yells out, "Dice!... I'm in the bathroom!..." and goes inside.

"Right! I heard you!" Dice answers back, looking up now in the direction of the bathroom. Then, he immediately heads towards Eternal's bedroom, opening the door and going inside.

A few moments later, Spike comes out of the bathroom, slowly walking past the whispering conversation in Eternal's room (he tries to make out a few words while passing), heading back to the front door, waiting there.

Eternal's door opens with Dice's back only visible at the threshold. Spike turns away from it, unconcerned in manner. When Dice exits the room she immediately closes the door behind him.

He walks over to Spike to leave the place in a hurry. "Ready?..." he asks, and Spike nods yes as they walk right out.

As the two walk down the empty block in the sun, Spike is looking at Dice with his mouth fixed as a smirk. Dice has his eyes set looking one way, ahead of him.

They keep walking, heading down the block without a word exchanged so far, with Spike still glancing and looking at Dice with the same smirk that's evident on his face. After some moments, Spike finally utters something with the smirk. "So..." he begins. "You obviously must've got over in a grandiose sort of way last night... huh?..."

Dice looks over at him with no yes or no on his face. Spike gives his hands a clap and laughs. "I knew it!... Ah shit!-- on the first meeting too! Without a night on the town even!..."

Dice's quick frown is hardly noticed by Spike as he goes on. "That's good tho!... That's good!... Damn, my dick is all riled up now `n shit!... I wish I could get over real quick like that..." And he grabs hold of the bottom of his pants where his penis is and slurps up the air one time.

Dice looks at him now with his frown diminishing. Spike continues. "But you know who I'd like to fuck tho?..."

"Who?" replies Dice, not looking at him.
"Nuns..."
"Nuns?
"Yeah man. The Catholic church has changed man. Some of the nuns wear shorter dresses now, have you seen `em?"

Losing some of his attention, Dice absently says, "Yeah, I seen a few of `em..."

"Man, I'd like to take some of them and..." He stops at a lamppost with Dice stopping a few feet ahead of him to look back. Spike simulates sex with the post, humping it "Mmph!... Mmph!..." on his pump strokes, then walk-running to catch up to Dice's few feet lead. They resume walking.

Dice asks, "And you wanna screw some nuns now, huh?..."

Spike looks at him and laughs goofily.

On they walk, now heading across the street for the bus stop that stands before the deep green leafy park for sitting that sits there. Soon after, a bus rolls up to the stop and they get on it.

It later pulls up to a stop where gingerbread brown brick two story structures line the blocks, wearing solid white gables over their windows, which are two to a floor. The buildings house grocery stores, card shops and thrift shops, along with a bakery, laundromat and other evidence of community and neighborhood there.

When the friends get out of the bus, Spike gives a vocal observation. "We gotta cleanse somebody in this area?... It looks like a two-parent town, where even mom serves sandwiches at lunch time."

"She said it'd be in another area tho," Dice says, as he looks around, up and over parked car roofs, trying to find the correct area. Then he begins to lead the way.

As the two start walking, they nearly reach the corner of a block where a flower shop sits. Around the other side of it (unseen) comes a grayish-brown woman, fortyish, with her head down, wearing a battleship gray wool overcoat and a faded print kerchief over her head, tied under her chin.

The friends and the woman walk into each other-- she stops back short, backs up, shifts her head up back to look at the two. Her eyes then bulge out terrified big.

Dice smiles soft and utters "Excuse me," and Spike starts to say something but is halted by her eyes.

The woman still stares wide-eyed terror at them. Then, she swings around and runs away, in the same direction she came.

Spike's words shoot out to Dice. "Hey, I think that chick knows us!..."

Dice's stare borders on a squint. "Nah... I don't think so man. She looks kinda freaked out..."

"Man... I'm tellin' you... I think that chick knows us. Her vision might've witnessed us from somewhere, man..."

Dice still watches the woman scurry-running down the block. "Nah," he hums with hesitation. "I think she's just a freaked out lady man... I'm not gonna read too much drama into that..."

Spike watches the woman as she fades into disappearance and says, "I got a feeling inside my stomach that's making me think... something..."

Now Dice's attention seems to sail like a boat away on the ocean. His eyes shift up to the left, looking somewhere. "Ehh..." he reasons, "she probably just thought we were somebody else..."

Suddenly, Spike woman-screams out a long siren loud scream-- Dice hunches back his torso from the shock of it. "Spike! C'mon man!!"

Spike chuckles, sort of to himself and to no one. "I was desperate... Your mind is sluggish and lovesick..."

Dice hands him a look like he's crazy. "Look man, if it makes you feel any better, we'll go in that restaurant over there and stay hidden like fossils. Fair enough?" And he immediately starts walking across the street, towards the restaurant.

Spike is looking at him. "Fair enough," he follows, and goes off behind him, walking with a bit of haste to catch up with Dice's lead.

Still walking ahead, Dice moves on making determined steps across the street, stepping up on the curb and walking into the restaurant with anger seen soaking through his calm expression. Spike is behind him.

Inside the restaurant is the hustle of waitresses, from the tables to the counters to the swinging-door back room kitchen. The friends take seats at the counter, rotating their heads slow from the left to the right to observe the place's entirety.

A white-opaque petite-built waitress sinuous in her movements approaches Dice and Spike with menus in her hand and a pleasant smile Dice places an order for two cups of coffee and two orders of dry toast. When the waitress jots the orders down in her pad, she steps away professional but drenched in pleasantness. Dice says to Spike in aside manner, "I think you're really stretching out what likelihood means."

"What chu mean?"
"I mean that woman... My senses tell me we're over reacting."
"Better safe than sorry."

Dice turns his face the other way after Spike says that.

A few moments pass before the waitress returns, carrying high above her head two trays (a tray in each hand), full of plates of piled high hot food.

The two turn their heads to see her coming and instantly, the trays in her hands slow-tilts downwards, with the dishes and food sliding down the same way, till all crashing on the floor, sounding in multiples of clangs. Everyone's head inside turns swiftly to the direction of the waitress, who quickly turns around and heads back into the kitchen void of expression.

Dice and Spike look at each other, then, instantly raise themselves up from the counter in simultaneous fashion. They immediately leave the restaurant casually with no will to look back.

Once outside of the place, they stand in the front of it as Dice reaches in his pocket for his cigarette pack, and flips out one. Spike holds his hand out for one himself, waiting. Dice tilts a look over to him and remarks, "Foreboding..."

Spike takes the cigarette Dice holds out to him, saying "I know..."

"Trays falling 'n shit. What else would be next, a buzzard instead of toast? A beer instead of coffee?… Charge me guilty I guess for leading us into there..."

Then he looks at Spike. "Hey man, would you say that your apprehension over that chick is about over, so we can resume the mission?..."

"Yeah," Spike sighs with an edge of frustration. "Forgive me Father for I have sinned..."

Dice looks back at him as they both begin to walk. "Cut the shit, Ramsey..." he says.

They walk away from the restaurant now and head in the same direction they were walking before they ran into the woman. Taking the same path, they approach the same corner, and reaching it, slam!-- they smack right into the same woman again.

Dice and Spike stop and stay still (their eyes bright with fright) while the woman is stuck there, moving nothing as her mouth is shocked wide-opened. She pronounces a horror-filled "EH!" for a scream, then turns around and runs down the block again in the same manner as before, disappearing.

The insides of Dice and Spike well up. "Oh shit!" their words burst out at the same time almost, then, they turn around the opposite way, and run for dear life.

The two continue down the block on the opposite side they were on. Gradually they slow down their running as they come to a moderate pedestrian pace of a walk. Out of breath, Dice admits, "I can't... I can't believe..."

Spike's breath almost mimics Dice's in its out of breath manner. "She scared... She scared the shit outta me..."

Coming back to normal as they walk, Dice soon realizes that they both have reached the bar and grill called Rudybell's. There it sits sandwiched between little stores and shops of various types, all with two-step stoops and black wrought iron banisters lined in front of them. These structures wear dull multi-colored faux brick facades, and almost look plaster of paris like in texture.

The entire block where the bar and grill sits is like an island, surrounded by open lots of auburn dirt, showing evidence of more to be built there by the wooden planks strewn about the areas.

Dice notices the sign over Rudybell's entrance and taps Spike on the corner of his shoulder with a swipe. "This is the place," he says.

Spike looks up and steps back. "Good," he sighs. "I was beginning to feel like I was in a new kind of maze... My head is feeling dreary from it."

Stepping back to get a full-sized view, Dice observes the front of Rudybell's which is closed like the other stores, due to the earliness of the morning. He folds his hands behind his back and strolls from the left to the right, looking over the place while Spike observes it with a professional expression. Dice remarks, "Let's go check out the back of the joint."

"Right."

They both walk, heading for the back of the buildings in a casual manner. Spike asks, "What's up with the back?..."

"Ehh you know... in case they got a graveyard waitin' for us inside there or somethin'... Somewhere to escape..."
"Okay."

Reaching the back of Rudybell's, they see on the ground in front of the back door of the place, a body-sized bulge of battleship-gray wool fabric between two trash cans.

Spike and Dice stop and stare at it. Spike says, "What the hell is that?..."

Dice goes over to it first to get a better look with Spike behind him. When Dice gets up to the bulge, he takes his foot and gently tips it with a slight touch of his shoe. The bulge slowly flips over, revealing the woman who they kept bumping into. Her closed eyes, faded print kerchief tied under her chin and motionless expression, gives the appearance of death.

Spike says "Oh shit" while Dice is staring down at the corpse with motionless surprise.

Just then, the back door opens up, and the friends just stand there stunned and waiting.

Emerging from behind the door is a pale-pink complexioned man of six feet one inch height and wet stringy black hair flipped over the right side on his eyebrow. His forehead is full of beads of sweat as he holds a cigarette between his pinky and his thumb, which keeps three fingers in front of his face when he takes a drag on it, grinning, trying to hold back a chuckle.

Beside him is a medium sized tan man of shorter height, wearing a tight black suit which is too small for him (white shirt sleeves stick way out underneath the suit jacket sleeves, with pant legs raised way high over the ankles). He looks at Dice and Spike with no concern showing, and bends down to move the body.

The grinning man steps a bit closer to the two friends as they watch him. He speaks. "Do you, see something unnatural here?..." he asks, holding in his chuckle and shaking from doing it, as he takes a drag from his cigarette (the three fingers are in his face as he holds it with the thumb and pinky).

Dice stares at him, not moved. "Depends on what's natural," he answers, as he watches the shorter man move the body by dragging it inside through Rudybell's back door.

The grinning man's whole face now shows sweat beads as he steps another step forward, holding his laugh in and trembling from it, with the three fingers in his face as he drags on his cigarette again. "Do you," he says, "… do you think that what you see is wrong?..."

Spike looks at Dice, waiting for his answer and Dice looks at Spike like he can't believe what the man is asking. He then turns to the grinning man, "Look man, I don't care what you're doin', okay?... Continue your chores and I'll continue mine..."

The man keeps grinning and lets a chuckle out through his nose that goes "Hmph" when he does it. The sweat beads begin to scatter-roll down his head and cheeks as he nervously brings his cigarette filter up to his mouth with his pinky and thumb, flicking the three fingers in front of his eyes. "Do you feel, that there is a body here?" the man asks, laughing silently through his nose now.

Dice looks far into his eyes and breathes deep. "Listen you fuckin' freak," Dice hauls into him. "I don't give a fuck what kinda production you're handlin' here, just go on and handle it!... If you're gonna do something about us mothafucka then go on and handle it!... standin' there askin' stupid-ass questions..."

Spike gives the grinning man an expression of That's right! as he looks into his sweat-ridden face. The man quivers from holding in his laugh. After dragging on his cigarette, he moves it away from his mouth, rigidly holding it with his pinky and thumb. Then he glances over his shoulder at the back door behind him.

The shorter man slowly walks out again, holding a Smith & Wesson model 59 semi automatic pistol calmly in front of him. He stands there looking at Dice and Spike with no expression, and Spike says to him, "What say you morose?... You taking action here or what?..."

The grinning man laughs through his nose again letting out an "uh-hmph!" through it as he brings the pinky and thumb holding his cigarette up to his mouth, and the three fingers in his vision again. His hand and head quivers as he draws hard smoke into his lungs. Then blowing it out smoothly he says, "My friend has his weapon... I have my own... What do you think it is?..."

And the grinning man steps back once with a quickness. Dice and Spike wait for what the outcome may be with their eyes not shifting-- stuck on the grinning man's next move. The shorter man stays looking at them all without moving nothing, holding his gun down steady.

The grinning man, suddenly swift, reaches in his pants pocket, pulling out an index finger-length grease-filmed dull gold knife. He flips up the blade open with his thumb, takes it, and cuts his wrist quick with it (the one with the hand holding the cigarette). A dribble-sized stream of blood draws up from it.

Then he looks at Dice and Spike as the shorter man behind steps back a bit more inside Rudybell's. Then the grinning man, slings the blood from his wrist forward.

Dice and Spike jump back hauling out "Whoa!" as the grinning man slings it again at them. Dice and Spike watch with stationary caution, as the grinning man now hacks up spit from the back of his throat, and when it comes up he shoots it out, landing on the ground a couple of feet from Dice and Spike, who say "Whoa!" again.

Spike yells, "What th' fu-- you got somethin' mothafuck??"

The grinning man chuckles through his nose again, as his pinky and thumb bring the cigarette back up to his lips for a smoke (him, dragging and quivering while doing it) with the sweat beads rolling down his face. He comments, "You two remind me of my pets." Dice and Spike are watching him carefully as he continues grinning, quaking, and dragging on his cigarette. The shorter man remains standing still in the back in Rudybell's threshold, holding the gun at his side pointed at the ground.

The grinning man decides to turn away from the two friends and slowly walks into the back of Rudybell's, with the shorter man moving out the way to let him in.

The friends continue watching the shorter man as he now goes into Rudybell's and closes the door behind him. Nothing sits on the ground outside the back of Rudybell's now, as Dice and Spike just stand there looking at the door. Spike says, "What-- did that mothafucka have?..."

"He had some kind of weaponry inside him, that's for sure," Dice remarks, still watching Rudybell's backdoor. "Now what kind of fear was that supposed to be he was administering? Does that mean we're not supposed to make a return here or somethin'?..."

"Oh fuck that!... Who does he think he is?"
"Oh absolutely. Believe me, I have no apprehension on subjects like that. ...fuckin' freak... He ain't man enough to end somebody in a traditional manner like everybody else."
"Here here."

Dice's face has the anger inside him coming out as damp perspiration as his body turns slowly to walk away, but his head stays facing the back of Rudybell's. Spike asks, "What chu wanna do now?..."

Dice still looks at the back of Rudybell's, thinking. "Well... I really seen all I need to see back here I guess..." And he finally turns his head around to face the proper direction so he can leave the area. In casualness the both of them gradually leave the place.

The two walk cautiously with silence, their ears substituting for eyes behind their heads. Spike asks, "What's your observation? You think he stands to be the owner of the place?..."

Dice looks straight ahead saying "It could be possible... But his status is nil to us is what I'm saying. What the hell do I care about who he's ending for? We got our own subjects to run and take care of."

"Exactly," Spike adds with a touch of firmness.
"But my insides feel like he's gonna start tailing us or something."
"Yeah?"
"Yeah... Like we better not forget the function of usin' our eyes right."
"Right."

And the two pass the faux brick multi-colored shops and stores that they passed when they came by earlier. They walk past a spot where the grinning man stands hidden inside an opening between two stores-- the three fingers up in his face as he drags on his cigarette, with the pinky and thumb holding it as usual.

Spike sweeps his face quick to that direction. Sees nobody between the stores. "I think I saw smiling boy," he says.

"Where?" says Dice, stopping at the same time. He swings his head to that direction. "You OVER THERE? FUCKA FACE??..." he shouts to the empty space between the stores.

Spike squints his eyes looking over there. "I know I saw that mothafucka..." he says, still squinting.

Dice's eyes remain watching the space there until his mind tells him to keep walking. Spike, following suit, says, "Maybe we should walk over there to be accurate.."

"Ehh... A barrel in my face is not what I'm after... Who says he ain't there waitin' for us to come in like that?..."

On they walk looking back at the same time. The space between the two stores becomes filled again with the grinning man who steps in it for a second, looking at Dice and Spike's backs, then stepping out of it leaving nothingness there.

Spike turns around again to look behind him. Dice sees him doing that and says "Forget seeking the drama over there, we got work to do."

"Yeah, I know," Spike heaves out, continuing to look back behind them in sporadic head turns. "I'm sure his ass is back there somewhere tho..."

Dice keeps his eyes straight with force while walking, focusing on that.

Suddenly a male voice bathed in a distant tone eases out a, "Yoo hoo..."

Spike slows his walk now to an almost stop along with Dice, who strains to not look back behind him. He says to Spike, "I know that mothafucka's not fuckin' with us now. Tell me that's not infectus, beckoning my soul, because it angers my soul that I can't BEAT the living SHIT outta his ever-loving ass..." Dice stops now sudden-like, turning his head slow to look back behind him, with Spike stopping to do the same thing the same way.

A male figure shoots by fast, past the opening between the stores where the grinning man was standing. He resembles the grinning man in color, stature and height slightly.

Dice and Spike shift their eyes along with the figure as it darts behind a corner of a shop. They look at each other with the same disbelief, with Dice asking, "Who's that-- that other freak with smiley?..."

"I dunno," Spike comments in a low tone. The figure now comes from behind the shop's corner, looking beige and teen-like sleek as he walks on ahead, swinging his arms and looking back at Dice and Spike, laughing.

Dice remarks to his friend, "What the fuck's the deal with this town, everybody laughs around here??... It's some kind of epidemic??..."

The man continues to walk as Dice and Spike eye him. He looks back at the two, laughing and swinging his arms way out in front of him with the pace of his walk.

Dice's face turns hot. "Spike... This is ridiculous! Does this asshole want me to suck his insides out?..."

"Our feelings are gone enough as it is," says Spike. "How much effort would it take to do that?"
"None what so ever... You think he's down with smiling boy?"
"I dunno. Could be. But where was he during the action tho?"
"I dunno..."

The man reaches another store and pivots around its corner, fast disappearing from sight. Dice and Spike look at each other with a shock of surprise. Dice mumbles "The shit fuck..." then declares, "He's baiting us."

"Yep."
"He's baiting us, and if I go over there to punch him in his neck, that smiling infecto'll make an appearance."
"Maybe..."
"Yeah, maybe."
"This shit is like the stock exchange."
"Exactly."

Casually, Dice leads the way in beginning to walk over to the store's corner, with Spike following his steps, moving his eyes in windshield wiper fashion. When they slowly approach that corner, Dice says, "Watch this. Watch what I said bears the fruit."

"I know."
"I feel like my sanity's being questioned."
"For days."
"And I'm feeling more heated for being subjected to this water torture."
"Water torture?... I think it's more severe than that."
"Well, that's exactly why his neck must be punched in..."

Reaching the store's corner, they take steps around it and stop in their tracks to look. There, a few feet away from them, stands the sleek teen-like man who cooed "yoo hoo," standing in conversation with a shorter pale olive man, who wears gold-framed faint pastel purple sunglasses, and an underwear white knitted Kangol cap.

The friends look at the two as they stand there chuckling and talking between themselves, with the one in gold frames, doing a swift head turn to Dice and Spike, flashing a smack of severe seriousness from his face.

Dice aims back with his stare while Spike shows the two men a look of damage intent. The man in the gold frames fires, "Fuck you lookin' at!?..."

First inhaling hard, Dice tells him, "Your friend right there's got a problem, right??..."

The yoo hoo man's anger swells up in him. "What problem!?" he daggers out to Dice. "I'll fuckin' bite your eyes out man!" And the gold-framed man immediately storms over to the two with short quick steps and a malice look.

Spike watches Dice watching the gold-framed man step up to him, with the one who said yoo hoo coming up behind him with meanness attached to his face. Dice lasers a vision into the framed man's eyes. "You got some kind of prerogatives with me, Dillinger?.. or somethin'?..."

The gold-framed man now engages in circling the two friends by walking, looking at Dice from his shoes to his face, with his own face folded into disgust for a remark. Then he chuckles with the yoo hoo man following the action, with a chuckled laugh in the same manner.

Dice knits his brow with the frown he gives him. "What the fuck's the deal around here--laughing's an infectious disease?..."

The gold-framed man stops abruptly (with his look remaining on Dice). Then he chuckles again, throwing his head back sharp with a jolt.

Spike swings a stare to his friend's eyes while the yoo hoo man guffaws loud and clear— the intent being twin to the gold-framed man's, as Dice seems to see it. Spike says to the yoo hoo man, "Death... What does it mean?..."

The yoo hoo man's face flashes on shock, as he stands there with his mouth way wide opened. The one in the gold frames shouts out, "Hey, who the fuck you gon' end?" he declares in a questioned tone.

With his forearm, Dice swoop-swings it into the gold-framed man's throat-- the man snap-tilts his head backwards and drops down to the ground on his back. The yoo hoo man's shock remains, watching the man down there with his mouth wide opened.

Spike is immediate when he grips his fist with his other hand, and lams them both into the yoo hoo man's stomach -- the wind whooshes out from him. And the gold-framed man starts trying to get up, until Dice takes his foot and smashes the bottom of it down in his face.

Before the doubled over yoo hoo man raises his chin up, Spike gives a strong punch to the side of his face, and he falls to the ground now. Dice bends his knees down to the gold-framed man and punches him in the neck hard one time. The man does a quick gasp for breath. Spike takes the grounded yoo hoo man's leg and lifts it up high, pulling it to the side. Dice catches a glimpse of Spike doing that and shouts, "The other way!..."

Nodding "yes" two quick times Spike takes the half-conscious yoo hoo man's leg, and lifts it way up over his head, pushing it backwards with one hand, and with the other, he takes the man's neck and chokes it. Keeping hold of the yoo hoo man's neck and leg (pushed back now all the way passed the man's head), Spike puts his feet together, jumps up, and, drives both his knees square into the back of the yoo hoo man's thighs.

Dice blooms out "Riiight... Riiight..." to Spike's way of executing the act, with the gold-framed man lying still on the ground in a moaning semi-consciousness. Dice leans back to raise his fist up but remembers. "Spike... we better straighten up and fly before passengers start coming 'round to be nosy..."

Spike stops, looking swift lefts and rights as if a crowd exists already. The friends stand up now almost together, with the position of their bodies hinting a getaway. With the gold-framed man and yoo hoo man flat on the ground with their consciousness gone, Dice and Spike take a step away, while two middle-aged women are walking forward, approaching the two but not seeing them.

Dice and Spike see them now and the women now see them. The friends standing there is similar to being caught naked, as the women jack their mouths open looking at the two men on the ground.

Tapping Spike on the elbow Dice says, "Let's start moving our asses outta here..."

As the two start moving, one of the ladies exclaims, "Oh my Gawd!" and gives birth to a squealing scream, while the other woman lets out one that's more mannish.

The friends walk fast now, vaguely following a route back to the bus stop where they came from. The women make more screams similar in sound, with the woman's mannish one honking even more male-like in her squealing. Dice and Spike take themselves across a street while looking back at the women as other passers-by now creep up to the scene where the beaten men lie. Spike says, "Look at that..."

    "What," Dice answers, "the people's brigade?"
    "Exactly."
    "Keep walkin'... even if they scream like widows..."

In the distant commotion a woman is heard ordering, "Somebody call the police," as Dice and Spike reach the bus stop. They stand there at the stop nervously, making sporadic shoves of hands in their pockets, and head turns to the right, left, and center directions. Spike spills out, "Man, we gotta evaporate or somethin'!..."

Dice searches around with his eyes a bit more urgently. "Listen... waitin' for a bus now at this stage of the game is less than kosher. We'd be better footin' it rather than risk our breath over this shit."

    "You think they were down with smiling boy after all?..."

Dice gives his friend a disbelief look but instead responds, "He makes me wish I'd swiped his breath from him..."

Coming from the beating scene's direction are three young men, looking around with their heads as they walk.

Spike taps Dice on his shoulder to show him the reality in his sight. Dice turns in that direction and sees the men coming. "Fuck the bus," he decides, "we better take the route of it and deal with it by foot..."

And the two head on down the street now, looking ahead of them. When Dice and Spike both dare to decide to look behind them, they see three more people (two women and a man) with the three men walking behind them. Although their closeness is marked by their distance, the friends can see the seriousness embedded in their eyes.

Spike asks Dice, "You think these guys practice vendetta justice?..."

"I dunno..."
"We ain't got a hint of an army in weapons..."
"Don't put an extreme on this Spike. Just continue the moseying on that we're doin', and fuck puttin' every single feeling that's trying to edge up into our brains, on the top of the list..."
"I'm not tryin' to, I'm not tryin' to..."

They continue their walk down the streets they assume to be the bus route they rode down. Spike thinks he hears a Hey you! from one of the people back there, but he ignores it. Then he sees Dice swinging a look at him. "What," asks Spike, not wanting to know.

Dice just looks at him. "Nothin'," he replies, relieved. The two keep going, nearly developing a rhythm about their steps as they also increase their speed a bit with each one.

They step and stride past landscapes and scenery that resemble the urban and the rural, with three and four-story buildings stripped bare of their previously painted advertisements, left chipped now against the dust-purple color of their bricks. Some buildings have long stretches of green lawns the length of two farm corrals or one city block, interrupting their adjoining positions.

Dice and Spike focus on keeping their silence firm to keep their ears wide open, while their eyes refuse the force to make them look back behind them. Suddenly, Spike thinks he hears a Hey you! again, but cuts his eyes over to Dice, who's already looking at him. With almost simultaneous sighs, the two gradually turn their heads behind them.

High in the air comes an empty beer bottle heading for their faces. Dice and Spike shift themselves to the sides, ducking it as it smashes.

Stuck in their tracks from the act, the two now see a slightly larger group of people behind them, standing almost triangular in shape from the back to the front, with a lead person before them now, whose short stature equals four feet. He smiles at the two with his upper lip (curled up) tucked against his front gum.

Dice tells Spike, "He did it"-- him, meaning the man with the curved smile.

Spike wonders, looking at the man. "Yeah..." he says aloud. "Probably..."

Dice angers out to the man. "Hey man, you did that??..." he spits.

The four foot man renders a raised but husky pitched, "Yeah! That's me! Did that!..."

Spike looks at Dice, expecting the appropriate answer. Dice says to the man, "Go `head. Name the problem to me..."

The man raises up his right eyebrow. "Problem?" he squirts. "You!... Neighborhood basher!..."

Then a short one toothed hunchbacked metal silver-haired pale woman, with white ankle socks and black cordovan men's shoes shouts, "Whadaya doin' comin' `round here... comin' down here in this neighborhood botherin' our townfolk!... like city folk comin' `round here, draggin' down-- we know you from the city..."

Spike looks astonished at Dice who frowns before speaking. "Look, those guys begged for wreckage... We couldn't even move our feet without your residents, trying to season up some fish to fry, for who knows what reason-- you know?..."

Spike begins to lower his head. "Maybe we should start leaving," he eases out, looking at the grayness of the sidewalk with his head up now.

Dice goes on. "And besides that, what committee is this?..."

The four foot man raises his eyebrow up again before speaking, while Spike says to Dice, "We better pretend to have fear and lose our presence..."

Then the four foot man pitches to Dice, "Committee?... None of your business!... Call it that!..."

Spike reminds Dice, "Come on man, we gotta come back here, don't we?..."

"Definitely," says Dice so his friend only hears. "And when we do I'll make sure we come like we're comin' to change history..."

The group just stands there behind Dice and Spike in the form of waiting, for whatever. Dice slowly turns back around to face the direction him and Spike were walking in. With his face a bit drawn in he begins his walk forward, with Spike readily following his movement.

As they keep walking, the two go back to not wanting to check behind them again. Their walk is a casual one in meter as they silently regard the sounds of no sounds behind them.

After some moments Spike finally says, "What d'you think Dice, think they still stand behind us?..."

Dice turns his head around to look behind him first, with Spike following second. No one is seen standing behind them now back there.

Spike percolates as he walks. "Just the idea of a fuckin' cowboy mob behind us... What the shit is that?..."

"That yoo hoo man was practically whistling at us back there, like we were girls," Dice declares. "I dunno man... My fuse is gettin' shorter and shorter... I guess... It seems like I don't have the ability to say Fuck it! no more... I dunno..."

Spike thinks about that. "Maybe we're gettin' older... But listen, some people have to be taken care of by a human hand right away..."

"Yeah," Dice drones out, looking off to the side with no regard. "We have that inside us already."
"I know... That's why... I wonder when we come back here if those mothafuckas're gonna be occupying my space where we gotta go..."
"It's probable."
"Probably right. That's why if we see any of `em they should be hammered down like flathead nails in a bookcase..."

They continue their walk, now past two-story buildings donned in cinnamon colored cobblestone-like bricks. One building they pass has a rusted metal door that squeaks like an elephant's shriek as it opens. Two arms missile out— snatching the two by their shirt collars, pulling them inside.

The basement grayness and emptiness of the cellar that they're in is the first thing Dice and Spike notice inside. Several naked light bulbs hang on long black single sooty iron extensions from the high ceiling. Above, along the sides of the walls, is a catwalk, and there, in the center of the floor with the friends, is the mob.

While two men hold the arms of Dice and Spike, the short hunchbacked metal silver-haired woman stands before them with scolding intent piercing from her eyes. The four foot man stands beside her with his one eyebrow up. The friends also spot the grinning man standing there-- his three fingers up in his face while the usual two fingers hold the cigarette that he smokes, quivering, letting out through his nose the "uh-hmph!" laugh that he does.

The silver-haired hunchback woman steps up to Dice. "So..." she sputs. "Whadaya wa-- Ya still here, ya know that?... `Course ya know that!... Why?..." Her voice echoes out en masse to prove the cellar's vacantness.

Dice stares right at her and all of them. "You saw us walking on our merry way outta here. It takes time to walk-- we're not electronic."

Spike uses the corner of his eye to glance at the grinning man's wrist where the open cut was made earlier. Then he says to the hunchback woman, "How fast did you expect us to walk? Did you want us to scurry?..."

The four foot man jerks his head quick to him. "Death!" he spears, nearly aiming the eye with the brow up at him. "That I see for you!... Why?... Tu boca!..." Then he takes his hand and imitates a yaking mouth, opening and closing it in front of Spike's face.

The grinning man laughs "uh-hmph!" through his nose as he smokes, while Dice says to the hunchback woman, "Look-- why create a convention outta this? We were on our way outta here, and guess what? We wanna continue."

She blares back at him. "Suppose'n I don't believe-- Whadaya take me for, noseyin' aroun' here like a bunch a sailors or somethin' with-- We know what ya come aroun' here for... We're not a sex town anymore!... And we don't need no more publicity than we got awready. Did you know that-- The hell with it!... fuckin' sex hunters..."

Dice frowns at her. "Sex?... Look, what we do is our business, and sex ain't even on the agenda... Keep your ways and traditions. We ain't concerned with that shit. We're here for business and that's the long and short of the deal..."

The hunchback woman oozes up closer to Dice until she reaches his face, then says "Haw, haw!" to it, with a take-that! style.

Dice returns with "I don't need no entertainment. You guys can do whatever ya want, play post office, whatever... But me and my friend here's got business to take care of, so you've got a mistake on your hands. We're not sailors..."

The grinning man's face is beaded with sweat as he brings his cigarette up to his mouth for a drag, and when he gets the filter there via his two usual fingers, he trembles as he draws the smoke in, the three other fingers also trembling. "They're like cookie cutters," he says to them all. "So delicate when they slice..."

Spike rears back, trying to swing a punch at the grinning man (who steps back backwards in mocking little steps). Now two men are holding Spike's arms. The four foot man says

"Easy... Easy..." to everyone, as the tension relaxes in the form of only one man now holding Spike's arms.

Suddenly, the grinning man slings his cigarette down hard on the ground, snatches his index-finger sized gold dull knife out his pants pocket-- the mob sees this and their eyes splay wide open. The grinning man now holds up the back of his wrist, makes a slice on it with a grunt, and the mob jumps away from him.

The four foot man urges the grinning man. "Robert!..." he says. "Please!... Please!..."

Robert (the grinning man) drops his arm down to his side with some blood dripping from it, and a damp smidgen of solemnity on his face. Then, he grins his usual grin, standing where he is, and places another cigarette in his mouth, holding it with his usual pinky and thumb, quivering and trembling as he does it. "Uh-hmph!" he laughs through his nose again calmly.

A sigh of relief is heard from everyone as they don't show themselves watching Robert, who steps back from them a bit. The four foot man turns back to the captured Dice and Spike. "Now!..." he settles, as he starts to resume his speaking, but shuts himself off when he remembers that the hunchback woman was talking to the friends earlier. "Mayzy?" he asks her. "You wanna resume with the questioning?..."

The hunchback woman, Mayzy, scowls a look of scorn at Dice and Spike. "Sex addicts in town," she mutters to them. "We need that like a hole-- How many minutes should--" she turns to the four foot man. "Would you say it takes less than five minutes ta get outta this town?..."

The four foot man wastes no time before aiming his face at the two, then his eye, then his raised eyebrow. "Less than five minutes!" he lances into them.

Mayzy scowls back angrily at the friends, while beginning to slowly bring her hand down to her inner thigh, slowly rubbing it there, nearly touching her vagina. "I hate little sex furrows like you two, you--" Then she turns to the others. "They need guidance!" she shouts, and taking both her hands, she rubs her vagina with a quick swipe.

Robert the grinning man shakes from holding in a guffaw, and trembles while dragging in smoke from his cigarette. Dice says to Mayzy, "Awright. So you're a tribunal... What the fuck do you want us to do? Can we leave now, if it ain't too much trouble to ya?..."

The four foot man fires, "We!... What're we gonna do wit ya!..." Then, he snaps his finger like he hatched an idea. He turns to two men standing in the mob. "Go get Rosaletta, and Morris!..."

The two men immediately head to the back of the area while the four foot man smiles his curved smile with his upper lip tucked against his gum, satisfied at Dice and Spike. "What we do wit you?" he asks with the answer inside him. "I show you what!..." Then he takes his hands and puts them together, slanting them as he rests his cheek on them. "Qué lástima!..." he whimpers. Mayzy is smiling at the friends as she eases her hands back down to her vagina, then back up again.

The two men now return. One carries in his arms a white and caramel colored basset hound. The other carries a machete.

Looking pleased, the four foot man cheers "Bravo!... Bravo!" while the rest of the mob begin to applaud for a quick moment. Dice and Spike look at each other.

Coming up to them, the four foot man says, "What're we gonna do?... This is what we do!..." And he turns to the two men. In Spanish he says, "Haces!..."

The man with the basset hound holds it up to his chest while another man grabs the dog's head. The man with the machete raises it over the dog's neck. Addressing Dice and Spike, the four foot man declares, "That is Morris!" while pointing at the machete. Then to the men he says, "Do it!..."

The machete swings down and slices the hound's head off. (The man in front of it jumps back quick one time, letting the head drop. It thumps on the floor.)

Dice shuts his eyes, unable to look at the headless dog, as the blood from it johnny-pumps out onto the floor. He keeps his eyes closed as Spike stares at Dice, unable to believe his friend's response.

The mob applauds for a quick moment again, pleased with the act, as Mayzy comes up to Dice's face as he cautiously opens his eyes. She asks, "What's the mat-- Too chillin' for ya, huh?..." Then she takes her hand and pets the right side of his cheek.

As Spike still stares at Dice in disbelief at what he did, the four foot man smiles his smile, then asks Dice, "So!... "You think what!..."

Dice gradually brings his head back around to face him, hearing Mayzy say, "He looks sick..." to those who would listen. Dice now looks at Robert, who quickly shifts his legs real close together at him, mockingly. Robert then fake laughs, "Ha ha ha... Uh-ha..." and brings his cigarette up to his lips with his two fingers, quivering as he drags the smoke in.

The four foot man looks at Dice, then Spike, then turns a look over at Mayzy expectantly. "Mayzy!... What's the verdict sayin' inside you?..."

Mayzy flicks on her angry face to look back at the two friends. "Verdict?" she half-hollers. "I can't stand no sex fiends comin' to hunt aroun'-- We need respect known in this--" She then looks at Dice, slowly creeping her hand back down to her vagina, this time, opening her legs wide to massage it with the flat of her fingers.

A male in the mob shouts out, "You gonna penalize `em Mayzy!" and everyone else in the mob yells, "Yeah Mayzy!" "Do it! Do it!" "Penalize `em, Mayzy!" "Go `head and penalize `em!"

Mayzy has stopped her motions with delight, as her eyes brighten up while she moves her head in all the directions where the encouragement comes from. Happy with the suggestions, she shouts back to them, "Ya want I should--" And the whole mob almost answers "YEAH!" in precise unison.

Then she turns to the four foot man and orders, "Hold `em down!... One by one!..." The mob goes ballpark crazy with cheers as the man holding Dice leans to the side to let two others assist with holding him. Then, the three of them pull Dice down to the floor on his knees as Spike looks on with concern.

The mob continues cheering like a sports arena, as Mayzy lifts up her skirt with a wide-armed hoist, showing her pale muscular boney legs. She stoops down and jumps staying stooped over to Dice, standing over his face, pulling down her panties. One of the men now holds Dice's head tight like a vice as the crowd begins a rhythmic chant, shouting "Go!... Go!..."

Staring down at him maliciously, she takes her hand and places it on the back of Dice's head and pulls his nose into her vagina (with the help of the men holding him). "So," she starts, "you're conduct canNOT be--" and pulling his head even closer, she moves herself up and down, up and down, letting out a coarse sound of "Oooo" as she does it.

Dice struggles to free his head, moving it from side to side, but can't, nearly suffocating as he tries. His sounds of breathing are hard and pronounced, as Mayzy continues her rhythm, moving herself up and down up and down, sighing a rough "Aahhh" along with the "Oooos" she still emits.

The mob has ceased chanting but continue their cheers in a scattered manner, still sounding like a stadium crowd.

Spike is watching with his face twisted in disgust as Robert looks at him, quivering and chuckling as he holds his cigarette with his pinky and thumb. Spike looks at Robert, then looks back down at his friend.

Mayzy is moving herself up and down faster now, harder, and harder, with Dice struggling with all his might to get away with no luck. The men holding his head help Mayzy pushing it into her more, as they detect the sound of the orgasm approaching in her tone.

Mannishly she groans, "Ugh!... Ugh!..." faster and faster, then she stomps her foot, cries out "OHHH!... OHHH! you cocksucker!..." using both her hands now to grasp the back of Dice's head, moving it all around in her as if she were scrubbing with it.

The four foot man smiles with his tucked lip and applauds Mayzy's orgasm. The others in the mob follow his applause with their own, as Mayzy slowly stands (pushing herself up with her hands atop her thighs).

Dice shows full fatigue on his face with cellophane wetness glistening from it, as he tries to catch his breath now. He sees Robert, bursting out cigarette smoke from his mouth, chuckling at him-- quivering while he holds the cigarette away from his mouth, with the three fingers standing up tall over the pinky and thumb.

Mayzy takes the heel of her hand and wipes her female lubricant all over his face, as the mob applauds again approvingly for a brief moment. Mayzy's hand massages her fluid well into Dice's skin. Suddenly she stops, pivots her head over to Spike. "Where's the other who-- Is that him?..." she asks the four foot man, with her face bagged in seriousness.

Before he releases a word, Mayzy stoops down again, and jumps (still stooped) over to Spike, as the man holding him brings him closer to her, and two other men come over to assist him. (Those holding Dice pull him back now away from the others.)

The mob begins to chant again, "GO!... GO!... GO!... GO!..." as they pull Spike down to his knees on the floor. The four foot man hollers over the chanting, "Learn `em Mayzy!..." as she spreads her legs open, swiping Spike's head like a flash of light, shoving it into her vagina commandant style.

Spike manages to snatch his head away. "I'm gonna remove your CHEST, bitch!!" he plunges.

The four foot man quickly, with the back of his hand, SLAPS the side of Spike's face. "BASTA!!" he fires, as he takes his hands and helps Mayzy push Spike's face back into her vagina. (The men there take over holding it as the four foot man moves his hands away, and stands there in overseeing fashion.)

As the men grab a tight hold of Spike's head, Mayzy begins moving it up and down in her vagina. "Oooo," she sighs, "Look at this... What the fuck ar--" and she pulls his head into her harder, yelling "Push it!" to the men, who grimace as they push Spike's head harder into her.

The mob cries "Yayyyy!" as Mayzy moves Spike's head up and down, up and down in her. She moves it, cooing out, "Youuuu fuckin' bastard--" then, grunting violently, moving Spike's head up and down in her, with Spike gasping violently for air. (The men can hardly keep up with her motions.)

Then she takes his head and thrusts it away from her. "You worthless shit!..." she jabs, raising herself up to stand again with her hands on her thighs.

The mob howls out "Whoa!" and giggles and chuckles at Mayzy's comment and action, as she stands there next to the four foot man staring down at Spike, who hangs his head down showing exhaustion.

Mayzy says, "This is a respectable town, my fr--" Then she looks around as if she's waiting for an agreeing cheer from the mob. Both Dice and Spike (still being held by the men) stare wearily at everyone, with Spike's face showing more and more anger in seconds.

Continuing Mayzy says, "We know who we are and what kind of people we-- We've sired our own way of life here... What is, is what was, and if you sailors wanna keep comin' `round here for sex... Well, who th--" and she looks at the mob again for crowd assistance. "My name is what??" she asks.

"MAYZY!!" they thunder back with a bit of immediacy.

She nods her head with assuredness. "That's right... They gotta pay Mayzy..." Then she looks at the two friends, then over at the four foot man. "Release their asses," she says, "the goddamned--"

And the men holding the two instantly drop their hands, letting Spike and Dice's arms drop loosely.

Mayzy, Robert and the rest of the mob begin to walk out of the area, most of them, appearing to not even notice the two as they walk past them in an almost funeral procession.

Spike and Dice (still looking hazy) hear a voice call out in Spanish, "Mira!..." They look up and see the four foot man still standing there. "Your departure is still being timed!" he marks. "Get started!..." And after that, he leaves with the rest of the mob behind them.

Spike fumes as he watches them all leaving the area the same way they came in. Then he takes a look at Dice, who seems almost dazed as he looks one way at blankness. Spike says, "Hey man..."

Dice gradually glances over to him. "Don't say it... I don't know what type of pussy that was. It smelled like somethin' inhuman... It was very unknown to me... Was that a person?... Jesus Christ!..."

"Nah," answers Spike. "That ain't even inside my brain right now..."
"Ain't in-- What're you talkin' `bout?" Dice replies.
"I'm talkin' `bout the dog..." says Spike.
""Dog?... What about him?... They killed him..."
"Yeah, but you laid eyes on it like it was sensitive to see. Even brutal."
"Man... You fuckin' got that female impersonator's cum on your face... How do you think you looked?..."
"Man, I know how I looked. And it wasn't like, `Oh God, please save the animals, and the birds, and the trees'..."
"What-- you tryin' to say I had a dress on or somethin' Spike?..."
"I'm sayin' my eyes ain't lied to me since I was born, and not even then."
"I think you better analyze yourself. Since when I don't know how to shed blood mothafucka?"
"You turned away!... When they sliced the fuckin' dog you turned away!"
"Your eyes frolicking with you now?... They frolicking with you now. Or you're gettin' old."
"Hey, I know how the truth smells when I see it."
"Right."
"I know how truth moves when I feel it, and you turned away--"
"You're wrong."
"--you turned away when they sausaged up the dog!"
"Right."
"I know what I saw."
"I didn't turn away, but if I did turn away, what does that mean to you?..."
"It means... It means you ain't fit for the job no more, of bounty huntin', that's what."
"Man, you're the wuss in this duo! You forgettin' that?"
"That was the bullshit your fantasy was creating inside you!"
"No, you, are the wuss in this duo!... How you gonna declare you're so gladiatorish now?... Check the centuries... You ain't never heard about no strength like yours in history, have you?"
"You turned away, man. You turned away when they sliced the dog, Dr. King!"
"What?"
"Mr. Gandhi... Dalai Lama... You're the fantasy man, `cause you're trying to deny that violence is only a tool..."

"Oh-- now you gonna teach me the facts of life?"
"No."
"I taught you mothafucka!... I tolerated you!"
"Tolerated me--"
"That's right. And now look... Who showed you that you even had strength?..."
"You?"
"Right."
"Listen, I already knew what was inside a me. Your fantasy wanted you to believe that I didn't."
"That, is bullshit, spoken in true politician fashion."
"Right..."

Spike pushes himself up from the floor right away. He reaches in all his pockets until he pulls out a tissue, then he wipes off his face all over with it. "Hey man," he says as he wipes. "I'm through..."

Now Dice rises up, holding his hands out as if they wore contamination. "Oh, you leavin'?" he asks with the tone of I-dare-you.

"Damn straight, I'm gonna pursue this profession like a professional. That calls for guts and hard-on stamina. Remember that? It left you."
"You got a problem with reality Spike... Your eyes gave you a mistake--"
"My eyes gave me the truth!... You turned away. Definition?... Cream puff, whip cream, oatmeal strength... Your wisdom's off too I bet, `cause I bet you that bitch ain't gon' pay you..."

Dice swings a look of anger at him. "Hey... Eternal... ain't no bitch, understand?..."

"Whatever... It's your change of life. Me myself, I'm stayin' on course, with my wisdom intact. As for you muhfucka... You retreated!..."

Spike starts walking out of the place.

Dice looks at him with disbelief stained over his face. "Right," he utters, "you gonna finalize Eternal's husband?..."

Spike stops in his tracks. "I'm not even touchin' that. That's your adventure, man. Your payment for that is `she loves me/she loves me not'... Payment for this for you was secondary in the first damn place."

"Oh, so you know her financial status now?" Dice daggers.
"I know one thing that's called definite, and that is, money ain't comin' from that girl, `cause, you ain't made it a priority in the first damn place."

"Right. So begone muthafucka! I don't need you to do a job for me. Case closed. I'm glad to know you're a seer man..."

Spike throws his hand at him with a sweep of disregard, and walks out of the area without looking back.

Dice stares at him leaving with his mouth making an attempt to open up, with a word stuck behind his tonsil. He starts to make a move and makes one step behind him, then finally gets out, "Go `head! I'll get the muthafucka myself... and the money!..." His look expects Spike to come back in, but he walks out of the place before it might happen.

When he gets outside he sees Spike's figure walking way ahead in the distance. He stares at Spike, as his image gets smaller from the straightahead walking that he continues. Dice yells to him, "You're the one that's got all the feelings! They're ruling you, not me!... Look at how pissed you are!..."

Spike is a dot now, engulfed by the distance.

Realizing that he now stands in this neighborhood alone, Dice begins to start walking, heading for the bus stop where they both entered the district.

When Dice arrives there after a number of minutes, his face shows surprise at not seeing Spike standing there. (Only an elderly woman, who's shivering from the sight of him there by herself.) He stares beside her at nothing as she looks at the side of his face. After some moments the bus finally pulls up and the two move to climb aboard it slow.

Soon after, Dice arrives back at Eternal Jones' house. After his knocks on the door, Eternal opens it with her usual gentle motions, then sticks her head out the door and looks behind him. Dice watches her doing it and says, "He's not there," while entering her place. "He went home." Then he immediately heads for the bathroom.

Eternal's responding "Oh" has an element of surprise in it as she closes the door behind him, looking at him.

When Dice comes out of the bathroom (after the rushing sound of running water stops), his face is damp and his bland expression is granite in emotion as he goes over to the couch, and slowly drops himself down in it. Eternal watches him with concern as she goes over to him. "Why did he go?" she asks.

"Ehh, he said he had to go and check on his mother or somethin'," replies Dice with disregarding tone.

"You look like you've been molested by a lot of confusion with him going..."

Dice looks at her with a speck of surprise on his face. Then he turns his head back around to look at the tv that shows a weather forecaster pointing at a lightening bolt on a map. "Molested..." he repeats. "Every man's got his own priorities I guess..." Then he turns to look at her. "My priority tho is you Eternal, and I mean to harvest bouquets for you the rest of your life..."

Eternal's face shows sunshine when she hears that, as she quickly comes over to Dice and plops down next to him on the couch, embracing him. He gives her a quick full kiss on the lips. Then they sigh pleasure almost together as they relax in their embrace and watch tv.

On the screen is the news, with the anchor there reporting on a double homicide. As the pictures on the screen show the outside areas where the crimes took place, Eternal immediately closes her eyes and covers her ears with her hands. "Sometimes I get physically sick from hearing about those kind of things..." she says.

Dice doesn't really hear all of her as he stares into the kitchen while she watches him. Smiling she calls out, "Diiice..."

"Hmm?" he replies with quickness.
"You didn't even hear what I said," she says cheerfully with a chuckle.
"Yes I did... Listen... I want you to know that by the time the next sun rises up there, this animal you had will be nothin' but history in your life..."

Eternal smiles satisfied from being next to Dice.

As the day grows into afternoon, and from there, into night, Dice steps into the kitchen after Eternal puts away the last dinner dish that she dried, walking out. She asks him, "You want something else to eat?"

"Nah," he replies. "Just some water... I can get it..."

He kind of turns his head to watch her as she walks over to the couch to take a seat, just as he opens the cabinet drawer there to remove a butcher knife. Still looking over his shoulder, he gets two sheets of paper towel from the towel rack there, wraps it around the blade, bends down, raises his pant leg up, and inserts the blade inside his sock, slipping on two thick rubber bands to keep it in place against his ankle. He then raises up and takes a glass to get some water.

After that, Dice then slowly walks into the living room where Eternal sits watching tv. He approaches her with a bit of caution in his steps. "Um..." he begins. "I think I'm a get ready to end your problem now..."

Eternal looks up at him. "I know that you're a better man than him darling," she remarks. "Much better... And I know I won't have anymore fears of him after you confront him." She stands up to hold him while she entirely kisses him on the lips. Dice keeps his eyes open as she does it, then takes his arms and drops them over her shoulders for a hug while looking at the picture of Eternal, her children, and her husband on the bureau.

A few moments later Dice heads for the door. He puts his hand on the door knob, then turns to give Eternal another kiss on the lips before leaving. "I'll be right back," he tells her as he opens it and leaves.

Dice hears his footsteps echo off the Urdsville concrete as he walks to the bus stop. Nighttime darkness had blanketed the sky some time ago. The twinkle of stars can be seen now when Dice looks up. Noise is no where to be heard he notices.

At the bus stop he stands there and blends with the sparseness of traffic on the streets and the sidewalk. He alone waits there for the bus as he stares down at the street where litter is not known. He breathes in air deep into his lungs and breathes it out. His vision stays stuck on a fire hydrant across the street.

Suddenly before he knows it the bus is there in his face with its doors open. He quickly snaps out of it and climbs on before it decides to leave him.

On the bus, two middle-aged people sit inside-- a woman reading a newspaper, a man avoiding slumber. Dice gives them a quick look, then his sight becomes fixed on the bus seat's metal bar in front of him.

It travels its course rolling moderately, making its scheduled stops with a simple opening and closing of doors. Dice is not remembering to follow his whereabouts through the window as the bus continues on, passing spots that may be his stop. He takes his fingertips and rubs his forehead while looking at the bus floor's galaxy design.

A passing car horn does a polite beep at another passing car outside, which makes Dice look out the window. His eyes recognize the district of Rudybell's, so he jumps out his seat quick to pull the stop cord. When the bus slows down for the stop, he leaves it.

His face as he walks looks mission-bound, while his eyes are doe-eyed wide open, and fixed on the structure of Rudybell's that he sees not too distantly. His vision is on the sign of Rudybell's-- no surroundings exist in his sight which is tunneled towards the bar and grill. He hears the faint sound of Jr. Walker and the All Stars' soul music emanating not too far away from his ears.

He walks. The sound of get-together party music gets closer to his ears, as the image of Rudybell's begins to spread, filling his eyesight. The butterscotch yellow hue light in front of the place looks warm, covering the patrons who are standing outside, smoking, talking and laughing.

Dice steps up to Rudybell's looking only at the entrance of the place, as the patrons out there sort of glance at him and sort of stare at him, while "Shake And Fingerpop" continues to play from Jr. Walker and the All Stars. He walks past them all, seeming not to see them as he passes. He pushes the saloon-styled door open and enters while some eyes watch him.

Inside Rudybell's "Shake And Fingerpop" pounds hard in the chest as he surveys the inside of the place, seeing a curtain of tobacco smoke in front of the crowd there, that dances and sits on bar stools, drinking and talking. Some people walk from one side to the other, almost to the beat of the music, and as Dice stands there examining every body, some of them begin to notice him standing there.

He walks more deeply into the place, staring at every person in all areas at each table on every bar stool. Some look up from their drinks at him, then drop their eyes back down on their drinks or food.

Finally, Dice sees a bald muscular man with a thick mustache, sipping on a drink. Dice alerts himself with a jerk of his body and walks over to him.

Reaching the man, Dice gives him a light tap on his left shoulder, which makes him swing his head in Dice's direction. Dice says "Hey, what's happenin' man. You Mr. Eric Jones?..."

With a frown of anger on his face the man retorts. "So what!?"

"Nothin'," Dice replies with innocence bathed in it. "Listen... your wife sent me here. She's got a message for you, but she told me not to give it to you in here... She said to give it you outside..." And Dice turns his body that way towards the door, with a benevolent expression and gesture of will-you-come-out-with-me?

Eric Jones looks at Dice like so much garbage. "That hoe you mean!... That's a hoe you talkin' `bout!..." And he turns back to his drink and takes a sip of it, while Dice invisibly cringes up hard with anger. Eric Jones slightly slams the bottom of his drink down on the counter and gets up, preparing to follow Dice outside.

Dice forces his facial muscles to create a pleasant look right away as he heads to the saloon-styled doors, going through them, with Eric Jones following haphazardly. In the back of the place, Robert comes out of a room, closing the door behind him. He has his usual cigarette between his pinky and thumb, and stands there, appearing not to see the two.

Outside Rudybell's, Dice passes the couple of patrons left standing outside the place and steps over to the corner of the buillding, where he pulls out the butcher knife from under his pants leg unseen, and waits.

Eric Jones wanders out of the place, looking around with the same frequency of anger on his face. Dice sees him come out there and steps back more to the side of Rudybell's, as Eric Jones shouts out "Hey!" not seeing him. He walks to the corner where Dice waits for him.

More anger shows up washed on Jones' face. When he turns the corner, his eyes bulge out shock seeing Dice standing there with the butcher knife. Dice slides it into his stomach with a jab-- it goes in easy like it went through a tub of butter. When he pulls it out, it comes out robotic and smoothly. Then Jones' stomach drains the blood out, staining his shirt in a full circle.

Dice turns away quick from Jones-- standing sideways from him, but eyeing him out the corner of his eyes, waiting for him to drop dead. Jones' face shows complete gaped surprise as he holds his stomach with both his hands, looking at Dice the same surprised way. Suddenly, his eyes freeze and he tilts over, stiffly falling on the ground like a board. Dice never turns his head to look at him. He immediately walks away from there sternly with oak emotion.

Some time later, Dice walks through Eternal Jones' door with his eyes in expectant mode. She is standing there looking at him with the status of her eyes matching his. Her arms want to stretch out to greet him uncertainly. Dice helps her decide by immediately embracing her tightly, sliding his cheek against her hair, then kissing her on the side of her neck.

He then takes her by the shoulders and extends her back to look into her eyes. "It's done," he says with relief.

"It's done?" Eternal replies, with a tone of not knowing.

"Yeah," he comes back, with more relief in his uttering. "It's over for you now..."
"What did he say when you told him?..."
"He didn't say anything... There wasn't any time for him to say nothin'. I did it nice and easy, like a baby pulling out flowers..."
"Did what nice and easy?..."
"Th-- His ending baby. What's the matter with you?..."

Eternal gasps back sudden with a swing of the back of her hand to her mouth. "You... you killed him??..."

Dice looks like he doesn't recognize her. "What's the matter with you? You're scarin' me like I'm in the wrong house..."

Eternal steps back from him with a firm stare of shock. "You killed him??... You killed him??..."

"Sweetheart... What'd you think!?... That's what you wanted, right??"
"What I wanted??... I never... You're horrible!..."
"What'd you think I went huntin' for him for... to talk??..."
"You killed him!... My God!!..."
"What'd you think! What'd you want?..."
"What did I want??... I thought... I thought you would talk--"
"Talk to him??... What the fuck would I do that for??..."
"You're a murderer!!... You're just like him!!..."
"Him??... How you gonna stand there and match me up with--"
"Murder is the worse thing you could do! You're worse than him!!"
"Worse than him??..."
"You're horrible!!... You're a murderer!!... HELP!!... HELP, poLICE!!..."
"Bitch, you disheveling now??... Aww!-- my mind is fucked up!... I've been taken!..."
"HELP!!... HELP!!... MURDERER!!..."
"YOU fuckin'..." And Dice shifts his head here and there to find what to do.

Eternal throws the door open and runs out into the street screaming. "HELP, poLICE!!... POLICE!!... MURDERER!!... MURDERER!!..."

Dice looks up, sees her outside and, quickly runs out of her house, running past her. She sees his image whizzing by and yells out even louder. "HERE HE IS!!... THE MURDERER'S HERE!!... HE'S HERE!!..."

Dice keeps running fast, heading for the bus stop, as people begin to trickle out of their two-family wood-framed houses. He runs and runs and reaches the stop with an awkward halt. He feels eyes on him from all directions as he hears distant "There he is"s and

"Over there"s speckled throughout the air, with the screams of Eternal Jones underneath that. In a second's time he decides to keep running.

Far away sirens sound towards him, coming closer as his footsteps rush head-on to their approach. He stops clumsily, and begins to see red lights rotating and circling the spot where he stands, trying to figure out what to do next. The sirens cast their blare all over him as seven patrol cars pull up and screeching, stop in staccato pops, like popcorn popping screeches. The doors swing open. Cops come out-- guns drawn.

Dice stands there stiff and wide-open with his eyes and posture, as the officers walk towards him with their guns aimed at his body. Haze starts settling into his head and voices sound echoey and metallic as the officers throw him against a patrol car. They frisk and handcuff Dice like rodeo cowboys, and hold his arms out in cattle branding fashion. His sight of two other officers in a patrol car on a radio (holding his wallet i.d.) is gauzy and glass-smeared visible.

His flesh feels multitudes of people around him and he senses a stadium of conversation and mumbles. Then, he suddenly makes out a gray-eyed officer staring in his face. "You're wanted for the murder of Michael Stanapopolis," he says with a smidge of anger.

Dice squinches his eyes from not making out the name. "What?" he replies, as his head tilts round as if unscrewing.

"Michael Stanapopolis," the officer repeats. "Your landlord..." Then he addresses his fellow officers. "Throw his fuckin' ass in the car before I gut him!..."

And the officers surround Dice like a football huddle and haul him into a patrol car, slamming the door behind him with thunder god strength.

All the other officers enter their own patrol cars as scores of onlookers continue to look on and talk amongst themselves. Then, the cars start up individually, and slowly head down the road from which they came, with their rotating red lights still circling round in a streamlined path now down the street.

Chapter Ten: A New Place

The plant green prison bus slowly climbs the short hill outside of the federal court building underneath the sun's light. It crawls onto the six-lane roadway, which leads to a battleship gray suspension bridge that's a few miles away.

The roadway is filled with tied up vehicles that creep along forward as the prison bus slides into a space in between them. Male heads are visible in silhouette through the caged windows of the bus. One of them is Dice, who stares out the window blankly now at the pedestrians who walk past a small park he sees, where benches surround a neatly manicured grassy lawn.

As Dice continues to look out the window, he notices a tall male figure slowly walking with a bent gait and a black-brown wooden cane, with a farmer's straw hat on top of his head. He sees that underneath the hat, his medium-sized Afro is completely old-aged white.

Dice's delight opens his eyes wider because he realizes that the man is Lube. He puts his mouth through the opening of the window's caged wiring. "Lube!" he yells out, with excitement coating the call.

Lube comes to a stop and gradually turns his head over to the prison bus that sits in the tied up traffic. He looks through the bus windows and sees Dice's face. "Dice!" he responds with surprise. "By God man!-- what are you doing in there?..."

Dice stares out at Lube and notices the whiteness of his hair, and the cane. He realizes that Lube is not wearing his make-up and usual bone through his nose, and that he seems to have aged nearly forty to fifty years. "Lube," Dice calls again, as the bus moves up a couple of notches in the traffic. "How'd your hair get so white man?... You look so old!..."

Lube chuckles. "My word man," he replies. "I have always looked like this... Perhaps your eyes needed glasses all along... Good God!-- how did you wind up in there?..."

Confusion strikes Dice's face as Lube's reply sinks into his head. Then he remembers Lube asking him about his predicament. "Huh?... Oh... I dunno... I fucked up somewhere along the line..." The bus rolls up a distance the length of three cars.

Dice has to turn his head now, as the bus's movement has placed Lube almost behind him. He sees Lube feebly walking forward with the help of the cane and can't believe the image his eyes are giving him. Lube calls out louder now because of the distance. "Perhaps you will discover another profession more worthy... I have faith that you will find your niche soon... I am optimistic..."

"Yeah," Dice responds with uncertainty. "You always had a way with words Lube..." Then he stares at him with the same degree of disbelief on his face over Lube's appearance. As the traffic lets up a bit leaving more driving room, Dice yells out with concern, "Lube!... What happened to your bone?..."

"What?" Lube replies, as the bus begins becoming more distant as it moves on. "The bone the bone!..." Dice yells. "What happened to it?..."

Lube takes his hand and cups it out over his ear in I-can't-hear-you fashion, as he watches the bus travel easily down the roadway now, heading for the suspension bridge that's ahead.

END

Bensonhurst, Brooklyn 1996
Williamsburg, Brooklyn 2020